D1521365

Swipe Left

For

Love

Happy Reading

Lynn Stevens

Lynn Stevens

Swipe Left for Love Copyright © 2019 Lynn Stevens

All rights reserved, including the right to reproduce this book, or portions thereof, in any form without written permission except for use of brief quotations embodied in critical articles and reviews.

Copyright 2019 by Lynn Stevens
This is a work of fiction. Names, characters, places, and incidents either are the product of the author's imagination or are used factiously, and any resemblance to actual persons, living or dead, business establishments, events, or locales, is entirely coincidental.

Published by Lynn Stevens
www.lstevensbooks.com
Cover design by Premade Book Cover Shop
ISBN: 978-1-698853-39-0

For Dave

CHAPTER ONE

Beads, so many beads. Too much white silk and satin. And sequins. Ugh.

Macie Regan wanted to be anywhere but Morgan Bridal. Even Hawt Yoga next door sounded like more fun. And that wasn't much of an option. The last time Macie tried a pose, she let out enough gas to evacuate the room. Not a moment she wanted to relive. She swiped across her tablet and hacked into the shop's Wi-Fi. It took her less than two minutes to figure out the password—weddings. Obviously not designed for security.

She stared at the Blind Friends app with a white background and a B and F in blue. It wouldn't hurt to check. Yeah, she'd just heard from him this morning, but it was possible he'd already responded to the last message she sent a few hours ago. Every message came in fast, like he couldn't wait to talk to her. Macie smiled. She couldn't wait to talk to him either.

"Mace?"

Macie's head jolted up, and she remembered the real reason she was in sateen hell. Lauren Tamm would be Lauren Coleman in a month. Her best friend since freshman year was getting married. And damned if Macie wasn't going to do everything she could to make sure Lauren's wedding went off without a hitch. Even if she

1

thought the whole thing was a terrible idea. When Macie hadn't reacted with excitement after Lauren told her about the engagement, they had a fight, then a long talk with plenty of wine. Lauren understood Macie's hesitation about marriage, but she had also pointed out that those feelings were Macie's and not hers.

"Wow," Macie said, with just the right amount of envy and awe. She'd practiced before Lauren had picked her up. Macie should've known that was unnecessary. "You look amazing."

"You really think so?" Lauren spun around on the small platform in front of a trio of mirrors. The dress shimmered in a blush so light most people would mistake it for white. The satin clung to her slim body in all the right places. The halter elongated her neck. Lauren was already beautiful, but she was a goddess in the simple dress. The first time Macie met her in their dorm, she thought she'd hate the girl. Lauren was the opposite of her in so many ways. Blonde to Macie's cinnamon brown. Blue eyed to Macie's dark chocolate. Model thin to Macie's curves. Lauren had hugged Macie immediately and had told her new roomie that she was jealous of Macie's then purple streaked hair. They'd been inseparable ever since. Lauren stepped off the platform and stopped beside Macie, spinning again for the full effect.

"It's perfect." *And no beads.* A ding sounded from her tablet, and Macie's gaze dropped to see the app had loaded. A red number one appeared over the blue M icon, and her pulse kicked it up a notch. Macie tried to hide her grin and glanced at the salesperson who hovered ten feet away, ready to tackle Lauren. She'd been trying to upsell accessories Lauren didn't want. Macie smirked and said, "You're going to give that woman a heart attack if you don't let her do her job."

"She'll get over it." Lauren leaned over the screen and shook her blonde head. "When did you get unlimited data?"

Macie snorted, and that was enough of an answer.

"You didn't?" Lauren giggled as she made her way back onto the platform.

"They need to upgrade their security. Besides, you're the one who taught me how to figure out passwords. It's not a true hack. You never taught me *that*." Macie stared at the Blind Friends app. Lauren created it with her fiancé for their final projects. Hers for programming and his for student counseling. It was only open to people enrolled at Lafayette University who had the password, and most of the campus had signed up. With a population near four thousand, that was a lot of pen-pal possibilities. Macie went to press her finger over the icon and stopped at the sound of Lauren's voice.

"Talking to your pen-pal?" Lauren straightened herself and smoothed her hands down the dress. "You should just meet him. The app's probably going to come down after graduation anyway. Tell him you want to hook up before you lose your chance."

"Hook up? With a complete stranger?" Macie set the tablet on the table beside her.

"It wouldn't be the first time," Lauren said, spinning back around to admire her angles in the mirror.

"That happened exactly once, and it won't happen again," Macie said, grabbing the tablet and closing the app. She opened the camera and took a few pics.

"Hey," Lauren snapped. Her eyebrows furrowed, and her nose wrinkled.

"Bring it up again and I'll show these to Ford." Macie raised her eyebrows in challenge. In reality, she'd taken the photos to send to Lauren's mom who was in Atlanta on yet another business trip. "You know that's bad luck."

"He's out golfing with Zac."

Macie scowled at that name. Zac was a prick.

"You know how he is with his phone. He probably wouldn't even see the text for three days. More than enough time for me to delete them." Lauren shook her head and slipped off the too-high heels. "What do you think of the shoes?"

"Hate 'em." Macie shrugged when Lauren glared at her. "The dress is you. Shoes of any variety are not. Go barefoot."

"I'm not walking down the aisle barefoot." Lauren held up the offending stilettos. "But I'm not going to kill myself either."

Lauren stepped down from the platform and headed toward the salesperson behind the counter. Macie smiled. Lauren came across as timid and innocent; but when she was on a mission, get out of her way. Macie attached the photos and emailed Lauren's mother, wondering for the millionth time why Sylvia couldn't have stayed in town *one* weekend. Then Macie went back onto Blind Friends.

Lauren didn't want to make a new dating app. There were enough of those out there. It was Ford's opinion that making friends was harder than finding true love. Of course, Lauren met Bradford Coleman at a freshman orientation party their second day on campus. Love at first sight and all that bullshit. Ford wanted a way to keep the users' profiles private, no way to upload photos. That way people could 'meet' and get to know each other before they met in person, if they chose to do so. Macie had not. Keeping with the spirit of the app, they had agreed not to exchange names or any personal information like her major. She only knew that her pen-pal was male. Other than that, he could be anybody on campus.

Macie opened the message and began reading

You mentioned not understanding football. I have a better question. Why do people golf? I don't get it. My father is a big golfer, but he's terrible at it. Whenever I go with him, and I have to go more than I wish, he spends most of his time in the sand traps rather than the green. Maybe that's the point. Golf itself is one big sand trap. You have to play to make deals in the business world. I wonder if you stepped onto a course and asked every golfer to take a lie detector test, how many would you catch lying about their love for the game?
Obviously, I'm not a fan.

But I digress. You also mentioned pets in your last message. I've never had one. I always thought I would be a dog person but reading about your love for your cat makes me wonder. Am I a cat person? I honestly don't know. Maybe one day I'll find out. But if I ever get a dog, I'm not taking him golfing.

Macie smiled. She'd told him about the cat her mother adopted when Macie was still a baby. Tabby died a little over a year ago, and her mom sunk into a deep depression. Over winter break, Macie adopted a kitten that looked nothing like Tabby and gave it to her mom for Christmas. Reba was her mother's constant companion, and the light that had dimmed in her mother's eyes started to return. Reba would never replace Tabby, but she could help heal her mom's heart.

She tapped on the screen to bring up the keyboard.

Macie glanced over to where Lauren stood with the salesperson. The shoe collection in front of them was vast, and Macie had no doubt Lauren would want to try on every pair. She should just go barefoot. It would be more natural, more Lauren than any shoe on the planet. Shaking her head, Macie began to type.

✐ ✐ ✐

Zac Sparks leaned on a golf club, waiting patiently for his father to putt. Of course, he had to be more patient than usual considering the circumstances. His dad was recovering from surgery, but he refused to miss their monthly outing. Gall bladder removal wasn't life threatening by any means. Zac would've happily skipped the game and taken his father out to eat, instead.

"He's moving pretty good," Ford Coleman said beside him.

"Yeah, not too bad." Zac watched as his father bent over the putter and took aim. Again. "His doc wouldn't be happy if he knew."

"Like father like son." Ford laughed and slapped Zac on the shoulder.

Zac shook his head and smiled. He'd broken his wrist during a drunken skateboarding flip sophomore year. They'd inserted a plate in his arm to make sure it healed. "That wasn't major surgery."

"No, but you were on enough pain meds to kill a horse. Didn't stop you from hitting the beer bong."

"Which I regretted." Zac tilted his head and stared at Ford. His friend was in an unusually good mood. Not that Ford wasn't in a good mood most days, but today more so than normal. "What's up with you, anyway? Win the lotto?"

Ford's grin widened. His perfect white teeth gleamed in the Louisiana sunlight. How many times had Zac wondered if Ford would've been better making it as an actor in California instead of studying music education and student counseling at Lafayette? Ford's dark hair and dark eyes were the current standard in LA. His demeanor reflected something calmer, more serene. As much as Zac knew Ford could trade off on his good looks, he also knew his friend's desire to teach music ran much deeper. Cuts in music departments across the country led Ford to tack on student counseling as a major. If he couldn't get a job teaching, he'd take care of the kids another way.

"Spill, buddy." Zac's father finally tapped the ball, sending it toward the hole but not in. A few swear words flew from the elder's mouth. Zac was the younger version of his father, except for the eyes. Both had dark blond hair and a square chin, but Zac had been blessed with his mother's light blue eyes. He saw his future whenever he stared at his father. It wasn't bad. "Dad might make this putt before noon."

"Lauren's trying on the dress." Ford's eyes lit up at the mere mention of his fiancée. "I've just been thinking about it. What she picked out. What she might look like."

It took everything in Zac's power not to roll his eyes. Ford was like a puppy who'd found his furever home when it came to Lauren Tamm. Since the day they met, she was all he ever talked about. Zac didn't want to admit that he was envious, but he was. Four years of dating and he hadn't even come close to looking at a girl the way Ford looked at Lauren.

"Macie went with her." Ford flipped his putter on top of his shoulder as he kept his eyes on Zac's dad. "She promised to send me pics if Lauren got out of line."

This time Zac didn't bother to hide his reaction. He scowled openly at the mention of Lauren's best friend. "That sounds like Macie, ruining everything. It's her M.O."

"Man, you guys are going to have to get along until the wedding. After that, you can hate each other all you want. At least until we have a kid." Ford turned toward him, all joviality gone. "You know you'll be my first kid's Godfather. And there's a good chance you'll share those duties with Mace."

Zac didn't know what to say to that. Best man at Ford's wedding, sure, no problem. Godfather to an unborn child? That was not something he'd ever planned. Or even thought of to be honest. The last time Zac stepped into a church was for his grandfather's funeral four years ago. "Wait. Lauren's not —"

"No, she's not. But we're going to have a family." Ford beamed again. A low rumble of jealousy filled Zac's gut. "Maybe in a few years if all goes well."

Zac swallowed hard. It wasn't like being a Godfather was being a parent. All he'd have to do was stand there when the kid got baptized. Right? Zac pulled out his phone to Google it. He hated being unprepared for anything. His gaze caught the Blind Friends app Ford and Lauren had created together. Another thing he hated to admit was that he was still talking to someone on there. And that he anticipated getting her messages the minute he sent his. Zac opened the app. A red number one appeared over the blue M of the mailbox. All thoughts of Godfatherhood disappeared. She'd replied.

"I thought you quit that last month," Ford said, peering over Zac's shoulder.

"Yeah, well…" Zac didn't bother to come up with any other excuse. He'd tried to quit, but when he went longer than a day without talking to *her*, he missed her. He didn't even know her name. It was stupid. He'd never even met this girl, if it even was a girl. What if he'd been talking to a guy for the last five months? The thought made him shudder. He shoved the phone back into his pocket and watched his dad pull the golf ball out of the hole.

"Meet her, Z. Just send a message to meet." Ford shoved his putter back into Zac's golf bag, a gift from his father at Christmas. "There's obviously something there."

"Maybe," Zac reluctantly admitted. In the four years they'd known each other, Ford had become the brother Zac never had. He loved his two younger half-sisters and would do anything for them, but Ford was what Zac imagined a brother would've been like. And Ford was the only person who knew Zac's dreams and fears. So, he had no problem sharing them now. "What if she's a he? What if she's ... a complete bitch in person? What if she's —"

"Perfect for you?" Ford shook his head. "Then wait. Don't meet her. Don't put yourself out there. Don't even try." Ford raised his eyebrows. "Quit before you get hurt. That's your norm."

Harsh words, but Zac knew brutal honesty was what he'd get. Ford didn't hold back his psychological mumbo jumbo. "Maybe after graduation."

Ford harrumphed, but he didn't say anything else as Zac's father strolled up to them. They moved onto safer conversations about investing and money. The two things both Zac and his father were good at. Ford had already let Zac start investing what little he could. When they entered the clubhouse for lunch, Zac sat at the table alone while Ford hit the restroom and his dad talked to some friends at another table. He pulled out his phone and opened the app.

Dogs are great, too. I never had one, though, so I can't say if I'm a dog person for sure. But I'd be more than willing to try. Maybe I should get one this summer to run with. Or not to run with but to hang out with or something. What do people do with dogs? I see them walking all the time and running, but do dogs plop across your lap like cats? Wouldn't it be like having a kid in animal form? Maybe I won't get a dog. Sounds like a lot of responsibility and life is crazy busy with everything.

I'm graduating this spring. I know we agreed not to give details about our lives too much, but since we both go to Lafayette and around a thousand people are getting their diplomas, this little bit of information shouldn't be much of a surprise. Wow, that was a ramble. I'm not deleting it, though.

The truth is, and I haven't even shared this with anybody, not even my best friend. The truth is, I am terrified. What if I made a huge mistake in my major? What if I take the wrong job? What if I move into the wrong apartment? What if I fail?

That last one, that's the kicker. What if I fail?

I don't want to fail. But does anybody?

Zac reread the message. Ford was right; he needed to meet this person. Even if she ended up being only a friend, he needed to have this girl in his life. But he didn't want to rush into it blind. He wanted to wait until the right moment. With less than a month to go in the semester, he had too much going on. He wanted to meet her, just not yet.

Just not yet. That was his new mantra. He wasn't too crazy about it either.

CHAPTER TWO

Macie stepped out of the arts building into the heat. She'd spent all weekend talking to Lauren about the wedding, and she'd never been happier to go back to class on Monday. It was wedding-overload.

It wasn't technically summer, but Mother Nature gave zero shits about the seasons in Louisiana. It was either mildly hot, hot, or oh-hell-no hot. That was all they got. Not that Macie complained too much. She'd rather have hot than a blizzard.

Her phone buzzed in her hand.

Come over around nine. Lauren was always polite when she wanted Macie to come over. This was more of a command. That meant something was up. Macie texted back that she'd be there.

It was only twelve-thirty. Her work study at the library started at one. She had to walk across campus to her dorm and drop off her bag. Hopefully her bitch of a roommate would be nowhere in sight. Macie had lucked out with Lauren through her junior year. When Lauren and Ford decided to share an apartment for their senior year, Macie got screwed. Jackie had been a nightmare since day one. She was messy, loud, and had no problem putting a white towel on the doorknob when she was screwing the basketball team. Macie couldn't care less about who Jackie entertained, but it made it almost impossible for Macie to get anything done in her own room. She'd spent far too much time at the library these past two semesters.

"Hey, Mace. Wait up," a voice shouted behind her.

She turned around and smiled. Kyle Capshaw was in most of her classes. Like her, his major was graphic design. Unlike her, he wasn't that great at it. Also unlike her, he already had a job. She hadn't figured that one out yet. Then again, Macie was holding out hope that her internship at Rivot Design would turn into an offer. Macie wasn't afraid of a gamble. She'd only applied to Lafayette, knowing she'd get in. She just knew in her heart that Rivot Design was where she belonged. She was all-in, even if it wasn't the smartest move.

"What's up?" Macie asked as Kyle fell into step beside her.

"Can you believe we're almost done?" He huffed as if the short distance between them had stolen his breath. Kyle wasn't exactly in shape. His form leaned more toward basement dweller than athlete, but over the last few years he'd started to trim down, and his face cleared up. His glasses even shrunk in size to something more fashionable than the Coke bottles he wore that covered his pale green eyes.

Macie chided herself for being so damn judgmental. "Crazy, right?"

Kyle nodded and shot a glance at her from the corner of his eye. She knew that look. Too well. He'd asked her out twice this semester. He was due. Sometimes she wondered if he asked because he had also asked out Meghan Hanson, another graphic design major. Meghan also shot him down multiple times. She shook it off, though. Kyle wasn't that big of a dick.

"So, what're you doing later?" His voice hitched on the last word. Hope filled his face, making her smile.

What could it hurt? One date. That's all he ever asked. In a few weeks, they'd probably never see each other again. And he wasn't *that* bad. He was sweet, kind of like a lost kitten. "I'm heading over to the library for a shift now." She paused as his face dropped. "But I'll be free later. Coffee?"

Kyle's eyes widened. "Serious?"

"As a heart attack." She stopped in the middle of the sidewalk and put a hand on his forearm. "Java Junkies at eight?"

"I was thinking something more … date-like." Kyle dipped his head as a blush covered his cheeks. "Dinner? I'll pick you up at seven, and we can go to Peking Palace?"

That was a little more commitment than Macie wanted to make, but why the hell not? It wasn't like she had any other plans. Except to stay home and message a virtual stranger on Blind Friends. Of course, that was more complicated than her friendship with Kyle. Over the last week, she'd thought about nothing other than meeting Guy, as she'd started calling him. They'd been communicating for months. Why shouldn't they meet? It wasn't like she didn't want to. But it was that fear of failure buried deep inside her. The same fear she'd already shared. She didn't want to fail with him.

Kyle smiled as worry crossed over his face.

"Sounds good," she said at last. A night out wouldn't kill her. She could just pretend it wasn't a real date, because it wasn't really, and be friends with a nice guy. "But I'm paying for myself."

"Great. I'll pick you up then." Kyle back away. A huge grinned covered his face. "Oh, and Macie, I miss the purple hair."

Macie faked a smile and realized her mistake. He'd want another date. Then another. Then another. That was something she couldn't give him. Not that Macie didn't want a boyfriend. It wasn't in the cards for her. Just like her mom who'd raised Macie on her own and never asked anyone for help after her biological father split when Macie barely had a heartbeat. Macie never knew him. She never wanted to either.

Besides, there was Guy. The messages between them were more real than any relationship she'd ever had. Even if he wasn't real. Well, real in a virtual way, and Macie knew he was flesh and blood, but it was easier to think of him as code sometimes. That kept him at a safe distance. Sometimes it felt like he was programmed for her and her alone.

She wanted to learn more about Guy. Kyle wasn't even slightly interesting. God, she felt like such an asshole for accepting. Macie glanced toward where he had gone. She should cancel. In the two minutes since she accepted, he'd disappeared.

Her phone buzzed. She glanced at the message and almost laughed.

Are you seriously going out w/ Kyle? Lauren asked.

Let me guess. Facebook? Macie texted back.

Twitter. Lauren added a winky emoji.

Word gets around fast. Yes, but I will be at your place by nine. Macie hit send and checked the time. She was going to be late for work.

Zac washed his hands and stared at himself in the bathroom mirror. He had a date tonight. The problem was he wasn't sure if he wanted to get out of it or not. Emily's legs stretched longer than the Pacific Coast Highway and were just as gorgeous. She was an all-American blond hair, blue eyed bombshell. They'd met at a bar a few weeks ago and he'd asked her out then. If he really wanted to admit it, he'd been a little drunk and had felt rejected by his pen-pal. Which was stupid. She hadn't responded to his message, and he felt dumped. To make it worse, when he got home after his debauchery, there was a message waiting for him about her love of cats. He didn't even know his mystery girl, and yet, she knew him on a deep level. Even if she wasn't aware of it.

His. He needed to stop calling her that.

The doorbell rang, and he closed his eyes. To make his current situation worse, Macie had arrived at Lauren and Ford's apartment. That woman infuriated him just by being in the same room. Unfortunately, she was Lauren's best friend and her maid of honor. He shook off his doubt and strolled down the short hall just in time to see Macie step past the door. She may piss him off, but she was damn fine to look at. Her cinnamon brown hair flowed around her elegant face and highlighted her brown eyes. Macie Regan exuded darkness, but her smile brightened an entire room. When he'd first met her, he thought she was perfect with her exotic looks and purple hair. He thought she'd be fun and exciting. Her personality shot down that theory.

"Great," he said, stuffing his hands into the pockets of his jeans. "Gang's all here. How's it going, Chomper?"

"Peachy keen." Macie's gaze iced over as Zac shot her a fiery glare. "Thanks for the warning, Lauren."

Lauren held up her hands. "If I told you he was going to be here, you would've made any excuse to get out of coming over. Besides, this involves both of you."

She sat beside Ford on the couch. That left their loveseat open. Zac preferred to stand. He leaned against the wall. "Then let's get on with it. I've got plans."

Macie rolled her eyes. "You say that like you're the only one." She shook her head, and Zac admired the way her hair swung around like a shampoo commercial. Macie turned her attention back to her friend.

"Wait, didn't you have a date?" Lauren asked, her face lighting up. "Tell."

"No," Macie snapped. Her olive skin reddened with a blush. Zac knew that look. He'd seen Macie get embarrassed more than once. "Move on."

"Oh, if you won't tell, I'll find out on my own." Lauren pulled out her phone and pressed a few buttons. Macie didn't try to stop her, much to Zac's surprise. Lauren's mouth twisted in disgust. "What an asshole."

"Drop it, Lauren," Macie snapped again, her eyes darkening.

"I can't believe he stood you up," Lauren said, ignoring Macie's order.

"Who?" Ford asked just as Zac let out a laugh.

Everyone turned to Zac. Wisely, he ducked his head, but he couldn't stop laughing inside. Macie didn't date very often since their sophomore year. Sure, she flirted a lot, but she rarely made serious plans with a guy. She wouldn't have agreed unless it was a sure thing. Zac knew he shouldn't laugh, but he couldn't help it. Macie hadn't stopped laughing in his face when a date stood him up before Thanksgiving last year. Zac had resigned himself to drinking alone at Hoof, a local bar near campus, only to find Macie serving drinks behind the bar. And she had laughed hard at him. A pillow hit him in the chest.

"Fuck off, Zac," Macie said. Her voice held all the anger she could muster as tears rimmed her eyes. He almost apologized, but Macie turned away from him and stared at Lauren. "Just tell us what's going on so I can get the hell out of here."

Lauren and Ford glanced at each other. Zac hated their silent conversations. And he envied them. They also had the kind of relationship only seen on TV. He'd heard them argue, but never fight. He'd seen them at a standstill, but they always found a compromise. Every flaw of Lauren's was treated as a quirk for Ford. And Ford's flaws just meant he was human for Lauren. They saw the bad in each other and loved anyway.

Ford cleared his throat. "We want ... look, we know as best man and maid of honor, you're in charge of the bachelor —"

"And bachelorette—"

"—parties." Ford shrugged and glanced at Lauren. "We'd like to have ours together."

Zac glanced at Macie, watching her already tense body as it wound even tighter. She swallowed hard but put on her obvious fake smile she wore like a badge of honor.

"If that's what you want," Macie said.

Lauren relaxed and slipped her hand onto Ford's knee. "Thank you."

Zac hadn't said anything yet, and he didn't really plan on chiming in. The deal was already done. He just had to make the best of it. Which, in his opinion, meant letting Macie do whatever Lauren wanted. He'd stay out of the way.

"Z?" Ford asked. Lauren stared at Zac with concern and determination. There was no way she wasn't getting this. Ford's expression remained hopeful. If he wanted a joint bachelor/bachelorette party, Zac had no clue. For Ford, Lauren's happiness was all that mattered. "You in?"

Zac felt Macie's gaze burning into his skin, but he wasn't stupid enough to look at her. "If Chomper's in, I'm in."

"Stop calling me that," Macie whispered in a low growl.

A smile tugged at his lips. "Never."

Then she punched him. His upper arm throbbed where she'd hit him. He wanted to rub it, but that would mean admitting she'd hurt him. Never going to happen.

"You should get your money back from that dojo," Zac said, turning toward her until her face was eye level to his chest. He loved that Macie was half a foot shorter. Not that anything intimidated her, but she hated people making an issue of her height. He bent down, resting his hands on his knees, and spoke to her like the errant toddler she could be. "It's clear you can't throw a punch to save your ass."

Macie pulled her arm back, but Ford grabbed it and spun her toward him and away from Zac. Ford glared at his best friend. Zac felt bad for about two seconds, give or take, but no more. Just last week Macie had announced how small he was in front of a girl he was on the verge of asking out. The girl giggled and cut out faster than a cheetah toward an antelope. Macie smiled and strolled away, swinging her hips a little extra just for him. Okay, he may have imagined the extra swagger.

"Why do you guys insist on provoking each other?" Ford asked as Macie pushed past him, leaving Ford the only person between her and Zac.

Lauren rose from the couch and stood beside her future husband. "We hate it."

"Hate's a strong word," Ford said gently.

"No, not in this case." Lauren grabbed Macie's hand and pulled her toward Zac. "We've put up with this for almost four years." Lauren glanced between them. Macie avoided her friend's gaze, and by default, Zac's. "I don't care what happens after the wedding. You guys can avoid each other as much as you want. But for now, at least learn how to fake getting along." Lauren squeezed Macie's shoulder. "Mace, you've been more than my best friend. You've been my sister, and I can't stand the thought that you'd let Zac come between us."

"What?" Macie roared. The lioness had returned. Zac enjoyed the way her face lit up with indignation. "That's ridiculous."

"Is it?" Lauren remained calm, but her hands shook in front of her. "Are you going to avoid me for the rest of your life?" She pointed at Zac, and Macie's gaze followed her finger. "Zac knew you were coming tonight, but that didn't stop him from showing up."

"He's the one who started all this," Macie snapped.

"Whoa, whoa, whoa." Zac put his hands up in defense. "I didn't start anything. You did, Chomper."

Macie turned her fiery gaze at him, sending Zac back a step. "Stop. Calling. Me. That."

"Look, guys," Ford said, always playing the intermediary. He put one hand on Macie's shoulder and the other on Zac's. "We're not asking you to become friends, just be friendly. No more hitting." Macie raised her eyebrows. "No more name calling." Zac smirked. He loved calling her Chomper. It pissed her off. "No more anger. Just … fake it if you have to. After the wedding, you can go back to hating each other. Okay?"

"Sure," Zac said, offering his hand to Macie.

Macie scoffed, but she didn't agree or disagree.

"Come on, Macie," Zac said. "It can be their wedding present."

Macie dropped her hands to her sides and stared at the ceiling. "Fine."

Then her gaze fell to meet his. Zac saw the passion, the hatred, and the anger. He hated to admit that he admired anything about her, but her passion for life was one thing he couldn't deny. Macie gripped his hand, shaking it firmly. The contact was brief, but Zac noted the silk of palm and the soft callouses on her fingers. His pulsed kicked up a notch, but he shook it off. Macie had surprised him by conceding. It was a rare occurrence.

There were two things Zac was certain of in that moment: it was either going to be fun or it was going to be a nightmare, but Lauren and Ford would never know which.

CHAPTER THREE

The waiter was more interesting than Emily, or was it Emma? Zac couldn't remember, and he'd picked her up for their date ten minutes ago. And this girl was smoking. She was athletic and defined just enough without being overly built. Her blond hair hung down her back, and her blue eyes were wide like she'd just downed five energy drinks. Except that she was always in constant wonder. God blessed her body, but not her brain. She agreed with everything he said to the point he started making bold, and utterly false, statements.

"Did you see that UFO last night?" he'd asked.

Emily's smile dropped for a moment before returning. "Yes? Over the north end of town?" She slapped the table excitedly, knocking over her empty water glass. Her gaze dropped to the glass and she giggled. "Wasn't that amazing?"

"Yeah," Zac said, dragging the word out. She either really saw a UFO or she faked it well. If she was faking it, she deserved an award. "So…" He thought about his pen-pal and a real smile crossed his face. "Dogs or cats?"

"Both?" Emily sat the water glass back upright.

"Is that a question?" Zac asked. Emily's eyebrows rolled together like a Shar Pei. Zac shook his head and glanced around the generic chain restaurant he'd brought her to. The walls were lined with imitation antiques. It was like the chain took the restaurant out of a box and plopped it in an empty lot. Instant food and money. This wasn't his best move, but he couldn't get a reservation as his go-to place. Plus this was close to campus. "Do you prefer cats, or do you prefer dogs?"

Her lips thinned into a stressed line. "What do you prefer?"

"I…" Zac shook his head. What did it matter what he preferred? He wanted her opinion. Giving up on this conversation, he pulled his phone out of his pocket and stared at the locked screen. "I'm sorry. I need to take this. Will you excuse me?" He stood from the table and pretended to answer the call. "Hey, Ford. What's up?"

Guilt twisted in his gut. The right thing to do would've been to tell her outright that it wasn't going to work, but that was also the hard thing to do. Zac stopped at the bar and leaned against it, nodding at Emily when she glanced his way. She waved her fingers. Zac faked a large smile before turning his back to her.

"Need a drink?" the bartender said.

Zac grimaced. "No, an escape route. Got one of those?"

The bartender glanced over Zac's shoulder. "From her? You're nuts. She's ripe."

Zac followed his gaze. Emily sat with perfect posture and reapplied her lipstick using a silver compact. "Yeah, I know."

"Just tell her work called—"

Zac faced the bartender again. "I'm in college. No job until after graduation."

"Okay then, one, you're a lucky sonofabitch, and, two, tell her one of your parents needs something." The bartender shrugged then leaned closer. "Whatever lie you spill, make sure you tell her your buddy Mick," he pointed at his name tag, "will take her home when his shift ends."

Zac glanced back at Emily. He could use his dad's recent surgery as a reason to bolt. But that wasn't right. And he certainly wasn't leaving Emily behind with a complete stranger. Although, what the hell did he know about her? They'd met once and Zac got her number. They didn't even text or chat before dinner. Zac knew nothing about her other than she was a sponge who soaked up information to please him. He wanted a challenge. He wanted someone with their own opinions.

He let his phone drop from his ear and stared at the screen. The Blind Friends app glared at him. A white box with a blue, shadow boxed B and F had a prominent place on his front screen. He pressed the icon. A list of suggested friends popped up, but his gaze moved to the upper right corner where the envelope was. No new messages. He hadn't heard from her since yesterday. It was insane to think she'd get back to him with any sense of immediacy. They didn't even know each other for crying out loud.

Then a red one appeared, and his heart slipped into overdrive.

Zac knew it was time to go. He headed back to his table with a swift nod to Mick.

"Everything okay?" Emily asked, her doe eyes seemed concerned, but Zac wasn't sure.

"Yeah," he motioned to the waiter as he passed. "Check please?"

Emily's smile turned sultry. "Your place or mine?"

He slipped into his seat. *She is so clueless.* He debated how to answer that when the waiter appeared like an apparition with the check. "Hold please," Zac said as he pulled his wallet out of his pocket and put the credit card into the black bi-fold. He didn't even look at the bill. Zac rolled his finger in a circle to indicate he was in a hurry and the waiter nodded.

"Well?" Emily asked. She squeezed his thigh under the table.

"Not here." Zac pulled his leg away from her firm grip.

"But later?" Her head dipped, and she stared at him through her lashes.

Jesus, maybe she just wants to get laid. Not that there was anything wrong with that. People had needs. Zac started this evening with that possibility in mind. He knew she wasn't anything more than a one or two date deal when he asked her out. Clearly she felt the same way. But there wasn't even a twitch from him. Not an ounce of desire.

His phone vibrated in his pocket. It wasn't *her.* That wasn't how the app worked, but the idea it could've been sent his heart ablaze. He'd have to meet his mystery girl. Sooner rather than later. Zac took his phone from his pocket as if it was something important. Just a text from Lauren about the tuxes. Nothing that couldn't wait.

The waiter brought back the card. Zac signed the receipt, giving a twenty percent tip. "Let's go," he said to Emily.

She followed him out of the restaurant. "Slow down, tiger. We'll get there."

Zac kept his face forward, so she wouldn't see him roll his eyes. He must be an idiot to pass up a quick lay. She was willing, and no doubt ready. He could probably just push her against his car, have his way with her, then send her home in a cab before they even left the parking lot. He unlocked his car and turned to face her.

"This isn't going to happen," he said without a single hint of remorse.

"Excuse me?" Emily stepped up to him, pressing her hand against his crotch. He stepped back, but her fingers squeezed too hard. Zac winced. He didn't want her touching him at all. Her pretty mouth dipped down into a frown. "You're soft."

Zac swiveled his hips to free himself from her grasp. "You're a nice girl, but—"

"Seriously?" She stuck her hip out and glared at him. The sweet innocence from the restaurant disappeared when they left. The come-and-take-me expression she wore shifted into full rage mode. Anger turned her ugly. "I went along with your stupid bullshit all night, and you shut me down now?"

Where had this vixen been all night? She had passion, flare, and style. The Emily he'd had dinner with was nothing but a facade. He preferred the real one standing in front of him. But it was too late. He'd already discovered her secret. She'd do whatever it took to get what she wanted, including faking her personality. He didn't need that kind of headache in his life.

"You know what? Whatever." She turned on her heel and stalked back toward the restaurant. "I saw at least four guys in that restaurant who'd love to spend the night with me. I'll go rock their world instead."

All four? he wanted to ask. But he really didn't want to know. "Don't forget Mick the bartender. He said he'd take care of you."

She flipped him off above her head but didn't bother to glance back. Zac shrugged as he opened his door and slid into the seat. It was no skin off his nose. Where did that saying come from anyway? He never really understood it, but he knew the minute he got home he'd Google it. Stupid things like that nagged at him until he had the answer. Last fall he had a date who kept saying 'peachy keen'. It drove him nuts until he looked it up online and got into the etymology of the saying. Unfortunately, his timing wasn't exactly peachy keen. The girl stormed out of his bedroom and he never heard from her again.

To make matters worse, Ford told Lauren and Lauren told Macie who used it every single time she had a chance. Like she had earlier in the night.

He drove a few blocks to The Grove neighborhood. His father hated all things considered hipster, but Zac didn't mind. It was simply old-school thinking on his dad's part. Besides this section of town had the best craft beers around. As much as Zac liked a good bar scene, Crafts Cafe was the opposite. It was more like a coffee shop with relaxing music, mismatched furniture, and bistro tables. There wasn't even a bar.

Zac parked in the lot behind the building. He'd learned before that his Nissan Armada, in serrano red, stood out by the ten notes on his windshield about environmental consciousness and driving. It wasn't a gas guzzler, but it was still a big bad SUV. His father had given it to him for his high school graduation. It wasn't Zac's first choice, but who was he to look a gift horse in the mouth? Zac loved the history, or lack thereof, of that cliché. It was also one of the first he researched.

Crafts was busy as usual. There were soft murmurs of conversation and waitresses quietly navigating the large dining room like ninjas. Solo guitar music played through the speakers, and the lighting was soft and warm. Not too dark, not too bright. Everything about the cafe whispered 'just chill with us'. Zac loved it. He spotted an open table in the corner and headed toward it. He set his tablet on the menu mat just as someone else did the same.

"Not you," a too familiar voice said.

Zac looked up and stared into the eyes of his worst nightmare, Macie Regan.

✐ ✐ ✐

Macie had come to Crafts to plan a new mixed media piece and drown herself in an overpriced beer. She needed some form of distraction after Kyle stood her up. After she had left Lauren's, she went on Kyle's Instagram. Probably the same thing Lauren had done. Kyle had posted a selfie with Meghan Hanson. He'd gotten the real target. Macie had just been a means to an end.

Crafts was one of her favorite new places. She loved the ambiance of the place, even though most of the beer was shit. There was an ale she didn't mind. Besides, she wanted to get used to this area. She was still waiting patiently for a job offer at Rivot Design. They *had* to hire her. She hadn't applied anywhere else. Rivot was innovative, state-of-the-art, and open. The environment was everything she wanted in a job. And they'd given her rave reviews when her internship ended. There was no way they wouldn't make an offer before graduation. The internship had been enlightening. She thought she fit in with the other designers.

The Grove was the best neighborhood within walking distance, and that would save money in the long run. She'd spent the last few hours looking at apartments online. Most were out of her price range. One was not. She'd printed out the application for residency, dropped it off at the building manager's office, and now just wanted a quiet place to sit down and draw plans for a new piece of art.

So why was Zac Sparks here? This was not his country-club style.

"Hey, Chom—"

She glared up at him, and he grimaced.

"Sorry, Macie." Zac's expression never changed. It was always set at cocky asshole, which was too bad. He was a sexy cocky asshole. His dark blond hair always looked like he'd just rolled out of bed. And those eyes, most women would kill for those bright blue eyes, and plenty paid extra for contacts to fake them. Her neck strained as she stared up at him. He was at least half a foot taller than her, and she loved tall guys. If only he didn't have such a shit personality.

"Just go," Macie said as she sat down. To her horror, Zac joined her. "What're you doing?"

Zac scoffed. He pointed around the room. "There isn't another table, so I'm sitting here. You're more than welcome to wait for a different one to open up."

Macie closed her eyes and pinched her nose. Lauren wanted them to get along. At least until the wedding was over. This was a good place to start. Macie opened her eyes and stared at Zac until he shifted in his chair. "Just be quiet."

"Ditto." Zac opened the blue case of his tablet, ignoring her completely. She glanced over to see what was on his screen, but he had it turned so she wasn't able to snoop. "And no hacking."

"What makes you think I'm going to hack into your..." She waved at his tablet, "what type is that, anyway?"

"It's an iPad. Why?" He tapped on the Bluetooth keyboard without looking at her.

"The latest version?" She wanted to take it from him and play with the features. Macie loved technology, but anything that would improve her future as a graphic designer was something she longed to get her hands on. At this rate, she'd be able to buy his at a pawn shop in a few years.

"Yes, why?" Zac stopped typing and glared at her.

Jealousy and disappointment battled for dominance. She went with jealousy, her voice sandpaper on her throat. "Lucky you. Must be nice that Daddy buys you everything you want."

Zac's gaze shot to hers. "It was a gift from my stepmother."

"You had a perfectly good iPad." Macie knew she was whining and on the verge of a toddler-esque tantrum, but she hated that her mother worked her ass off just to survive whereas someone like Zac got everything handed to him.

"Yes, I know. And I gave that to Ford." Zac leaned over his screen. His eyebrows furrowed in irritation. "Despite what you might think of me, Mace, I'm not a complete jerk."

"Everyone has their peachy keen moments." Macie sneered. Her blood boiled at his privilege. Giving his old iPad to Ford was a decent thing, but they were best friends. He wouldn't do that for just anybody. She was certain he had an entire closet at his parents' house stocked full of laptops, tablets, and computers she could use or donate. There were plenty of students at Lafayette who could use them. She'd even started a campus-wide computer charity her sophomore year to get the tech into the hands of students who needed them.

"They do, Chomper." Zac's face remained blank despite her little jab.

"I told you not to call me that." Macie's anger burned beneath her skin.

"Then stop using peachy keen."

"Fine." The one thing she held over him was something she didn't really believe happened. Who would stop in the middle of sex to look up a catch phrase? But she never knew the truth. Friends tell each other the truth. And they were pretending to be friends so maybe that was close enough. "Did that really happen?"

"What?" Zac had refocused on his screen.

24

"The peachy keen thing."

Zac's face twisted into ultra-asshole.

"Did you really stop in the middle of screwing Amanda Billard to Google?"

"What?" Zac's laugh erupted, and several people turned to glare at him. He held up his hand to apologize then faced Macie. "Is that what Lauren told you?"

Macie's face burned, and she hoped the dim light kept him from seeing her blush. "Yeah."

"No, that's not what happened. I had the decency to make sure she was ... satisfied before I Googled. She still wasn't ... pleased. She expected more, I guess." Zac shook his head and went back to whatever he was working on.

Macie watched him for a few seconds until she decided that was stalkerish and opened a spreadsheet about the wedding shower. Zac's presence had sucked the creativity out of her so she figured she might as well focus on something else. Lauren hated white, and the colors for the wedding were light pink and black. She had the guest list, the invitations, and a list of party games for the wedding shower. What she needed were decorations. Crafts didn't have free Wi-Fi, but she'd cracked their password two weeks ago on the first try. Nine letters, microbeer, and they hadn't even bothered with numbers or making sure it was case sensitive.

"Macie?" Zac asked quietly. She glanced up, meeting his gaze. "Did you figure out the password?"

"I would never—"

"Liar." Zac's eyes brightened with mischief. Macie's pulse sped up. If this Zac was around more, she probably wouldn't hate him as much. "My service isn't working great. Can I get a little help?"

"Despite what *you* might think, I'm not a hacker."

"But Lauren taught you her trick on how to figure out Wi-Fi passwords." Zac raised his eyebrows.

Macie held out her hand and Zac handed over the tablet. She ran her fingers over the small keyboard, envious of the damn thing still. Zac didn't need such a perfect computer. Top of the line, too. Not just the newest model, but a fully loaded new model. Lauren was the IT geek, but Macie could still appreciate a fine machine. Zac didn't need it, not with a career in finance. Lauren needed it more. Hell, so did Macie. She shook off the thoughts. Not wanting to get into another argument, she typed in the password and handed it back. Lauren asked her to play nice. She could do that. She *wanted* to do that.

"Thank you."

"You're welcome."

Macie shook her head and opened the Blind Friends app, instead. Guy, as she called him, had written that morning. With all the wedding planning, job hunting, and her finals she had shot back a brief note, but he hadn't responded yet. He'd lamented about a fishing spot he enjoyed as a kid and how he longed to get back there. She understood why he hadn't been there for a while. College was a lot of work. The cabin actually sounded romantic. As she reread his note, she imagined a cool winter night in front of a roaring fire, just the two of them on the floor with a blanket covering their naked bodies.

Problem was she didn't know what he looked like. Each daydream involving her mystery man conjured up a different look for him. One day he was blond, the next ginger or brunette. Once he was bald, and it was sexy. He was always taller than her, but his build varied between muscular and slightly less muscular. She had a thing for a nice set of pecs. She only hoped her imagination wouldn't leave her disappointed in the end.

Macie clicked reply to his message and began to type a more detailed response.

Do you ever feel like you're utterly alone? That there is not one person on this planet who gets you? Or, if there is, they live on the opposite side of the world?

My best friend is fantastic, but sometimes she doesn't understand where I'm coming from. Her life has been so different from mine. There are times we both forget that and then something reminds us. For fictional example (since we promised no details about our lives), she was given a car for her sixteenth birthday. It was a few years old, but it was an amazing car. I was given a spare key to my mother's beat up truck.

Macie grimaced at her lie but not-lie. Sure she told Guy it was fiction, and a small part of it was. The part that Lauren's car was a few years old. Everything else was true.

I loved that truck. But what would it have felt like to get a car? Or anything for that matter? My mom did her best, but there wasn't enough to go around. That might be too much detail, but there have to be plenty of people who were raised by just their mom. On campus, I mean. It's just a way to show the difference between me and my friend. Her parents are happily married. The whole American dream thing with a white picket fence and two-point-five kids seems like a myth.

Is there really someone out there who's my soulmate? Does that really exist?

Sorry to get so philosophical, but I'm in deep-thought mode. It's one thing that drives people crazy about me. Well, that and my constant sarcasm. I don't deny it. I have a sharp tongue and a quick wit. Someday I'll learn to use it for good instead of evil. ;)

Your cabin sounds like a small piece of heaven. I can tell you love it. It's too bad we tend to let life get in the way of living, you know? I hope you get there sooner rather than later.

Macie reread her message. She hadn't gotten this emotional in anything she'd sent him before, but melancholy had been her friend the last few hours. Especially since Lauren and Ford asked her to get along with Zac.

If she was going to offer to meet Guy in the next few weeks, then she needed him to see this side of her. His reaction would be the tipping point of their anonymity. If his response didn't feel genuine to her, she'd keep it platonic. If it felt real, she'd offer to meet him.

Everything was riding on his response.

Macie ordered another microbrew, the strongest on the menu. She needed the liquid courage. Then she hit send.

CHAPTER FOUR

Zac read her second message. The first had been a blow off note, but then a second lengthier one came in while he sat at Crafts. He read it again. Then again. Each time his pulse kicked it up a notch. As much as he wanted to respond immediately, doing so with Macie sitting across from him felt wrong. This was intimate. Most of what they'd written had been just skimming the surface of their personalities, but mystery girl had opened a vein and let herself bleed. He'd wanted to shout 'Yes, and I'm right here' but that wouldn't have gone over well at Crafts. Or any other place for that matter.

He looked at his half-finished pint. Eight bucks for something that tasted like gym socks. What a waste. At least he'd tried something new this time. Zac was a creature of habit. He wore the same brand of underwear as long as he could remember. He woke up at the same time almost every day. He drank the same beer since he tried it at fourteen. Everything had a place, and everything was in its place.

One of the last lines of mystery girl's letter came back to him.

It's too bad we tend to let life get in the way of living, you know?

Was that what he'd been doing? He'd made an effort to try new things lately. His last girlfriend had told him he was stale. He'd laughed at her, but over the last few months her words haunted him. He went to a Thai restaurant, tried a yoga class, and even went to a clothing optional party a couple of towns over. Each was a fail, at least by Zac's standards. The Thai food was too spicy, the yoga too

28

boring. And the party, well, the party wasn't what he'd expected. He preferred meeting people with their clothes on. He liked the mystery, the discovery as he took each article off one piece at a time until the blessed fleshy reveal. Besides, staring was rude and near impossible not to do when everyone was already naked.

Zac glanced at Macie. She was lost in her world of who knew what. Probably the wedding. The only thing he'd ever liked about her, besides her body, was her loyalty to Lauren. If he was honest with Macie, he'd confess that he thought she was gay for the first year. Actually, he thought Macie was in love with Lauren. When Macie dated a football player during sophomore year, Zac realized he'd been wrong.

Macie sighed and closed her laptop. She left it on the table as she scurried toward the restrooms.

He leaned back in his chair and started his response.

I've been contemplating this for a long time, myself. If I hadn't seen true commitment, true compatibility, true (dare I say it) love in person, I probably would agree more with you. My parents are one example. My grandparents another. And I have a few friends who are so madly in tune with their significant other that there are times they just don't speak. They have these mental conversations and it drives me insane. Not just because I don't have a clue what's going on, but, to be brutally honest, because I'm jealous.

The truth is I've been looking for her, for the proverbial ONE, and I haven't met *her yet. But I know she's out there.*

As for the cabin, you're right. I need to get there soon. It's only a few hours away, and I could use a break from the reality of life about now. Maybe I'll take off this weekend, spend some time with the wilderness. It wouldn't hurt to stay away from the internet, either. LOL

It's time I start living more and going through life less.

I'll start, though, with this.

When can we meet?

Zac's finger hovered over his screen. He wanted to send it. He wanted to meet her and see if she was everything he believed her to be. But what if she wasn't? What if she was nothing like her online self?

Out of the corner of his eye, he spied Macie stalking toward him. It was now or never. He pressed the screen behind the question mark and deleted the last two sentences. He meant what he said. He needed to start trying new things like the warm gym sock microbrew he had been sipping for half an hour. Maybe step one was getting along with Macie. A sort of redemption.

Before Macie sat down, he pressed send.

"So, how're we going to do this bachelor/bachelorette party?" he said the minute her butt met the chair.

Macie glared at him over her own monitor. "Let me get through this week and planning the bridal shower. Then we'll talk. I'll show you everything I've already gotten done."

"Thought we were supposed to do it together?"

"In theory, but I'd already started working on it." Macie held her fingers over her keyboard, her gaze intent on the screen. He marveled at her new look. Macie had always colored her hair in crazy ways, whether it was completely red or streaked with purple. But, since the beginning of the semester, she'd gone back to her natural cinnamon brown. And she had started dressing less like a skater girl and more like an adult. He wasn't sure it suited her. "Just let me figure out a few things, Zac. I'll get back to you, okay?"

Zac flashed his best smile. In return all she did was glare.

This was going to be harder than he thought.

✒ ✒ ✒

Relief flooded Macie's bones when Zac excused himself and left. She'd made a cardinal mistake. She'd left her laptop unguarded when she rushed to the restroom. He didn't get in. Well, she didn't think he got passed her PIN number, but his sudden pleasantness twisted inside her. There hadn't been a day in the last four years that Zac hadn't tortured her in some way, shape, or form. And if he ever called her Chomper again, it would be his last word on earth.

The memory was as raw as fresh rug burn. Macie had let her new roomie dress her in a too tight skirt and a shirt that barely buttoned around her breasts for the freshman mixer. She hated it. Macie was more of a jeans, t-shirt, flip-flops kind of girl. Not that she was opposed to skirts or tight shirts, but Lauren was more money than style. Macie wanted to get along with Lauren, so she caved. They weren't at the party for five minutes when Macie spotted the hottest guy she'd ever seen. He was tall, blond, and had a California surfer appeal about him.

She'd nudged Lauren. "Wing me?"

"Huh?" Lauren had tilted her head. Her eyebrows rolled together, meeting in the middle.

Macie had fought the high school eye roll. She was in college now. College girls didn't eye roll. "Be my wing girl?" Macie had nodded toward the blond. "You know? Help me pick him up."

"Oh," Lauren had said as it dawned on her. "Okay. Got it."

Macie led the way, snaking through the crowd and never taking her eyes off her target. He stood with someone, smiling and talking. Clearly an old friend, in Macie's opinion. Macie made snap judgments based on his body language. He was smart, confident, and had an easy smile. Getting to know him wouldn't be too difficult. That was all she was after anyway. Well, for the moment. If it led to something later, even an hour later, she was fine with that, too.

Lauren had tripped, falling into Macie who in turn fell into the hot guy. Her face burned as he grabbed her arms, but it was too late. She'd lost any sense of cool she had tried to emit.

"Ow," he said, pushing her off him. He grabbed his lower arm and rubbed. "Did you just bite me?"

Macie's hand shot to her mouth. Her teeth throbbed from the impact. "I'm so sorry. I didn't —"

Lauren laughed along with everyone else in the vicinity, but Macie just wanted to sink through the floor. "I'm Lauren," she said to the blond.

"Zac," he said. He pointed to his friend. "This is Ford." Zac's steel blue gaze met Macie's. "And you must be Chomper."

Even now, Macie's face burned at the memory. The funny thing was it was Lauren's fault and she never even realized it. She was too busy fawning over Ford to remember what had happened. If Lauren hadn't tripped, and hadn't pushed Macie into Zac, things might've been different. But not much. Zac was a condescending asshole. He cared only about himself. And he reminded her about it every day since by calling her that horrid nickname. It took months before she'd finally gotten other people to stop, but Zac flat out refused.

She shook thoughts of him out of her head and focused on the task at hand. An hour later, the bridal shower invitations were done. Macie patted her own back. The personalized graphics would've cost a ton, and Lauren wanted something even her mother's money couldn't buy. Macie wasn't about to take a penny from Sylvia. Besides, it wasn't hard, just time consuming. Macie was the best graphic designer in school. She just hoped Rivot realized that and offered her a job.

Two weeks until graduation. It felt like she'd waited forever to get to this point in her life. Macie had never backed down from a challenge, but she'd always had to live by other people's rules. Even in college, she had rules. Stupid dorm curfews as a freshman. Stupid participation points by some profs. Stupid floor rules her sophomore and junior years. Once she was out on her own, those wouldn't apply to her anymore. Oh sure, she'd have rules at her job, but that was different. She wouldn't have anyone breathing down her neck at her apartment or on the floor of her building. She wouldn't have demands on her time outside of work.

Work.

If she had a job. Panic tightened her chest until she had trouble breathing. She couldn't wait on Rivot any longer. What if they didn't offer? What if they did, but it was only part-time? She needed to blanket resumes to every design firm in the area.

A quick scan through her system showed nothing had been tampered with. She checked all her social media pages. No unauthorized posts. Then she checked Blind Friends. One new message. As anxious as she was to hear from Guy, she needed to make sure there wasn't anything in her outgoing mail first. That would be right up Zac's alley. Sending a random message that made her look insane, totally his style.

But there wasn't anything there, either.

Macie wasn't entirely sure if she was disappointed or relieved. Zac had never missed an opportunity to screw with her head before. And this had been a prime chance. It was out of character. Then again, maybe Zac took Lauren and Ford's request to heart. She hadn't, but if he was willing to try, she would, too.

There was no way Zac Sparks would beat her at this game. And that's all this was, a game.

Too many thoughts about Zac and not enough focus on Guy. Macie shook her head to clear it. A move that was both useless and habit. She pressed on the virtual envelope and smiled. It was from Guy. While she'd hoped it was Guy, there was always a possibility that someone else had contacted her through the app.

She read through his message quickly and sat back in her chair. Had he really just said that? It wasn't a request to meet, but there was an indication he wanted to meet someone. The key word was 'yet' and she assumed he meant her. Excitement bubbled in her veins until she swallowed a giddy giggle.

Macie stared at the screen, reading his words slower and with more caution.

Then she began to type.

Maybe. I don't know though. I'm in the same position as you. I've seen people madly in love with one another. And with themselves.

She smiled as she typed because Zac was definitely in love with himself.

But that doesn't mean there is someone in this world who was crafted just for me. I'd like to think so. I know I'm still young and all that, but I'd be considered an old maid by Jane Austen's standards. LOL. I suppose I should keep the dream alive. If not, I may never meet him. Wow, that's depressing. Honestly, I shouldn't be thinking about this right now, anyway. I need to focus on school and graduation.

Taking a break from reality sounds great. Unfortunately, my reality includes sending out more resumes this week. The company I interned for this past semester hasn't come back with an offer. They said they'd let me know by graduation, but I can't wait that long. If they don't offer, then I'm up a certain creek without a paddle. So I'll be grinding away at building my next life. One day, I'll relax. One day, I'll take time off to smell the roses. Unfortunately, that's not in my near future.

Can I ask you something? Which looks as stupid in text as it sounds in person, but still… Have you landed a job yet? I know that's personal and all, so you don't have to answer if it makes you uncomfortable. It's just that I've heard a lot of others panicking that they haven't found anything. The market's tight and it's a little scary. So, yeah, I just thought I'd ask. And I feel like an asshole for asking, but I'm not going to delete the question. That wouldn't be me. And me IRL would bluntly ask.

She almost signed her name. Almost.

After pressing send, Macie pulled her resume up. She sent it out to every graphic design firm in Lafayette. She still had two weeks on Rivot, but she putting her eggs in one basket wasn't going to work. And there was another avenue she hadn't tried. Her mentor, Dr. Byrd, had suggested the local news stations. He even gave her a lead that the PBS station needed somebody. Macie glanced over it, making a few adjustments to the verbiage. She then pulled up her portfolio and rearranged a few graphics, removed a couple, and replaced them. Working at a TV network wasn't her dream job, but it was a job. She opened her cover letter and rewrote it with the station in mind. Then she copied it into the body of an email, attached her resume and portfolio, and sent it off.

The stress of the job search weighed on her more than anybody knew. She couldn't go back home. That wasn't an option. Too many classmates, teachers, and alleged friends had expected her to come home with her tail between her legs, and that was the last thing she wanted. Macie had let that part of her life go. It was time to move forward not back.

Her phone dinged a text message. Macie smiled when she saw it was from her mother.

I'm proud of you, it read.

Macie thumbed the six-year-old smartphone. *Thanks, Mom. Love you, too.*

She said a little prayer. She couldn't fail.

CHAPTER FIVE

It had been three days since Macie sent her resume off in another round of desperation. Crickets were louder than her phone. The only bright spot over the last week was Lauren. Every single thing Macie did for the wedding was exactly what Lauren wanted. Except for one problem. Lauren wanted the bridal shower to be co-ed. Macie winced, but she didn't hesitate to change the invitations to "Wedding Shower" and add Ford's name to it.

Then Ford insisted Zac help Macie plan the party. Macie gritted her teeth and agreed. Because that was what Lauren wanted.

"It won't be that bad," Lauren said across the table. They sat in the small dining room of Lauren and Ford's one-bedroom apartment. It was a cookie-cutter place with a small fireplace in the living room; a dining room that fit a four-person table, a galley kitchen ran along the hallway led to the bedroom and bath. Macie hated the white walls, the stereotypical first apartment. She hated the singularity of it. Lauren loved it, if only because she shared it with Ford. Lauren grinned as she tapped the table with her nails.

Macie glared at her over the laptop.

"Come on, Mace," Ford said, as he flipped the pages of his guitar magazine. He tossed it on the coffee table and stood from the gray couch. A smile curled on his lips as he walked to Lauren's side. "Zac's a good guy once you get to know him."

"Oh, I know him." Macie went back to the graphic and adjusted the font on the invites. It didn't look right. Wedding had one more letter than Bridal and the 'g' threw off the entire balance. She sighed, deleting the word completely.

"You really don't." Ford squeezed Lauren's shoulder and stared at Macie. "Just talk to him without insulting him."

"Then I'll have no fun." She pulled out the stylus and began to draw the letters onto the screen. "And remind me why we're doing this again. The invitations were already finished."

Macie knew she was being a bitch, but she had worked her ass off on creating something unique for Lauren. There were other things that needed to be done, like finding a job and putting a hefty deposit on an apartment and getting through her finals. The PBS station hadn't called. Rivot Design hadn't called. Nobody had called. She was going to end up back in her mother's small two-bedroom trailer and waiting tables at the same dank bar her mother worked at.

"We just wanted to do this together. I mean, men don't get a groom's shower." Lauren gazed at Ford with so much love in her eyes that Macie almost let her lunch make a reappearance.

"No, they get bachelor parties," Ford said. His gaze matched Lauren's. "And we're doing that together, too."

"Together forever," Lauren whispered.

Macie couldn't stop her eye roll. "Guys, I'm still in the damn room."

They at least had the decency to look embarrassed. Macie ignored them as they talked about their honeymoon. One thing they weren't doing was taking a honeymoon straight away. Ford's teaching job at Joseph Academy, an all-boy's private school, began a week after the wedding. The school wanted him to start immediately to work with the kids who had summer school. Lauren's life was going to be insane before the wedding. She'd agreed to work for her mother rebuilding websites for Sylvia's vast media empire and doing who knew what else Sylvia decreed. That was Lauren's way of paying her mother back for college. And Macie was going to do whatever it took to help Lauren get her dream wedding and ease the pressures off her friend. Macie knew Lauren would do the same for her.

Lauren also had other things going on. Blind Friends had gotten some attention from a couple different companies. The money they'd offered at first was minimal, but the bidding war had only gotten started. Macie finished drawing the new version of the shower invites and added a cursive font. It looked damned good too.

Why wouldn't someone hire her? She was more than capable of every aspect of graphic design.

Maybe she should freelance, be her own boss. It would take time. She could keep working at Hoof, slinging drinks while she built her business. Hell, she'd probably have to do that anyway.

"Here," she said, turning the screen around to face them. Lauren's face lit up, but Ford's didn't. In fact, he looked disgusted. Macie's heart sank. "What now?"

"You can't read it." He had the decency to look sheepish. "Sorry, but the letters are only outlined."

Macie dug her nails into her palms, but Lauren jumped in to save her. "Hon, that's just a sketch of it. She'll fill it in with the same coloring as before." Lauren turned to Macie. "We are sticking with the silver, right?"

"Of course. That way they match the save the date cards and the wedding invites." Macie turned the screen back toward her and filled in the *W*. She chided herself for letting Ford's critique get to her. He didn't understand the process. Lauren had been around Macie and her work long enough to get the idea. If she did get hired at Rivot Design, the clients would probably do the same thing on the mock-ups. She needed to work on that. A lot. Macie turned the screen back around so Ford could see the *W*.

He smiled. "Okay, I get it. That's great."

But his stilted voice gave away one fact: he didn't like it. Well, Macie wasn't going to change it. The invitations needed to go to the printer as soon as possible. If they weren't mailed out by the end of next week, they wouldn't get to people in time to RSVP. Macie had learned a long time ago that people rarely RSVP anymore. Maybe they would for wedding showers. Everyone was too wrapped up in their own lives to bother.

Macie finished filling in the letters and cleaning up the lines. The art calmed her. Besides, people would show for Lauren's shower. That was just the way it worked for her friend. And another reason she planned on eloping if she ever met Mister Right.

"Have you heard from *him* lately?" Lauren asked.

Macie glanced up from the screen. At some point Ford had left the table. Macie looked around their apartment. He may have even left completely. Weird. She didn't remember hearing him move. She turned her attention back to her friend.

"No. The last message said he would be off-line a lot because of finals." Macie shrugged and went back to her tablet. She smiled at her work. Not bad for an unemployed graphic designer. She attached it to an email, sending it to Lauren. "Get that invitation to the printer."

Lauren's phone dinged a new email, but she didn't take her eyes off Macie. "Have you asked to meet him yet?"

"No." Macie left it at that. She wanted to tell Lauren everything, but she also enjoyed watching her squirm.

"Why not?" Lauren smacked her arm. "Stop playing. Just tell me. What's going on?"

"Once graduation is over. There's just too much to do right now." Her head dropped to her chest. "If I'm even in the city. I still don't have a job. Or even an interview at this point. You know I'll have to go home if nothing opens up."

"We'll figure that out." Lauren squeezed her arm. Macie laid her head on her friend's shoulder for a moment. They stuck by each other, even after some of their more monumental arguments. They always came back to this point, this friendship. Macie couldn't lose Lauren. "You can stay with me for a while. Ford's going to live with his parents until we're married. That'll give you a few months."

"Wait. What? Why's he moving out?" It didn't make sense to move out after living together for almost a year. Plus, the looming wedding.

"Oh, it's the school he's going to work for." Irritation covered Lauren's face, but she closed her eyes and took several deep breaths, a technique she'd learned when she thought she was going to be a yoga instructor. Macie helped put the kibosh on that. Lauren was a programmer first and foremost. "I get it, though. They don't want any improprieties by the teachers. Even if it is the twenty-first century." She pursed her lips. "And you know Ford, he's so straight and narrow he might as well be a tape measure."

A snort escaped Macie's lips. It wasn't intentional but comparing Ford to a tape measure was too accurate. Lauren's lip quirked up, but she never let her smile show. Ford was a man of his word, and that was one of the most attractive qualities about him. He was loyal and cared about everyone. Macie envied that about him. Years of cynicism made trust hard for her.

"Thanks, Lauren," Macie said. Her phone vibrated on the table.

It was still early for a Monday, but she wasn't expecting any calls. Her mom was at work for the evening and Lauren was here. The number was local and...a job? It had to be. This could be huge.

"Answer it," Lauren snapped.

Macie pulled herself back to reality and swiped the phone to answer. "This is Macie Regan." She closed her eyes. That sounded so fake, she expected the person to hang up. Or worse, say they'd made a horrible mistake, *then* hang up. Or even worse, it was a damn telemarketer.

"Ms. Regan, this is Nancy Carter with NewsFirst Six." The woman's voice was sharp and demanding. Macie liked her already. "Our graphics department has an opening. HR handed me your portfolio, and I'd like you to come to the station at two tomorrow."

"Two sounds great." Macie's hand shook as Nancy Carter gave her the address and directions. It wasn't far from campus or the area she wanted to live. But it wasn't Rivot, either. "Thank you for the opportunity."

"I look forward to meeting you." Nancy Carter hung up without allowing Macie a chance to reply.

Her eyes wide with fear and excitement, Macie turned to Lauren. "I have an interview."

Lauren squealed, and they jumped in the air like sitcom teenagers.

Macie had to repeat it just so it would seem real. "I have an interview."

"I heard," Lauren said. "With?"

"Channel six." Macie's face screwed up as she thought about it more. She hadn't sent her resume into channel six. A budget cut crisis ten years ago shut down the news division. They'd only recently started it back up about a year ago. Her business management class spent three weeks reviewing the situation last fall. Macie thought they'd make the same mistakes and close shop again. That was why Macie didn't send her resume.

"What?" Lauren asked.

Macie shook her head and smiled. It wasn't a big deal. A job was a job. But she still needed to answer Lauren. "What am I going to wear?"

Lauren held up a finger. "I've got that covered."

🖊 🖊 🖊

The cabin had been nice, but it wasn't what Zac remembered. It was more of a shack than the home away from home he'd imagined. The one room building was weakened by years of neglect. At night the light breeze off the nearby lake felt like a hurricane inside. Zac half expected the walls to fall in on him.

Instead of relaxing by the lake, he was too busy swatting mosquitoes off his skin. His father enjoyed it more, and that was worth the bites and Bactine. His dad's health worried him more each day. The weekend getaway gave him some color in his cheeks. Zac hated to admit it, but he kept waiting for a heart attack. His father worked too hard and too many hours. The board should have him slow down.

The time away had given him some perspective on his mystery girl. They'd both used finals as an excuse to curb their conversations. Their last messages had been brief and nonchalant. Zac wondered why, but he took his cues from her. On the drive home, while his father slept, Zac replayed every step to see if he'd crossed a line somewhere. They would take two steps forward, three steps back. That was the epiphany he'd had in the cabin as his dad snored away while Zac sat on the couch unable to sleep. It hit him like a bullet train in the middle of the forehead.

"What's on your mind, son?" his father asked. They sat in the breakfast nook at his father's house, drinking coffee and having a doctor approved dinner of baked chicken and broccoli. His father speared a floret and sneered at it before popping the offending vegetable in his mouth. "You've got that look your mother used to get when something bothered her."

Zac smiled and dropped his head. His mom died when he was in elementary school. They only talked about her when his stepmother and half-sisters weren't around. Amanda didn't like it. Moments like this, they could. "What look is that?"

His father's face brightened. It didn't matter if it had been fifteen years, anybody could see he still loved her. Zac had no doubt that he'd leave Amanda in a heartbeat if his mom miraculously showed up on the doorstep.

"There's a girl," Zac began. He wasn't really sure where to go from there. How could he explain to his father that he'd never met her, but he thought he was already falling for her? Or was he falling for the *idea* of her?

"There's always a girl." His dad shook his head as he cut his bland chicken into minuscule bites.

"This one's different." Zac sighed and pushed his half-eaten plate away and leaned back in his chair.

His father stared at the plate, then met his son's gaze. His eyes widened. "I can see that. So what's the problem?"

Zac's gaze shift to the window and the perfect lawn outside. He would've loved this backyard when he was a kid. A large kidney shaped pool, a huge swing-set, and a trampoline dotted the lush green grass. Amanda refused to live in the old house, the one his parents shared. Zac couldn't really blame her, but that didn't mean he couldn't resent her for it. The old Victorian had been his mother's dream home. This place, while beautiful in its own way, would've made his mother sick.

"She doesn't feel the same?" his father prodded.

"I honestly don't know," Zac said, turning back to face his father and admitting the issue out loud. "I haven't exactly met her."

His father never judged, but he rolled his fork in a circle to encourage Zac to continue.

"Ford and Lauren created this app called Blind Friends." Zac tried to keep his shoulders relaxed as he talked, but it was hard. His dad believed in love at first sight, but would he believe love at first write? "It's designed as a way for people to get to know one another without knowing who the other person is. Ford and Lauren had a theory that it's harder to make friends as you get older. There are a million dating sites, but none for people just looking for other people to hang out with."

"Sounds dangerous, son." His dad set his fork down and stared at Zac.

"Yeah, there's always a risk, but they kept it strictly to campus. Ford helped Lauren create the psychological profile pages. A person fills them in, and then there's an algorithm that calculates who you'd get along with." That was the very basics of it, and Lauren's explanation was much more in depth. Most of what she'd told him shot over his head. "Anyway, I exchanged messages with a few guys and a handful of girls in the first month. Then I met this one girl."

"Met is a questionable word choice." Dad held up his hands so Zac wouldn't defend himself.

"Fine, I started messaging her." Zac sighed and stared at the ceiling. "I wake up every day and check the app for a new message. If there isn't one, I'm... crushed. If there is, I read it immediately and respond just as fast. Then I repeat the entire cycle. I ... need to get this out of my system. It can't be real."

"Why can't it?" His father sat back in his chair and patted his stomach. There was no way he was full. Zac knew if he left him alone, his father would find the cookie stash. Amanda and the girls would be back from ballet class soon. They could stop him from rummaging through the pantry for the sweets.

"What if she's really a horrible person? What if she's not interested in me? What if she doesn't want to even meet me?" Every question played through his mind.

"What if she does?"

Zac closed his eyes. He confessed the one thing he'd kept even from himself. "What if she meets me and runs the other way?"

"You're not *that* bad looking, Zac." His dad leaned forward and rested his elbows on the table. "Did I ever tell you your mother rejected me at first?"

His eyes snapped open. "What?"

"Yep." His father leaned back in the chair again, crossing his arms over his chest. He stared out the windows. The setting sunlight hit his irises, making them Caribbean green. Zac knew his father was lost in the memory. "We had English comp one together during our freshman year at Lafayette. The first day, I knew. I knew I wanted to spend the rest of my life with her." He chuckled and shook his head. "She had other ideas. I asked her out once at the beginning of the semester. She told me no. And she wasn't very nice about it."

"Seriously?" Zac had never heard this part of their story. "What about the New Year's party?"

His dad shrugged. "Still true, but with the context of the previous semester, it means more, doesn't it?" A flash of darkness scattered across his face. "I don't know what happened to her over winter break. She never shared that with me. I wish she had." His arms fell to his sides. "Whatever it was drove her into my arms. When she stormed up to me on New Year's and kissed me at midnight, I wasn't letting her go."

Zac watched the water in the pool lap against the side. His mom and dad had fallen in love fast and furious after that kiss. But adding in the information that his dad asked her out four months beforehand was depth he hadn't known. His father had always been a practical dreamer. He never went after what he couldn't have. He never gave up. If his target shifted, he shifted with it. Once a deal was in sight, he'd get it. He also dreamed big.

"Son, the moment I met your mom, I knew she was my end game. I knew I wanted to spend my life with her." His dad leaned his elbows on the table and gave Zac a hard look. "I never knew that I'd only get the rest of *her* life. People can slip away from you so fast. You never know how much time you really have with someone. I wanted more than the eleven years I got. I wanted more kids with her, gray hairs, grandkids. Cancer didn't care what I wanted. Life didn't care what I wanted." He stood from the table, leaving his plate. "It's the one time in my life I lost. Don't lose over something you can control, son."

Zac didn't see him leave, but he felt his absence. He wasn't sure what bothered him more, the talk about his mom or the fact his father was right. The hole in his chest ached as he remembered his mother's last days. Her hair was gone, her skin pale. She joked about looking like a vampire without fangs. Even through the cancer, she kept her sense of humor. And that was the worst part for him. Zac couldn't remember anything but the cancer. He never told his father that. It would hurt too much if his dad knew. Even staring at family photos before she was sick felt like he was looking at someone else's life. After she died, he lost his father for almost a year. There was a shell of a man who took him to school, fed him, and made him do his homework, but it wasn't his father. Not really.

That was what Zac was really afraid of. The realization smacked him in the chest. It wasn't about being rejected. It was about being left again.

But what if? That was the question circling his brain. What if she's the one? What if she's everything she seems to be? What if? What if? What if?

Zac opened up his tablet. No new message. He'd messaged yesterday about something trivial and hadn't heard back yet. They'd steered away from anything philosophical or deep lately. Not anymore. He needed to know if this could be real. He began to type.

CHAPTER SIX

The reception area was larger than the space for the anchors and their mirrors, which reminded Macie of a backstage theater complete with messy desks and makeup strung about. The anchors' desk space was slightly larger than an actor's though, more like a combination of an open office cubicle and a makeup table. It was odd. The graphics department was jammed into a large closet with three cubicles stuffed inside, one of which was empty. Could she see herself in that space? At this point, she didn't care. She just needed a job.

Macie didn't have to wait long after her tour before she was ushered into the office.

"Have a seat," Nancy said. "Dwayne at channel nine thought you'd fit in here. That's the reason he sent me your resume."

Macie swallowed hard and nodded. Nancy Carter was everything Macie expected. Strong-willed, determined, and a roaring bitch. Not that Macie minded. It was an interview, a potential job. If Nancy hired her, then Macie could suck it up and deal. The station wasn't as big as Macie thought it would be. It was incredibly small actually.

Nancy spent the first ten minutes asking standard interview questions, most of which Macie had prepared herself for, and then asked for Macie's portfolio. She handed it over with solid confidence. She'd spent the previous night reviewing the station's website and watching news clips from recent stories. The graphics they used were simple and clean. And not too difficult. The job wouldn't be hard. She could do most of these in her sleep.

"Ms. Regan, your portfolio is good. Very good." Nancy said as she flipped through the art Macie had printed. Macie made sure the ones she had available matched what the station was already known for. "But we're looking to add some…" Nancy rolled her wide hand in a circle as she searched for the word or paused dramatically, Macie wasn't sure which. "Pizazz. Yes, that's the word. They need to stand out more in this market. As you know, the news department has only recently been rebooted. We need to go the extra mile to knock our competitors out of the way." She leaned in and Macie fought the urge to lean back. "Do you have anything else?"

Macie didn't break her gaze and she reached down into her canvas messenger bag. Her tablet was so old Macie was almost embarrassed to let Nancy see it. But she bucked up and unlocked it and opened the file before handing over it over. She'd been working on a portfolio for freelancing work while she waited. Some were book covers, some book trailers, others were ads for small companies. Macie needed a backup plan to no job and that was what she had come up with. She'd also added some of her favorite fun graphics to the mix along with wedding invitations and such.

Nancy's face lit up. The hard lines around her eyes and mouth softened. A smile lifted her cheeks, taking ten years off. The station manager wasn't old by any means, but she was clearly battle worn with the lines to show it. By Macie's guesstimate, Nancy was only in her early fifties. Her potential boss cleared her throat and pointed at the screen. "Wedding invites?"

It was time to throw her cards on the table. "My friend is getting married in a few months. And since I haven't had a lot of job offers thrown my way, I thought I'd do freelancing work in the meantime." She cringed at how that sounded because it sounded like she wasn't good enough to get hired anywhere. "It would keep my work fresh as I continued to look."

Nancy nodded. "Smart. Do you plan on freelancing anyway?"

"Maybe. It would depend on my salary." *Stop talking. Stop talking. Stop talking.* Macie cringed again. "I had to take out student loans."

"Back up plans are always a good idea." Nancy handed over the tablet, and Macie's heart sank. The woman stared at her for a moment until Macie wanted to slip to the floor and slink out of the office. "Just don't let it get in the way of your work here."

Macie sat straighter as Nancy picked up the phone and ordered someone named Mark to her office. She waited while Nancy talked. Was she just offered a job and missed it? Nancy said 'your work here' so that had to mean she was hired. It wasn't like she asked Macie if she wanted the job, which of course she did. It was a job. In graphic design. No more bartending or waiting tables or working at the gas station. No phone center job. Pride surged through her. She was going to do this and do the best damn job they'd ever seen.

"You'll start immediately." Nancy set the phone back in its cradle. "Part-time until you graduate then you'll go full-time. As a part-timer, you'll be paid hourly but once you're full-time, you'll be salary like everyone else. Do the freelancing on your own time with your own tools. Don't use the station's systems for that. Any questions so far?"

Macie shook her head because she couldn't even open her mouth.

"Good." Nancy leaned back in her chair and clasped her hands together over her abdomen. "This place is fast-paced and can burn out the strongest person in a matter of months. If you're committed to the job, you'll be fine. If you're not, you'll be gone before the fall shows start running promos."

Macie nodded, again no voice to say a simple okay.

"You'll report to me and me alone until such time I see fit. I'll assign you tasks. Others will try. Ignore them. Even the talent. Sometimes they can be the worst." She shot forward in her chair. This time Macie leaned back. "The associate producers like to think they're me. They're not. If one of them comes to you, and they will, just refer them to me. If they email you, forward it to me. Same with the on-air personalities. If it's the sales department, refer them to my assistant. Got it?"

"Yes," Macie finally muttered.

"And the other designers will try to pawn their work off on you. Just tell them to fuck off."

This time Macie smiled as wide as she could. "Can I quote you on that?"

"Damn straight." Nancy stood as the door opened behind Macie. "You and I, we're going to make this station viable, Macie. As long as you listen to me and do what I tell you, success is within your grasp." Over Macie's shoulder, Nancy said, "Mark, get this lady on the payroll. She starts Monday in graphics."

"Nancy, you know we have to wait until the background checks and drug screens come back before someone starts," a deep voice said.

"You smoke anything lately?" Nancy asked Macie.

Macie snorted. She wasn't stupid. The last time she smoked pot was at Christmas with her mom. "No. I'm clean."

"Arrested lately?"

"Not since my freshman year." She smiled at Nancy who matched it with one of her own.

"Oh God, what for?" Mark asked.

Macie turned around and almost fell back into her seat. Holy hotness. Mark was at least six-one with lush dark hair and smooth olive skin. He pinched his nose, waiting for an answer.

"I'm kidding," Macie said. "I've always been the one to bail people out." Mark dropped his hand and Macie got a full look at his gorgeous face. With his sharp cheekbones and wide eyes, Mark could've easily been one of the reporters or even an anchor. Macie knew she'd tune in to watch him night after night. "Never even had a speeding ticket."

"Good." He smiled. One of his front teeth was crooked, but it was endearing instead of ugly. Damn, he was hot. "Then we won't have any issues."

"Take her to your office and get the paperwork done immediately, Mark. I'm not fucking around here. I need her in house on Monday." Nancy walked around the desk and stood beside Macie. She offered her hand, which Macie took and shook with confidence. "Macie, I look forward to working with you. Send your class schedule and any days off you need for your friend's wedding. We'll work around those dates. But be aware that you'll be required to work evenings, weekends, and holidays. Make sure you plan for that in advance. Okay?"

"No problem." Macie smiled as she followed Mark out of the office. She wanted to message Guy and let him know. The thought stopped her short. She had to scurry to catch up with Mark. Her mom should've been the first person she wanted to tell, then Lauren. She didn't even know Guy. Hell, that wasn't even his real name. And she hadn't heard from him in a few days. Yeah, there might be a message in her inbox, but she hadn't checked it since yesterday morning. Once she got the job interview, that had been her sole focus. Did that mean something? Macie really didn't know. And this wasn't the time to think about Guy or anything other than getting the job.

Toni, the receptionist who had given her a quick tour earlier, had shown her the administrative and sales offices, but only from the outside. They hadn't bothered to go in. Mark opened the door and Macie followed him into a large room with three rows of four cubicles. At the end of the long room were two doors to what she assumed were offices. Each cube was occupied by someone on the phone. Mark lead her into the office on the left and she settled in a hard chair across from his desk. Mark didn't say anything as he gathered up paperwork. He shoved it toward her.

"Do you have your license and social security card with you?" he asked.

Macie pulled them out of her purse and handed them over. She started filling out the forms. Mark mumbled about tax forms and I-9s on his side of the desk. She wanted to flirt with him, if only for the practice, but it wasn't a good idea. Not if she was going to work here for more than a week. He was very attractive, but he appeared to have the personality of a grapefruit. Regardless there had to be a policy about dating in the workplace. He took the paperwork and glanced over it.

"Where's Brickmeyer?" he asked.

"About three hours north of here." Not many people had heard of her hometown.

"Got family still there?" he asked as he scribbled something on a piece of paper.

"Just my mom. What about you? Did you grow up here?" Macie tapped her fingers on her knee.

Mark nodded. "Yeah, then I went to Tulane for school and came back. Just got my Master's from Lafayette last year."

"I'm surprised I never saw you on campus." Macie grinned and tilted her head. Was he flirting? Nah, he couldn't be. He was just being polite.

"Big school," he answered.

Silence filled the small office. So much for tame flirting. Macie glanced around the bland office. There was no personality to it. No photos, no art, not even a plant. Her mind drifted to Guy. Could someone like Mark be the person on the other end of her screen?

"Single or married?" he asked out of nowhere.

"Excuse me?" Macie wasn't exactly sure if he'd asked her that or if she imagined it. This day had been surreal enough already.

"For your tax forms. Are you single or married?" His gaze met hers and a small smile played at his lips.

"Single."

He nodded and marked something on the page. "Boyfriend or girlfriend?"

"Neither." Now he *was* flirting. Macie leaned forward because she'd played this game before. And there was clearly more to the grapefruit than she originally thought. "But I'm taking applications."

"And how does one apply?" Mark tapped his pen, keeping a serious expression on his face. Macie could get lost in those deep brown eyes.

"Usually with an exchange of phone numbers. Then a coffee interview. If that goes well, a second dinner interview can be arranged." Macie reached out and put her hand over his pen, careful not to touch his skin. "Who knows what could happen after that."

Mark smiled and let his pinky finger touch the side of her hand. "Sounds intriguing."

"It's a solid interview process." Macie pulled her hand away, wishing there'd been a tingle or a rush of anything where he'd touched her. That had been her goal, to get a rush. Chemistry either happened or it didn't. It was something she thought about a lot when it came to her Guy. And a reason why she'd never attempted to meet him. If there wasn't any jolt of heat or electricity, she wasn't positive she could handle that level of disappointment. Sure, they could stay friends, but that was easier said than done. She shouldn't meet Guy. Which was why she'd flirted with Mark to begin with.

"Here," he said, writing his number on the back of the card. He slid it toward her. "Consider this my application."

Shit. Macie smiled as she hid her real feelings. Maybe she was jumping the gun. Getting involved with a co-worker wasn't smart. Especially when she hadn't even started the job yet. She knew better, but she played the game anyway. That normally got her ass in the fire quick. "Accepted. But I'm not going to hold any interviews for a several months. Just so you know."

"Understood. Some things are worth waiting for."

Okay, she didn't feel anything when he touched her, but this man knew how to flirt because that was beyond attractive. But without chemistry, there wasn't a point. Her mind shot to Guy again. What if they didn't have chemistry? What if they did? Guilt warmed her gut. It was like she betrayed him even though she didn't even really know him. Guy could be faking those letters just to meet her and get in her pants. But if that was the case, he would've suggested they meet a long time ago.

They finished up the paperwork with minimal flirting and with Macie off to take a drug screen at the clinic down the street from the station. Mark handed her a water bottle from a mini-fridge behind his desk. "To speed up the process," he said. He walked her to the door leading back to reception. "It's been a pleasure, Ms. Regan," he said, bowing gallantly.

"Likewise Mr. …I don't even know your last name." She almost laughed. In all the flirting, they'd never actually introduced themselves properly. He'd gotten her name off her application.

"Sawyer." His grin widened. "I guess this has been a little…unconventional."

"A little." Macie waved her fingers and walked out the door. She'd text him tomorrow to thank him for helping her process, but that would be it. School had to come first. And she had to figure out where she stood with Guy before she considered dating someone else. Not that she was dating Guy. Or meeting him any time soon. Okay, or maybe never. She screamed internally. It was too complicated for no damn reason other than she hadn't stuck herself out there to meet him live and in person. She had to get him out of her head. Throwing herself into a new job would help. Planning to meet him would help more.

The clinic wasn't too crowded when she got there, but they still made her wait ten minutes. She opened her tablet and hacked into their Wi-Fi. It wasn't as easy as it was at most places, but it still wasn't secure enough. At least they added a number to their password: health1. She found the backdoor and looped herself in. Then she opened Blind Friends and smiled at the red one over her inbox.

We've been polite again lately, haven't we? Every time one of us opens up, the other pulls back. I have a theory behind that.

We're both afraid of this. I feel like I know you better than I've known anyone. But I still don't know who you are. That scares me. It terrifies me, really. I'm man enough to admit it. We obviously get along well, but is that because we aren't nearly as guarded being anonymous? Is it because I can freely say things to you that I can't say in person to others? Is it because I feel like there's nothing to hide from? I don't know. I wish I did.

I love talking to you. It's nice to be uninhibited and open. When I'm with my friends, I feel like I'm playing a part instead of being me. Certain things are expected, and I fall into those categories easier than if I'd let myself be real. I don't know if that makes any sense to you or not. I'm rambling now.

So I'll tell you a story instead. My mother died when I was seven. She was the love of my father's life. The one. He's remarried since and I have two stepsisters, but he's still in love with Mom. Tonight we talked about her. It's not something we do often. My stepmother doesn't like the reminder that she's not first in my father's heart. Don't get me wrong, he loves her, too, but I know it hurts her.

Anyway, Dad shared something new with me about their relationship. My mother rejected him before she finally caved. He had asked her out and she said no. Then something happened over winter break to change her mind. He never found out what that was, and he'll never know. It was love at first sight for him. The reason he shared this with me was simple. He never gave up. It's been my father's motto since I can remember. If he wants something, he never gives up.

It's something I should follow more.

There's a reason I bring it up. I think we should meet. I know this is finals time and we may have to wait until after graduation, but I'd like to meet you. I'd like to get to know you in person. If you tell me no, then I'll respect that decision.
But please say yes.

Macie's eyes watered. Meet? He wanted to meet? She didn't know how to respond and sitting inside a clinic wasn't the place to do it. Her instincts said hell yes. Her brain warned her to be cautious. As the battle played out in her head, the nurse called her name. She needed a clearer mind to think it over. Peeing in a cup wasn't giving her a clearer mind. She hurried through the test, grateful to Mark for the water.

When she got home, she read through the message again. There were so many changes in her life at the moment. She wasn't sure if she could handle another one. At least not yet. After graduation, maybe. She didn't want to put him off. But she didn't want to rush into it, either. She wanted to meet him, and she didn't. The last thing she needed was this emotional seesaw. Instead, she decided to do what she had done with Guy all along.

She was honest.

CHAPTER SEVEN

He'd hoped to hear from her rather quickly. Stupid hope. Zac regretted it the minute he hit the tiny paper airplane that sent the message. Too bad there wasn't an unsend button, because he really wanted to take it back. It had been almost twenty-four hours since he'd sent the message, and nothing. He'd scared her off. It was useless and stupid to torture himself like this, but he refreshed the app for the fourth time in ten minutes anyway.

Fortunately, his phone rang. He smiled at the name on the screen 'Good Catholic Boy', which was Ford. Zac had changed it when Ford accepted a job teaching music and counseling at an all-boys school. 'Not My Drug Dealer' wasn't nearly as funny anymore. Not that Ford ever thought it was, but it made Zac chuckle.

"What's up, Ford?" Zac answered. He leaned back on his couch and threw his arm behind his head.

"Macie, that's what's up."

Zac sat forward, dropping his feet off the coffee table. He'd moved into the one-bedroom apartment at the beginning of the month. It wasn't anything to write home about. The complex was full of the same shot-gun style apartments; a living room on one side, dining room opposite, a galley kitchen with a counter opened to the short hallway leading to a closet, a full bath, and a bedroom with a walk-in closet. It was similar to Lauren and Ford's place. The living room had a wood fireplace and sliding glass doors leading to a small balcony, which he didn't bother to use. His father decided it was time for Zac to be on his own, even though Dad was paying the rent until Zac could start at Sparks Investments. "What'd she do this time?"

Ford launched into a rapid-fire tirade. "I asked her to change the bridal shower invitations to wedding shower, and she got irritated and angry with me when I didn't see what she saw in her head on the graphic she changed, and she was clearly pissed that I even stuck my nose into it."

Zac kept his laughter in check as his friend caught his breath. Both Lauren and Ford were being ridiculous about the entire thing, but he wasn't going to tell them that. Just like he suspected Macie wasn't. She'd do anything for Lauren. "You want me to intervene, don't you? Tell her they're not neutral enough?"

"Please. Lauren loved them, but I don't want the guys to not show because they think it's not for them. Does that make sense?"

"Sure," Zac answered. He wanted to tell Ford to deal with it or to just let Lauren have her girly shower. "I'll talk to her. Okay?"

"Thanks, buddy. I'll check with you later to see how it went." Ford ended the call without saying goodbye, a sure sign he was stressing out.

The last thing Zac wanted to do was deal with Macie. He refreshed the app again just to check. This time he had a message.

His finger hovered over the screen. What if she said no? He couldn't think that way. He pressed the icon and the message opened.

You know what I call you? Guy. Because I don't know your real name, so I just made one up. I check my app constantly wondering if you've responded or sent me a new message. And I yell at myself for being so impatient. You have other things going on in your life. I'm sure you're not refreshing your app every two minutes to see if I've gotten back to you.

I'm sorry about your mother. It's not what you want to hear, but it's mandatory that I say it. That's what people do when they learn of a death. We apologize even if that's not appropriate because we have to say something and that's the only thing, we can think of to say. I don't know what I'd do without my mom. She's my rock. She's my inspiration. She's my best friend. Losing her would destroy me.

Sometimes when I write to you, it's just a string of thoughts in my head, and I'm afraid that it might scare you off. But you're right, we can be unbridled through messages. We can say what we think without worrying about how the words make the other person feel because we can't see each other's reactions. And we can think about how we're going to respond before we do. We can be open, and honest, and wild, and passionate, and free. Would I be like that with you in person? I don't know. Do I want to find out?

Maybe.

Yes.

Definitely yes.

But (isn't there always a but in life?) can we wait a bit?

With finals, finding a place to live, and starting a new job, I'm overwhelmed and terrified. I was afraid I'd have to move home until yesterday. I finally got an offer. It's not what I was looking for, but it's still in my field. Now I need to put the deposit on the apartment and move in. I'm just happy that I can get this place. It's not close to the dream job, but it's still close to the real job. And I want to live close so I can sleep in. LOL. Sorry, I like sleep and I'm not ashamed to admit it.

The bottom line is yes, I'd love to meet you. Can we plan something after graduation?

Zac's fingers froze around his phone. He swallowed hard. She said yes. His heart raced, and it took effort not to email her back and tell her where he lived. She could come over right now. As much as that sounded like a good idea, he knew it was definitely not one. She wanted to wait until after graduation. He could be patient. She wanted to meet. That's what mattered. He hit reply and responded that they would meet when she was ready. It was short, to the point, and fast. He almost added his phone number but decided against it. They'd kept up the game of anonymity for this long, why not wait a little longer? She replied just as quickly with an okay. He stared at the screen, at that one little word. It was on her, and he was fine with that. He could wait. The anticipation was thrilling and terrifying and annoying all at the same time.

Zac didn't want to lose this good mood, but he had promised Ford.

He picked up his phone and found Macie's number under the name 'Chomper'.

It rang three times before she picked up with a very pleasant, "What?"

"We need to talk," he said. No sense in beating around the bush. Another cliché he had looked up. Hunters still beat bushes to shoot birds flying out in this day and age. It was old and modern at the same time. He appreciated that. "About the shower."

"Not showering with you, Zac. We've had this discussion before." A sniffle punctuated her sentence.

Zac ran his hand down his face. She'd been crying. "Are you okay?"

"Yeah, why?" At least she hadn't lost her defensive tone.

"You've been crying."

She sighed loudly into the phone, probably so he would know she was irritated. Such a Macie thing to do. "Not that you care, but it's a good thing."

"Crying is a good thing? Since when?" He let the confusion fill his tone. Women didn't make sense and he wondered if they ever would. He also wondered if his mystery girl cried a lot.

"Since forever. Ever heard of tears of joy?"

"Yes, but I never understood it." *Why bother to cry when you could just smile?*

"You'd have to be able to *feel* joy to understand." She sniffled again. "Women have no problem expressing it."

Talk about an ice pick to his chest. He pinched the bridge of his nose. "Men can express their feelings just fine, Macie."

"Of course, how silly of me." Her bite was back. He could almost see her nostrils flare. "Thank you for mansplaining. My silly little female mind just can't comprehend such a thing."

One of the things they fought about most was women versus men. Macie always had to throw her feminist weight behind everything. Zac understood most of where she came from—women made less money than men in the same field, women aren't respected for their athletic ability, women aren't allowed to stand on their own. He got that. But he also hated that she made him feel like crap about it. It wasn't Zac's fault. He supported Macie's favorite causes on campus 'Lafayette Liberties' a women's rights group and donated to her technology drive for students who couldn't afford laptops or tablets.

Macie accused him of just throwing his money around.

"Can we not fight about this again?" He rubbed his forehead. How was he going to handle this for the next month?

"Fine. What do you want?"

"I told you, we need to talk about the shower." Zac stood from his couch and stretched. "The invites are too ... girly for a joint shower."

"Too girly? When did you even see them?"

I haven't. "Today." He paced the small hallway. "They're perfect for a bridal shower but since it's co-ed, they don't represent the couple."

"This is so stupid. Who has a fucking co-ed wedding shower? It's absurd."

"Oh, look, we actually agree on something."

Macie laughed. She had a beautiful laugh. He could listen to it all day. If she didn't have such a huge chip on her shoulder, they might be friends or tolerable acquaintances.

"Mace, I know it's a pain in the ass. I know you put a lot of work into designing those invites. But—"

"Here we go," she muttered.

"—can you just change the font to something less..." He didn't want to offend her by saying feminine, but it hung in the air between them.

"I already sent them to Lauren to send to the printer."

"So?"

"So, if she sent them to the printer, there's nothing I can do now. It's out of my hands."

"And you're not willing to make another neutral pattern for a small print run?" He knew he was pushing his luck, but he promised Ford he'd talk to her about it. One thing Zac never did was break a promise.

"You know what pisses me off about this entire thing?" Macie's voice cracked as if she might cry again. "I love Lauren and Ford, but they keep forgetting I'm doing this for free. Lauren at least thanks me, but Ford...I don't get it. He doesn't appreciate anything I'm doing here. It took me hours to make the shower invites and then I had to change them because they wanted it to be a wedding shower instead of bridal shower. And I changed it. Without complaining, I might add. Now you're telling me that you want me to change them again? No. Even if Ford and Lauren came up to me, I wouldn't. They need to go in the mail by the end of next week. And they still need to be printed. There isn't any time." Macie sniffled again, and this time Zac thought it had nothing to do with joy and everything to do with him. "I worked my ass off on those damn things. The least anybody could say is thanks."

He opened his mouth, but the silence filled in his ears. "Macie?" Nothing. The line was dead.

No one had hung up on him since high school. He wanted to call her back, but he knew she wouldn't answer. And what would he say? That she was right. He rewound his memories since Ford and Lauren started planning the wedding. Macie had volunteered to make the invitations and the graphics, so they would have something unique. She'd saved them money, which Zac respected. He couldn't remember a single time Ford thanked her. That was something he'd have to talk to his friend about.

✐ ✐ ✐

Mark called Macie the next day while she was in class. He needed her schedule for the last week of school and the days off for the wedding.

Her job. She loved the sound of that. She typed a quick text to Mark with her schedule.

He replied two minutes later. *How's my application looking?*

Macie smiled, but she didn't want to lead him on too much. *Interviews have been put on hold for the time being. The HR department is moving to a new location and needs more time to review.*

I understand. You do know I have my application in other places? he replied.

Of course, you can't only apply one place. Just let me know if you receive any offers so I can remove you from the candidate pile. This was easier, letting him down this way. He'd move on. She wouldn't have the awkwardness at work when it didn't work out. And it wouldn't. In her gut, she knew that even as she flirted with him.

She added the dates of the shower, the two potential party dates, and the wedding date in another text. Mark simply responded,

Noted, but doubtful all days will be approved.

That wasn't a surprise. Lauren would understand. If Macie was going to miss anything, it was the shower. Macie just didn't know when the party would be, but she was hoping for the weekend before. Her preliminary bachelorette planning had everything prepared for two weeks before and the week before the ceremony, but nothing had been settled. Macie wasn't sure if Lauren wanted that big of a break between the fun day and the big day. She just had to talk to Zac to confirm what would work best for everyone involved. The shower was a month before the wedding on a date pre-approved by the all-mighty Sylvia. Lauren's mom was out of town every weekend for conventions and conferences where she promoted her books, her healthcare products, or spoke to fellow health nuts. Lauren loved that her mom was finally following her dream, but she'd been heartbroken, too. Macie had held her friend the night Sylvia told Lauren not to marry Ford.

"His dreams, his life will be more important than yours. He'll want kids. Then you'll raise them on your own while he continues to live. Your life will be in suspended animation," Sylvia had said. "I know you love him. And I know he loves you. Just wait. Don't rush into this."

Macie understood and secretly agreed with Sylvia but for different reasons. She just didn't think it was a very Mom thing to say. Her own mother would've supported her unconditionally. Sylvia and Lauren's father were still married, but only because of years of intense therapy. Bitterness still seeped into Sylvia's voice. She'd put her own career on hold to support her husband. When she was ready to get back into the workforce, Lauren came along then Lauren's little brother. Sylvia was incredibly successful now as a health and nutrition guru, but she resented everyone for holding her back.

Maybe that's why Lauren kept Sylvia in the dark about her app. The bidding war was heating up. As it stood, Lauren would be able to do whatever she wanted after the summer she gave to Sylvia. Lauren had promised her mother she'd work for her to develop an app and to update her mother's websites. But Lauren had options too. The three standing job offers wouldn't go anywhere. She'd either start a job or freelance. Macie had a feeling Lauren had already decided, but she wasn't telling anyone yet. Not even her fiancé.

Macie strolled out of the art building and into the quad. The sun was high overhead and the air teased of a hot Louisiana afternoon. She tilted her head back, letting the sun soak into her skin.

Her phone vibrated in her hand and she smiled when she saw the name on the screen.

"Hey, Pete. What's up?"

"Do you have the notes from class today?"

"Be more specific. We have three classes together and you missed all of them." Macie held in her laugh. Pete was a good guy, but he tended to party too much and study too little. He wasn't anywhere near the top of their class and, yet, he had a job back in Baton Rouge already. How he landed it, she had no idea. He wasn't the only person whose grades weren't as good as hers who had jobs before she did.

"Okay, all of them." He chuckled under his breath. "You know that girl I've been chasing?"

Macie laughed. "You mean Cate with a C. You've only asked her out since sophomore year."

"Yep, that's her. Apparently, I'm not as suave as I think. She thought I'd been joking this whole time." He paused, and Macie heard a door close in the background. "She finally said yes a few days ago. We haven't left my room since."

"That is information I did not need to know, Pete." Macie wrinkled her nose. "But congrats."

"Thanks, and can I have your notes?" he asked a little more frantically then before.

"Yeah, but you're buying me lunch." Macie sat on the edge of the fountain and wrote herself a reminder on her hand to give Pete copies.

"Deal." Pete sighed. "And thanks, Mace. You've been a lifesaver these last few years."

Pete ended the call. Macie didn't even have time to think about Pete when her phone rang again. She was suddenly popular. That wasn't something she relished. She swiped to answer without looking at the screen.

"Hey, Mace," Ford said on the other end.

He never called her. Ever. Unless Lauren was in full freak-out mode. She sat ramrod straight. "What's wrong? Is Lauren okay?"

"Yeah, she's fine. I just..." He hesitated and sighed. "Look, I realized something, and I need to man up and apologize. I'm sorry."

"Okay. For what?" This was getting weirder by the second.

"You've done a lot for the wedding and I... I was a jerk about the shower invitations. They really are fantastic. You do amazing work. So thank you for doing everything. We... I really do appreciate it."

Macie wasn't sure what to say. "Wow, okay. Thanks. That means a lot."

"Good. I'm glad. I didn't want that hanging between us. I've got to get to class. Talk to you later."

"Bye."

Macie stared at her phone like it would answer all the questions in the universe. Mainly why Ford called her. She replayed the conversation. It was nice that he thanked her. She'd worked hard to get the save-the-date cards, the wedding invitations, the shower invitations, the place holders, everything. She was finishing up the final touches on the programs, too. And he was a jerk about the shower invitations, but he okayed the final draft.

Unless...

She wanted to slap herself. Zac told Ford what she'd said. Why would he do that? And should she be pissed or grateful? It wasn't like she told Zac anything in confidence. Why would he even bother? They weren't friends. She couldn't not thank him either. She pulled up his number under 'jackass' and sent him a quick text.

Thank you. You didn't have to do that but thank you.

He responded instantly. *For what?*

Macie shook her head. *For telling Ford he was being a jerk.*

No problem. He was being a jerk. It's always my pleasure to point that out to him.

LOL, she replied.

She slipped her phone in her bag and headed toward the student union for lunch. It was a small victory, but a victory nonetheless. And victories deserved pizza.

With two slices of extra-greasy pepperoni, she settled into a corner booth and opened her tablet. Her Blind Friends app had been silent since they agreed to meet after graduation. She missed Guy. There wasn't a message from him. Macie hated to admit being a little heartbroken by that, but she hadn't messaged him either. It took two to play the game.

> *Dear Guy,*
>
> *Now that you know, I'm going to keep calling you Guy. I'm not going to lie. This feels awkward now. Like, we've taken this huge step forward without actually taking it and I don't even know what to say. But I have to say something, right? I mean, this is what we do. We talk. We're honest with each other.*
>
> *But I also feel like we need to stay anonymous. I want to tell you everything about myself, but I want to do it in person. If I tell you my name, it will break the spell. Does that make sense? I hope so.*
>
> *My new job wants me to start before graduation. I'm meeting with the HR department to plan out my schedule until I can go full-time. It's only going to be for a few weeks, but I'll spend most of my time training, I think. Honestly I don't really know what to expect. This job isn't what I was going for. It was the only one that offered though, so I had no choice if I wanted to stay here. I need to make the best of it. And I'm terrified and excited at the same time. It's a lot to take in. I'm stepping blindly into this place. With the exception of us, I never do that. I research, study, prepare. There's no preparation for adulthood. Not really.*

Macie hit send. She'd almost told him about Mark. Almost. It wouldn't have served any purpose except to show him other men were interested in her. And she couldn't tell Guy that. It was pointless. She only had virtual eyes for the man on the other side of her screen.

She needed to just set a date to meet him and get it over with. One way or another.

CHAPTER EIGHT

Graduation day. It was both anticipated and dreaded by so many of Zac's classmates. Zac was indifferent. He had his life laid out for him since he could remember. And it was going to be a good life. One last party after the ceremony and he'd be on his way to wealth and, hopefully, happiness.

Things had gone somewhat back to normal with his mystery girl. They'd exchanged messages as if neither one had agreed to meet. He hadn't wanted to push and wondered if she felt the same way. But now it was time. Zac sat at his small dining room table and opened his tablet. He reread her last message.

Confession, I've never seen the ocean or been to a beach. We didn't go on vacations when I was a kid. As close as we are to New Orleans, I haven't even been there. Crazy, right? I think I would like the beach. I'm not someone who can sit still for any length of time, but I imagine long walks along the water would be nice with the tide covering my feet. Who knows, maybe I am the type to just sit on the beach. I'd like to find out. Maybe someday.

I'm moving into my new apartment. It's perfect for me. It's also scary. I've never lived alone. Maybe I should get that dog just for protection, but if I work insane hours, that's not really fair to the dog. I need an attack cat.

My new job is interesting. The company I interned for, the one I was waiting for an offer from, never contacted me. I called them, and they said they went in a different direction. Talk about a stab in the heart. I'll show them they made a mistake.

I'm sorry. I'm rambling again. I'm so uninhibited in my messages to you, sometimes I forget you don't necessarily need to know everything on my mind. LOL

That little bit of knowledge that she wasn't leaving, sent his heart into the sky. It was a weird sensation. He'd never felt anything close to it before and now it was with a girl who could have a wart on her nose and practiced magic in her spare time. It didn't matter if she did or didn't. He still wanted to meet her, warts and all. A smile crossed his face at the cliché.

Good morning,

Or afternoon, if that's when you read this. Today's the day. Graduation. It's such a long word with even longer implications. I've been mulling over what you said. What if we chose the wrong major? What if we've accepted a job we hate? What if we're not supposed to do what we think we're supposed to do with our lives? What if we're on the right path? What if everything goes right? I've never really considered any of it before.

I've known my career path for as long as I can remember. And I walk it willingly. It's a good life. I'm not ashamed to say I'm following in my father's footsteps. The real question is whether I'll be any good at it. I think so, but who knows? I'll find out soon enough, I guess.

So many of my classmates are either freaking out or overly confident in their next step. I know I shouldn't, but I find it amusing. Does that make me a horrible person? Maybe, but life is going to throw things at us no matter how confident or freaked out we are. I choose not to stress about it. That's something I've learned from my father. He juggles so many things and, if something falls, he picks it up and continues on. Because things fall. You can't go back to fix it, but you can move forward. But you know that's not the real reason I'm writing today.

We agreed after graduation. And, technically, it's not after just yet but it will be in a few hours. There's a party tonight. Well, there's a party every night around here, but there's one at the Epsilon house. I will be there in a red polo. Please come.

He read over his message. The only thing that didn't work was the red polo. What if she showed up and met some other guy in a red polo? He backspaced over it until it read *I will be there* and pressed send. They could plan other details when she responded. *If* she responded. He closed his eyes and leaned back into his couch. There was a chance she wouldn't get the message in time. It was something he needed to remember. There was a lot going on today, and a party may not be on her mind. It wasn't really on his, either. His phone buzzed, distracting him from the negative thoughts beginning to fill his mind.

"Hey, Dad," Zac answered.

"It's Amanda. Your father's …" She sobbed, and Zac's heart sank. "He's at Mercy."

He grabbed onto her use of the present tense and forced calm into his voice. "Hospital? What happened?"

Another sob and then rustling on the other end. "Hey, big brother," Lucy said. She didn't sound much better than her mom. "We just got here so we don't really know what's going on. They think he had a heart attack."

"But he's alive?"

"Yes. Mom hit the security panel, and Taylor called 911." She pulled in a sharp breath. Her voice dipped into his chest and tore at his heart. "I did CPR. The doctor said it maybe saved his life."

"Thank God."

"Zac?" Lucy's voice was small, making her sound younger than her thirteen years.

"Yeah, sis?"

"I never want to do CPR on Dad again." She broke into tears. He overheard Amanda say, "Oh, baby, you're a hero."

"Zac?" Taylor said into the phone. His youngest sister was ten but, like Lucy, more mature than she should be. "Is he going to be okay?"

"He'll be fine thanks to you and Lucy. You guys are both heroes." Zac loosened his tie. "I'll be there in a bit, okay? Just keep your mom calm."

"Okay. Love you." Taylor hung up before Zac could respond.

He set his phone on the table and bent over. His dad. His rock. His hero. He couldn't lose him. Not now. It was too soon. He needed to get to the hospital, but he couldn't move. He didn't want to see his father with tubes and wires coming out of him and an oxygen mask covering his face. He didn't want to see his father on death's door. He didn't want to watch his dad take his last breath.

He'd done that with his mom. That was all he could really remember about her. He didn't want to go through that with his father. Not today. Not ever. His little sisters needed him, and he had to get to the hospital. He glanced down at the tie he had on, his dad gave it to him the day before. It was a simple navy-blue silk, but the addition of the tie tack his father had worn at his own graduation was the real gift. It was a tradition. His grandfather had worn it, too. Zac touched the silver and sighed. He needed to get to the hospital.

He grabbed his phone and sent Ford a text.

🖉 🖉 🖉

"I'm so proud of you," Macie's mom said as she wrapped her arms around her daughter.

"Thanks, Mom."

"Now, how do we celebrate?" Mary Regan smiled as she held Macie by the shoulders. The mother-daughter team were often mistaken for sisters whenever they went out together. Both had the same dark hair and olive skin, but Macie had her father's eyes. Not that he would've even known it. Her mom had Macie when she was seventeen and still in high school. Macie's dad never bothered to stick around, and her grandparents helped Mary where they could, but they were old school. Once Mary became a mother, Mary became an adult. She started waiting tables and dropped out of high school. Macie became her life. Even though they didn't have much, they always had each other.

"By sleeping? I have to be at work in the morning." Macie lifted her hand to cover the yawn, but it was too late. "Sorry, Mom."

"I can't believe they made you work this morning." Mom scowled and crossed her arms.

"You know it was a last-minute thing. I've only been there a week. I have to prove myself." But Macie agreed with her mom. Nancy knew it was graduation day, but that didn't stop her from demanding an immediate revision on a sales graphic that morning.

Macie went in without complaining, did the graphic, emailed it and left. If Nancy didn't like it, she could have someone else fix the damn thing. In her email, Macie reminded her of the ceremony and informed her Macie's phone would be off the rest of the day. She still hadn't turned it back on. "I want a nap."

"Nap later. Dinner first." Mom checked her watch. "And drinks. I could use a whiskey sour."

"How about margaritas and Mexican food?" Macie threw her arm around her mom's shoulder.

"That works, too."

Lauren ran up to them with Ford trailing behind her. "We did it," she shouted as she pulled Macie into a big hug. "We made it, Mace. We actually made it."

Macie wriggled out of her friend's embrace. "Yeah, we did. Where's Sylvia?"

Lauren shrugged, but Macie knew that look all too well. Sylvia was a no show. Was she even going to make her daughter's wedding?

Ford reached for Macie and yanked her into an awkward hug. "Congrats, Macie."

"You too, Ford." She pulled away and glanced between them. Despite Sylvia's absence, there was a twinkle in Lauren's eye that also appeared in Ford's. "What's going on?"

The couple shared a glance, then both of them started giggling. It wasn't unusual to see Lauren break into giggles, but Ford? That wasn't right.

"Tell me or I might think the worst." Macie didn't want to hear the words 'We're pregnant' because it was way too soon for that in Macie's opinion, which didn't mean much.

"We reached a deal with MatchInHeaven, LLC." Lauren beamed. "They're buying Blind Friends and... well, I won't have to take one of the job offers for a while."

"That much?" Macie's jealousy soared. She stomped it back down and forced herself to be happy for them.

Lauren nodded. "It's enough. I'm going to work on the development for them as a freelancer after I'm done working for Mom this summer. That way I can keep my options open and work on other stuff, too. Plus..." She giggled again. "Now we can start a family like we really want to."

Macie hugged Lauren again, letting her jealousy slip away. It was stupid and childish to turn green over this anyway. Lauren worked her ass off on that app. It was fantastic and had brought her together with Guy. Well, sort of. "Wait, when will it go offline?"

"Not until the deal is settled." Ford wrapped his arm around Lauren's shoulder. "It's a tentative agreement, but we've made it clear that there are still some things to work out and we're in the midst of graduation and a wedding. After the dust has settled and things are ironed out, it should be done by the end of August."

"Plus, there's your role." Lauren's grin grew.

"Mine? What're you talking about?" Macie's eyes widened. She didn't have anything to do with the sale of the app.

"The graphics. They want to buy some of them." Lauren's grin stretched across her entire face. "They're going to contact you. I mentioned you might do freelance work, too. You're still going to do that, right?"

Macie nodded, barely able to keep her own heart from exploding. Even if it didn't pay much, she could add it to her resume. And right now a dollar was more than she had to her name. The deposit on her new apartment was astronomical. The minute she left graduation with her mom, they were going to eat too many tacos and then move her stuff into her new place. Hers. All hers. Macie couldn't contain herself. She lunged at Lauren and started laughing. "You're amazing."

"Yes, I am." Lauren squeezed Macie. "And this is only the beginning. I've got another app brewing in my brain. It's going to be a while before I can start working on it, but will you help with the graphics?"

"You know I will." Macie let go and pulled away from her friend. "Around my job at the station. They've got me in Wednesdays through Sundays with some Mondays thrown in for good measure. Any time after that, I'm yours."

"I knew I could count on you. It'll probably be closer to the end of the year. Still have a wedding to plan, a honeymoon to figure out. Mom…" Lauren's eyes glazed over, and she shook her head. "So much is changing, Mace. I know this is cliché but promise me we'll always be friends."

Macie smiled at the cliché and knew it was something that would drive Zac up the wall. "Of course. Just because we don't live in the same zip code doesn't mean shit. You're my best friend. Always."

"Lauren," Ford said behind them. Macie had totally forgotten he was even there. "We need to go."

"I know." Lauren's face turned somber. She squeezed Macie's hands and let go. "I'll stop by your new place this week."

"Sounds good." Macie smiled as Lauren turned around and strolled away with her arm around Ford's waist. They were going to be happy together. She knew it in her core. And it made her jealous. Ford wasn't a bad guy. He always put Lauren first. If she wasn't around, Macie wouldn't even talk to a guy like Ford. And by proxy, she wouldn't have to deal with Zac. Where was he anyway? It wasn't like Zac not to be around Ford for a big moment.

"Ready, kiddo?" Mary rubbed Macie's shoulder. "We've got a lot of stuff to move. And a lot of margaritas to drink."

Not really a lot of stuff. It was only one trip in her mom's truck. She didn't even have furniture. Macie smiled at her mom anyway. "Yeah, let's go."

✐ ✐ ✐

Macie juggled the box as she unlocked the door to her new apartment. It wasn't as close as she'd like to the station, but she could still walk and bike there. The old three-story brick school had been converted into apartments over the last year. Macie was lucky there'd been a vacancy. Lofts were the hot new thing these days. Her studio wasn't big by any standards, but it was perfect for her. Eight-hundred square feet with a small kitchen and bath in a safe building was exactly what a single girl in Louisiana needed. She wasn't far from Crafts and the BoHo district either.

The door swung in and Macie's breath stuck in her throat. A large futon sat against the exposed brick wall of the living room-slash-bedroom area. A coffee table sat on a plaid rug in front of it. Macie stepped further into the room. Under her lone window was a small desk and chair. Across from the futon was an oversized armoire that filled half of the wall. Her easel leaned against it with a large blank canvas, her paint case opened on the floor as if being displayed. It had been so long since she picked up her brushes. She missed them more than she realized.

Her heart surged when she saw the final item. A wingback chair and ottoman nestled into the corner by the desk. Mary had read to her every night in that chair. Macie had never told her mother how much she loved it, but Mary clearly knew.

"You're giving me your chair?" Macie asked. She set the box on the coffee table and settled into the seat. It molded around her as if waiting for Macie to sit in it again.

"Seemed appropriate." Mary took a spot on the futon. "This is comfier than I expected. I almost got a daybed, but a futon was more you."

Tears tickled Macie's eyes. "Mom, you can't afford all this."

Mary smiled at her daughter and shook her head. "You've always had it in your head that we had nothing. Maybe that's my fault, but it's not a bad thing. Kid, I'm not rich by any means. I work hard earning what I do, but we've never been poor in the traditional sense. I've been putting aside money for years."

Macie's eyebrows scrunched together.

"You rarely asked for anything, and I never offered you more than you needed." Mary smiled sadly. "It wasn't that I couldn't give it to you, within some limits, but it was more about you learning independence and earning your way. You learned a lesson I was forced into." Mary shrugged. "I'm proud of you, Macie Jean. You're making the world your own."

"So when I was seven," Macie said, still trying to wrap her head around this sudden change in her mother's financial situation, "and asked for an Itsy Bitsy Doll for my birthday —"

"Those dolls were fifty bucks a pop." Mary's face twisted in disgust. "And your friends were collecting them. I wasn't about to spend that much money on something that would just set on your shelf to collect dust."

Macie searched her mind for a time she might have played with the dolls. Her friends had done exactly what her mother said. Whenever she was at one of their houses, they played other games. The dolls never left the coveted shelves. "You bought me a skateboard. I still have that."

Mary laughed. "Fun and practical."

Macie pulled her knees to her chest and rested her cheek against her shoulder. She thought about her childhood. Her mother had done the best should could with what she had. That was what Macie always thought. Now, she wasn't so sure. Had Macie been denied stuff? Yes. Had Macie gotten angry about it? Oh, yeah. But had she suffered? Not in the least. Hell, she still used the skateboard. Her mom hadn't always given her what she wanted. She *had* given Macie what she needed.

"Thanks, Mom." Macie stood and sat next to Mary. "For the new furniture. For everything."

Mary's sad smile turned brighter. "You're going to be in debt for a long time, kiddo. This," she gestured around the room, "isn't much, but I wanted your adult life to start on the right foot."

Macie pulled her mother into a hug. "Thanks to you, it will."

CHAPTER NINE

The doctors sent his father home earlier than Zac had expected. Bed rest and meds, along with a follow-up with his regular doctor. Diagnosis: indigestion. No signs of a heart attack, but something wasn't right. His blood pressure was out of control and his cholesterol too high for someone who had taken good care of himself. Nothing had come up before his gall bladder surgery. Amanda freaked out. His little sisters did, too. Taylor's unwarranted guilt covered her face. She'd started CPR while his father was still conscious. Zac hugged her and told her she still did the right thing because most people wouldn't even have a clue how to do CPR. The ER doctor called it a symptom of growing older.

"What's going on?" Zac asked when they finally had a moment alone. Amanda had taken the girls outside to the pool to relax. Zac was grateful for the time alone with his dad. There was more going on than just indigestion. His dad's health scared him.

He bristled as he adjusted in his recliner. "Thought I was having a heart attack. Couldn't breathe. My heart raced. I thought I was dying."

"The doctors said you've been under a lot of stress?"

His father shrugged. "Just work. Nothing to worry about."

"Dad, I'm starting full-time Monday. If there's something worrying you, it's going to affect me, too." Zac cringed at how that sounded. "And look at how Amanda flipped. You scared the girls out of their minds. It's messing with your health, tell me what's going on."

"It's just some stupid in-fighting on the board. They want to go public and then sell out to one of the national firms." His breath hitched and he closed his eyes. "I'm fighting them with everything I've got, but they're going to win. Everything I've worked for, gone by their greed."

"Sounds like you've given up. That's not like you."

His father's eyes shot open and glared at him. "No, I haven't. I'm not going to, either. But they're forcing my hand. It's going to get dirty."

Zac smiled. "Then let it. I've got your back, Dad. Just tell me the plan."

"We need to get the employees on my side. Going public will hurt them the most. The board will claim it will help by creating stock options they can buy into, but the reality is the stock options will be gobbled up by the board then sold to the highest bidder. I didn't start this company to hand it over to someone with more money." He shook his head. "That sounds crazy even to me."

Zac laughed under his breath. "I get it, Dad. You told me you started it to help people not end up in shitty situations when they're older."

"Like your grandparents and great-grandparents."

Zac simply nodded. His dad's father had been boisterous and fun-loving until a stroke put him in a wheelchair. He ended up in a nursing home away from his family. It sucked the life out of him, and he died after six months. He was only sixty-four. His grandmother gave up after that and ended up in the same place, dying after a year. His great-grandparents lived in a hovel of an apartment after they lost their house. They hadn't saved for their retirement, only for their kids to go to college.

"I've always emphasized caring about the person investing and not the profit. Making sure they're getting what they need out of it." His father sat up. "A corporate buyout would ruin that. I'd have to start over. And we could do that, but it would be a lot of work and I'm not sure I'm ready for such a commitment. I want to save what I've built."

Zac patted his Dad on the arm. "If you have to start over, most of your investors will come with you."

"That's the only plus side." His father sighed and stared out the window overlooking the pool. Zac's sisters jumped in, splashing each other while Amanda sunned herself. "I wanted to spend more time with my family. Retirement in five years. Handing the reins of a solid company over to you. Send the girls to whatever college they want. Take Amanda around the world without worrying about work. But this fight might take it out of me. That's what scares me the most."

"Don't worry, Dad." Zac clamped his hand on his father's shoulder. "Let me fight. You just pull the strings."

"They'll listen to you."

I'll make sure of it. Zac sipped his soda and knew where, or rather who, to start with. He may be a 'new employee' on Monday, but Zac spent every summer interning at the office since he was sixteen. He knew the major players. He knew the lines dividing the office. He also knew who was the best person at spreading gossip: his father's secretary Maureen. That was where he'd start.

／／／

Macie settled into the wingback after work on Sunday and finally succeeded in hacking someone's Wi-Fi. Her internet would be set up on Monday, until then she needed a connection. The signal was weak, but it was a signal nonetheless. All she wanted to do was check her messages and maybe watch a movie. The eleven-hour workday had exhausted her. Nancy had her creating new graphics for the green screen. The old 'homicide' one the anchors used was stale and too similar to channel ten's new one. It needed a fresh look. After all, the news needed to make murder pop for the viewers. That took most of the day with tiny things popping up for sales and news stories. For the most part, she worked alone. Each designer taking a different shift that crossed over in the middle of the day and everyone was on staff. She was lucky she got the normal day shift for now, but in three months, she'd start working late into the evenings. In another three, she'd be stuck on the four a.m. shift. The rotating schedule sucked, but she didn't plan on working at the station for the rest of her life. It was just a stepping stone to the next thing.

She opened the Blind Friends app to see a red one in the corner. A smile settled over her face that quickly disappeared when she read it.

He wanted to meet? Last night? Fuck.

Macie began typing immediately.

> *I'm so sorry. I just got this message. Graduation was insane and I spent the rest of the day moving into my new apartment. My internet isn't up yet. This is the first I've had time to even log on.*
>
> *My job decided to kick it into high gear today. I knew this place would be a challenge, but I never expected everything to be so last minute. It felt like I spent my day working on one project until it was almost time to go home. Then I had five that needed to be done within the hour. When I finished those, five more were dropped onto my shoulders.*
>
> *Please forgive me.*

She didn't even read over it before she hit send. Her heart ached as she stared out the window at the streetlight. So close, yet still so far away. This anonymous man might always be anonymous. He might always be *the one that got away* or something like that. It was so fairy-tale-ish. How could she even think about there being anything more than what they already have? She glanced back at the screen. Another message.

> *No, I'm sorry. I dropped it out there with no notice, then I didn't even make it myself. Please forgive* me.
>
> *It's crazy now. One day after graduation and our lives are already upside down. My father had a medical issue yesterday. I didn't even make it to the ceremony. He's fine, but it scared the hell out of me. You once told me your mother's your world. My father is mine. He's done so much for his family. He's my idol, my hero. Seeing him lying in that hospital bed with monitors hooked up to him... It made me realize there will be a time in the future where he won't be there. That's not something I ever wanted to think about, but it's a reality I have to face.*
>
> *It also reminded me of something I already knew. Life is short. I can't let this fear of meeting you keep me from meeting you. I can't let the excitement overrule all common sense, either. They seem to be in constant battle with one another. And a frat party was not how I wanted to see you for the first time. Our*

relationship or friendship, whatever you wish to define it as, has been intimate. It's always been just you and me. That's how we need to meet. Just us.

So, how about coffee on Tuesday? There's a place on Chouteau called Spoons where they make an amazing latte. I work until five, but I can meet you any time after that. Just tell me when and I will be there.

Macie didn't hesitate. She didn't think. She just started typing.

I can meet you at six. But how will I know it's you? I don't want to trust fate.

She hit send and waited nearly ten minutes before he responded.

I don't want to tempt fate either. A red rose? Too cheesy? I don't know how to do this.

Macie sat back. It wasn't like she met men online all the time. This would be a first for her too. A rose was cheesy, but it was still something easily recognizable.

Me either. I'll bring a rose, too. We can be cheesy together. If it helps, I'm terrified and excited. What if this is a mistake? What if we're only meant to be the way we are now?

His message came back almost instantly.

What if it's not?

Macie smiled. He was right. There were so many variables in this equation that even Pythagoras would stumble over the solution.
I will see you Tuesday, she typed.
Grabbing her phone, she sent Lauren a text. Two seconds later, Macie's phone rang.
"What's going on?" Lauren asked, panic edged her voice.
"I'm going to meet him." Macie stomach rolled. She wasn't sure if she was going to be sick or if this was just some weird reaction to her excitement. They felt oddly the same.

"Who?" Lauren yawned so it sounded more like an owl than a person.

"Guy. From the app. Guy!"

"Holy crap!" Lauren screeched. Macie imagined her sitting upright so fast that all the pillows on her couch fell to the floor. Maybe she knocked Ford over in the process.

Macie pulled the phone away from her ear. "Yeah, holy crap. What the hell do I do now?"

"When? Where? What time?"

"Tuesday. And I'm not telling you where." Macie grinned. "You'll show up, and I won't go through with it."

"Spoilsport." Lauren giggled. "I can't wait to tell Ford."

"No, don't. If this is the fail to end all fails, I don't want him to know. He might tell Zac and I'd never live it down. Just... I don't want anyone to know." Macie's eyes watered as fear gripped her chest. "Please? Just between us."

"Okay, but you have to call me the minute you can. Even if it's the next morning," Lauren said.

"Believe me, if this guy is everything I hope he is, I won't call you for a week."

CHAPTER TEN

Ford sat at their designated table at Maciano's, a favorite restaurant they'd eaten at every Monday since freshman year. It wasn't anything expensive, but the Italian food was the best in the city. Maciano grew his own tomatoes, herbs, and peppers in a greenhouse on his farm an hour from city lines. It made all the difference in the world in Zac's opinion. Ford liked their prices, even though he'd never paid. Zac always picked up the tab. It was easier and Zac didn't mind. Ford refused at first, until they struck a deal. In exchange for the best marinara, Ford proofread all Zac's papers and corrected his grammar. For Zac, it was a fair.

"What's up?" Ford asked, standing to shake Zac's hand. "You look like you've either hit a bong or the lottery or gotten laid. I'm not sure which."

Zac shook his friend's hand, an old-fashioned maneuver but one he'd come to appreciate in Ford. "Wrong on all accounts." He pulled out his chair and settled into it, waving for the waiter who hurried over. "Vodka tonic please."

"Very good, sir," the waiter said as he dipped his head in a bow before scurrying toward the bar.

"So, what's with the good mood?" Ford sipped his water and raised his eyebrows.

"I have a date." Zac lifted his menu and glanced over it as if he'd order something other than the marinara. But it never hurt to look.

"Which is different from any other time you have a date?" Ford reached out and took Zac's menu.

Zac leaned forward so Ford wouldn't miss his words or his meaning. "It's with *her*."

"Her?" Ford asked, his eyebrows slanted downward into a V. He almost looked like a Vulcan.

Zac nodded, his grin stretched his skin to the point it actually hurt. Not that a little pain could wipe away this feeling of joy.

"The girl? From the app?" Doubt creased Ford's mouth, forcing it into a straight line. "Seriously?"

"Tuesday." Zac leaned back when the waiter brought his drink and a basket of fresh breadsticks. "Thank you," Zac said to the waiter. "We're ready to order."

When the waiter stepped away from the table with their orders, Ford asked again, "Seriously?"

"As serious as you are about marrying Lauren."

"This Tuesday? As in tomorrow?"

"Oh for crying out loud, yes." Zac downed his drink in one gulp. "Tuesday."

"Whose idea?" Ford freed a breadstick from the basket and set it on a small plate.

"Mine." Zac reached for one of his own and stopped midway. "Does it matter?"

Ford shrugged. "Guess not. Who picked the location?"

"Me. Why?" Zac drew out the last word. He didn't like what Ford was implying.

"Just asking." Ford ate his breadstick slowly, chewing every bit while Zac waited impatiently for more. "How're you going to know it's her?"

"Roses. Why?" Zac clenched his fists. He didn't like where Ford was going. It curled his stomach.

"Red?"

"Yes. Why?"

Ford smiled. "I'm just messing with you, man. You've never been this giddy about meeting a girl. It's an opportunity to screw with your head." He shrugged. "Couldn't resist."

"You're a jerk. I don't care how angelic you come across, you are a jerk." Zac relaxed, each muscle aching from where he'd tightened up. He stared over Ford's head at the mural Maciano painted himself. It was of an Italian hillside and Maciano claimed it was where he'd met his wife. The hills were a flat green and the people had no real faces. The buildings were white squares with red triangle roofs, but none of that prevented it from being charming. "I don't want to screw this up, Ford. She could be it. She could be the one."

"And they say I'm the romantic."

Zac threw a piece of bread at his friend. "You are. And it must have rubbed off on me."

Ford laughed. "I can't wait to tell Lauren. She's been wanting to set you up for years."

"No. No Lauren. It'll get back to Macie and I don't want to hear it from her." Zac's phone buzzed in his pocked. He pulled it free and groaned. "Speak of the devil. She wants to talk about your bachelor party."

"It's Lauren's party, too." Ford pointed at Zac. "Don't forget that."

"Man, I wanted to see your face when you got a lap dance." Zac glanced at his phone and tapped out a quick response. "I'll see if she's available this weekend or something. We can get the plans together then, okay?"

"I don't care when you meet her, but Lauren said she's working on the weekends. Fair warning."

The waiter arrived with their food and the topic of conversation turned to the wedding. Zac let Ford talk about all the little details, even though Zac couldn't care less. He was just glad Ford was investing his share of the sale of Blind Friends. It would make his and Lauren's lives easier in the long run.

"Did you even hear me?" Ford asked.

"What?" Zac's thoughts had trailed off toward money-land and work. He wanted to talk to Lauren about investing her share, but he hadn't brought it up to her yet. Or to Ford. Maybe he should talk to Macie about doing the same.

"I said that if it goes well with mystery girl, she could end up being your date to my wedding."

Zac sat up straighter. He hadn't thought that far in advance. A smile grew over his lips. "Yeah, she could."

Tuesdays were now laundry day. Macie didn't have time on the weekends to do much of anything. Mondays were reserved for cleaning, working on freelance projects, and watching Netflix. Unless she got called into work, of course. Fortunately, there was a laundry room in the basement of the building. She started early and finished just in time for Nancy Carter to call her in. At least her work clothes were clean. Not that the station had a strict dress code for her department, but Macie made it a point to look business casual. As long as it didn't require dresses and skirts. That was crossing the line. Her work attire consisted of black dress pants, dark button-down shirts, and black flats. It was a serious sacrifice of style, but Macie thought it was worth it. She preferred the shorts and t-shirts she wore every day of college. Her skater skirts were only for nights at the club. And she missed wearing her favorite Chucks, a red so faded that they looked vintage.

It took her less then twenty minutes to get dressed and get to work.

"Macie, thank God you're finally here." Nancy ushered Macie to her office. The news team geared up for the noon broadcast, which lead to chaos. Macie loved the craziness of it all. Nancy pointed to a chair in front of her desk, and Macie sat on the edge. "Ian quit. No notice. Just said *fuck this*, and left. Couldn't even finish out the damn day." Nancy shook her head and lifted her fingers to her lips. She fake smoked a pen. "I know it's your day off, but I need you to finish what he started."

"Sure, no problem. But I have to leave at five." Macie didn't want to come right out and say she had a date. It wasn't any of Nancy's business anyway. But she should've known better.

"Hot date, huh?" Nancy snapped forward in her chair. "Just don't let Mark know. He's still got a thing for you."

Macie grimaced. She regretted flirting with him like she had. It had disaster written all over it before it even happened, but once they started working together, it was worse. He'd hang out near her office just to say hi or make a point to talk to her about something they had broadcast or he'd seen somewhere. He was a nice guy, but they had nothing in common. Every interaction was awkward. Interoffice dating, never a good idea.

"I'll get you out of here by five." She handed over a file. "Ian's notes and computer access. Everything he was working on is on his computer so that will be easier for you."

"Great. And you're giving me a tetanus shot first, right?"

Nancy smiled. "Buck up, kid, and deal with it." Nancy pulled a can of Lysol from her desk drawer. "But this might help."

Macie took the can with a groan. "At least I get overtime for this. Remind me to kick Ian in the balls if I see him again."

"Beat me to it," Nancy said, but she'd already shifted gears to another problem. "Tell Barb to get her ass in here, too."

Macie didn't even bother to respond. She stepped out of Nancy's office and stopped at Barb's desk. "What happened to Ian?"

Barb glanced around, searching for prying eyes. She pushed her square glasses up on her long nose. "You know that new guy? Alex?"

Macie nodded. It was more like she knew of him, but either way.

"Well, he wanted Ian to do a graphic a different way." Barb glanced around again. It wasn't like this wouldn't be around the entire station before the six o'clock news. "Ian wasn't happy about it, but he agreed. Then Alex came back after Ian sent the new graphic and called him every name in the book. Ian took it until Alex walked away, then he said fuck this and left."

"What did Nancy say?" Macie wondered if her boss would have her back.

Barb shrugged and went back to whatever she was typing. Either Nancy wasn't surprised by this development or she didn't think twice about it and had already moved on. Barb knew everything that went on in the station. The older woman had worked there before they closed the news department. She was the first person they brought back, too. She was probably a better investigative reporter than most of the journalists on their team.

Macie shook her head. If Nancy didn't say anything, she probably didn't know the entire story. Then again, Nancy knew everything that went on inside these walls. Something else was going on. As long as it didn't directly affect Macie, she really didn't care. Ian was an alright guy, but he was a subpar designer. He half-assed everything and only did what he needed to get by. And he was a colossal slob.

"Oh, Nancy wants you asap," Macie added as an afterthought. Bara rolled her eyes and shot out of her chair like a rabbit.

When Macie got to the graphics department's closet-sized office, she immediately backed up all of Ian's files. Even his keyboard was sticky. Macie shuddered. How could one person create so much trash and just leave like that? She didn't even want to think about what his apartment looked like. Macie used a Clorox wipe on her fingers and sprayed Lysol around Ian's cubicle. Housekeeping didn't even bother cleaning his desk. Hopefully they would now that he was gone. They should get hazard pay for it, too.

Ian's phone rang. Macie glanced around the office, but she was the only person there. With a shrug, she picked up the receiver. She didn't even get a chance to say a word.

"Look you little rat fuck, I don't know what your problem is and I don't really care. Get that damn graphic done in the next two minutes or I'm going to come down there and beat your lazy, fat ass."

Macie raised her eyebrows and pulled the receiver away from her face. She did the only thing any self-respecting woman would do. She hung up. The minute her butt hit her chair at her desk, Ian's phone rang again. And again. She thought about unplugging it, but then she had a better idea. She grabbed her cell phone and rolled across the floor into his cubicle. Before picking up the phone, she pressed record on her voice recorder.

"You little fuck. I'm going to make sure you never work again, Ian. No employer will hire you after I tell everyone I know what a worthless piece of shit you are. Just do your damn job and do it right for fuck's sake."

Macie waited until Alex hung up. At least she assumed it was Alex. Unless Ian had other enemies among the crew. And, if she was honest, that was entirely possible. She didn't disagree with Alex's opinion of Ian's work, but she fumed at the way he treated her former co-worker. She rolled back to her desk and pulled up the graphic. It actually wasn't bad for Ian. That surprised her. There were several things that needed to be tweaked, but nothing needed a major overhaul. It was for an ad about an upcoming charity walk the station sponsored. Alex was the designated local celebrity leading the way. Of course, he wanted it to look good. That didn't mean he needed to be a dick.

The door to her office flew open. Macie didn't even turn around. The heavy breathing and stomping would've been creepy if it wasn't for the fact she knew who it was and she knew she had his balls in a vice. He just didn't know it yet.

"Where's Ian?" a very familiar and very calm voice said.

"Quit." One word answers usually pushed people over the edge. She had a gut feeling they would do the same to this guy. From the rumors about his temper, it wouldn't take long. She'd been grateful she hadn't met him based on what little she'd heard. He wasn't popular and he wasn't nice, but he was great on camera. That was all that really mattered.

"What do you mean he quit?"

Macie turned around in her chair, crossing her legs and smiling as politely as she could. "Guess someone pissed him off. He walked out."

Alex's gaze slid down her body in a way that did creep her out. He wasn't a bad looking guy with highlighted brown hair and light green eyes, but there was a menacing undertone in his voice and a deliberate sneer. Macie didn't want to run into him in a dark alley. But here, at work, she could handle him.

"And you are?" Alex asked, crossing his arms over his chest.

"Macie. I report only to Nancy and do exactly what she tells me." Macie uncrossed her legs and sat straighter in her chair. "If you have any questions or concerns about my work, talk to her. Now if you'll excuse me, I have plenty to do."

Alex smirked and leaned toward her. "Oh, you'll do what I tell you, or you won't be here."

Macie shook her head and turned around in her chair. She wanted to show her cards, but laying them on the table now would be a major mistake. She'd hold her hand close and wait to show it when Alex pushed her too far.

The door clicked closed behind her. Macie ignored the sinking feeling in her stomach that sent shivers down her spine. She fixed a few minor issues with the graphic and forwarded it on to Alex with a blind copy to Nancy. Alex didn't email her back, but Nancy did with six other projects that needed to be done by five. Macie glanced at the clock on her monitor. Only four hours to do it in. It was going to be close.

CHAPTER ELEVEN

It was almost five-thirty when Macie finished retouching Alex's smug photo. Apparently, that was where Ian went wrong. Alex wanted to look like a movie star, and Ian made him look like a news reporter. It was high school jock versus nerd all over again. She thought that shit was over, but obviously not. She read through the email exchanges again. They were almost as abusive as the phone call. Alex had managed to keep a string of cuss words out of the text. Smart move on his part. If he'd done that to her, she would've blind cc'd Nancy in everything.

"Macie," Nancy shouted from her office as Macie hurried past. "A moment, please."

It took every ounce of energy she had not to slouch her shoulders and act like she'd been called into the principal's office. Because it felt exactly like the time her high school principal pulled her in for some creative decisions she'd made on the school's mural. Apparently, he didn't like the overly large nipples on the school's mascot. She took her suspension in stride. Totally worth it.

"What's up, Nancy?" Macie asked with fake nonchalance as she stepped inside the office.

"Have a seat." Nancy pointed to the chair Macie occupied most.

"I really need —"

"This will only take a minute." Nancy pointed again. "The hot date can wait a few. Besides being fashionably late is still a thing, right?"

Macie knew if she argued, she'd be stuck in Nancy's office all night. Date or no date, Nancy would talk until Macie passed out. Macie sat as smoothly as she could without plopping.

"Alex has asked for you to do all his work." Nancy tapped her pen against the desk. "I'm inclined to agree."

Macie closed her eyes. "Please, no."

"Do you know who he is?"

"Nope, and I don't really give two shits. I only met him today," Macie said as her eyes snapped open. She pulled out her phone and set it on Nancy's desk. She pressed play on the clip of Alex's verbal abuse. A triumphant smirk fought to explode across her lips. Surely Nancy wouldn't make her work with Alex after hearing that. Hell, he'd be lucky to keep his job. "Imagine what he'd do if I pissed him off. Nobody should have to deal with that."

Nancy took Macie's phone and replayed the message. She didn't grimace or shake her head. Instead, she deleted the recording.

"What the fuck?" Macie fell back against her chair.

"Alex's father owns the station." Nancy slid the phone across the desk. "He's a spoiled brat who needs to be bitch slapped by every person on the planet. Even then, I don't think it would help him much." Nancy shook her head, resigned to the losing hand she'd been dealt. "Look, I'm sorry, Macie. You're off to a great start here."

Macie nodded. She knew a power play when she saw it. This was Alex's first move.

"He'll still have to go through me first. I'll be your buffer. I'll be your sounding board." Nancy's gazed dropped. "I'll do whatever I can to keep him in line."

You know I'm going to start looking for a new job, right? Already. After only a few short weeks? Or I could make his life miserable. There's a thought. Macie didn't say any of that, though. She gritted her teeth and stood from her seat. "You know, Nancy, he's not going to get to me. And he's not going to beat me. I won't let him."

Nancy smiled and waved her out of the office. Macie glanced at her phone. It was five-forty-five. She looked like hell and had zero time to even glance in a mirror. As it was, she was going to be late.

But there was one last thing she had to do. She opened her cloud. There in a file marked 'Just in Case' was the recording of Alex. Macie wasn't stupid. She knew to back her shit up, especially something that could come in handy later. Nancy had to realize

Macie would back up everything. If she didn't, then her boss underestimated her. Just to be safe, Macie downloaded it onto her phone and emailed herself a copy. She'd put it on her computer at home in case she was hacked. You could never have too many backups.

Spoons was a good twenty-minute walk from the station in the opposite direction of her apartment, which was fifteen minutes the other way. If she went home to get her barely drivable car, she'd have to find a parking spot and could be half an hour late. If she walked, she'd be maybe five to ten minutes late.

Walking it was.

She didn't hurry, though. Showing up like she'd just ran a marathon wasn't a good idea. The heat and humidity would certainly ruin her hair if she rushed. She reached into her messenger bag to check for her makeup kit. At least she'd had the foresight to pack that before she left for work. It wasn't much, just powder, lip-gloss, and mascara. Macie had never been a big girly girl, but she liked the basics. She pulled out the ponytail holder, fluffing her hair with her fingers.

Sure, remember the makeup but not the hairbrush, she thought as she passed a boutique. Using the window as a mirror, she fixed her hair into a messy bun, touched up her mascara and lip gloss. Only a few more blocks.

Something nagged at her. Something she should've remembered, but she couldn't quite put her finger on it. A block from Spoons, it hit her. A rose. She'd forgotten the damn rose. A small florist shop nestled between a law office and a chocolate shop caught her eye. She crossed the street, getting a few honks as she dodged traffic.

"Look where you're going, lady," one guy shouted with a thick creole accent.

Macie waved at him, but never took her eye off the prize. She got to the door at the same time as the clerk inside flipped the sign.

"Please," Macie said to the forlorn woman who stared at her with disgust. "I'm sorry. I just need one rose."

The woman rolled her eyes and opened the door. "You sound like a guy who was in here about twenty minutes ago."

"Really?" Macie stepped into the small shop, inhaling the smell of roses and lilacs that filled the air. Had Guy bought his rose here? Macie's heart swelled. Sure, it could've been any man on his way somewhere, but she wanted it to be her man. *Her man.* He wasn't her man. Not yet, anyway. Macie didn't even know him. She had to keep reminding herself of that tiny little fact.

"Yeah, really." The clerk opened a cooler filled with roses. "Any color?"

"Red."

"Of course." She pulled out a single red rose and wrapped it in thin green paper. "Red is universal. I prefer the white myself. There's something about the purity and innocence of the color. It blends, bends, and flows with light. And white goes with everything."

"So does black," Macie said as she pulled out the cash and handed it to the woman.

"Very true. Black has a negative reputation, but I've always found depth in it." She handed Macie her change and the rose. "Have a great night."

"You, too," Macie said. She clutched the rose tightly to her chest and strolled out the door. The woman's words reverberated in her ears. The artist in her wanted to explore the depth of white. She wanted to feel it on her brushes, between her fingers, on the canvas. She wanted to stare at the paint and let it tell her what to do. During the last semester, Macie's time had been stretched thin. She hadn't picked up her palette since January. Her focus had been school and the wedding. Painting was her zen, her love, her need. How did she let it slip away?

Macie stopped to take a deep breath. She stood outside the entrance to Spoons.

Just go in, she chided herself. *Woman up. You know he's in there. You know he's fantastic. Walk through the damn door.*

Her internal pep talk turned into an internal argument. One with a logical solution. *Peek in the windows. See if you can spot him.*

She was already ten minutes late. If he was there, she could catch a glimpse. She could see what he looked like, how he sat, if he looked as nervous as she was. Drawing in another breath for courage, Macie tiptoed past the front door and glanced through the windows.

Spoons was packed, but there were only two tables with single occupants. One was a girl around her age typing frantically on a laptop. The other was a blond man. Macie's heart skipped. She couldn't see his face, but there was a red rose on the table. His fingers played with the stem, rolling it between them. The light glinted off his watch. She'd seen the gold face and worn leather band somewhere before. Where, she couldn't remember. Her heart skipped a beat as he chatted with the waitress. The woman smiled warmly as she tapped her pen against her fingers. He threw his head back and laughed. The waitress smiled.

Guy turned away and glanced out the window.

Macie couldn't breathe. She couldn't move. She couldn't fucking believe it.

Zac Sparks.

Of all the people in the world, she had been flirting with Zac fucking Sparks.

Macie turned on her heel and headed back toward her apartment, dropping the rose in the trash along the way.

✐ ✐ ✐

Zac checked the time on his watch again. She was almost fifteen minutes late. He'd done some work while he waited, running numbers and planning Ford's investments. And he'd checked the Blind Friends app every minute to see if she'd canceled on him or at least messaged to say she was running late.

As much as he hated to admit it, Zac knew he'd been stood up. It had been foolish, childish even for him, to dream that he'd meet his future partner over a stupid app. It wasn't like he didn't have time to find someone. It wasn't like he was pushing fifty and still single with no family. He was twenty-two. He wasn't bad looking. What if she thought he was? What if she glanced through the windows and took one look at him then left? Zac didn't think that would happen. She wasn't that shallow.

The door opened, and he steeled himself as he looked for a rose. The woman who walked in didn't have one, but she did have something. A serious attitude problem. Macie was the last person he wanted to see. She turned toward the dining room and caught his gaze. Zac expected to see the usual hate mixed with anger, but her shoulders drooped as if resigned. She held her head high and strolled over to him.

"Can we talk?" She sat down, glaring at the rose on the table. She picked it up and twirled it between her fingers. "Or am I interrupting something?"

Zac reached out and plucked it from her fingers. "What do you want, Macie?"

"We need to plan the party." Her gaze glanced at the rose still in Zac's hand. He pulled it under the table, away from her prying eyes. "How's she going to know it's you now? Or is she late?"

"We can meet this weekend. Preferably Saturday afternoon," Zac said, ignoring her question and the rising bile in his throat. "I'm taking Dad to the club in the morning."

"How's he doing?" Macie rested her elbows on the table.

"Fine. It wasn't anything major." *Not that you'd care.* Zac searched Macie's face for any sign of insincerity. He was surprised to find the opposite. "Thanks for asking."

Macie smiled, but it looked more like a grimace. "I have to work on Saturdays. It would have to be in the evening. Same for Sundays. Right now my Mondays and Tuesdays are open." She bobbed her head. "That might change, though."

Zac squeezed the rose in his hand, the thorns biting against his skin. "Saturday evening would be fine. Where do you want to meet? Here? Crafts? Some place else?"

Macie bit her lip. "Sure you won't have a hot date? I mean, the suave Zac Sparks has never had a Saturday free since I've known him. Or were you so confident that you never expected to be stood up tonight?"

"Pretty sure I'm free." Zac leaned in, glancing at the spot where she'd sucked her lip into her mouth. "And to answer your smartass question, I was supposed to meet someone. Said someone did not show. Does that make you feel superior? I know it's killing you not to laugh. And I know it's killing you not to make a sarcastic comment. So just get it out, Macie."

She sat back in her seat. Her mouth stuck open as if he'd just slapped her across the face. "Is that really what you think of me? That I'm that big of a bitch?"

Zac couldn't believe it. Macie actually looked hurt. Guilt welled in his chest, but he pushed it down. She'd never been nice to him, never bothered to get to know him. Yeah, they'd gotten off on the wrong foot, but that was four years ago. They'd both grown. They'd both matured. Well, he had, but that wasn't the point. "No, I—"

"Just forget it. It doesn't matter, anyway. Once the wedding's over, we'll never have to see each other again." She stood from the chair and pushed it in. "It would be easiest to meet at my place. Then I don't have to lug everything with me. I'll text you the address."

Zac didn't stand. He didn't try to stop her as she walked away. Why would he? She was right. They could finally be done with each other soon enough. Out of each other's lives except for the occasional meeting at Ford and Lauren's. That didn't stop him from feeling like a jerk. Zac normally kept his composure. He was always polite, respectful, and kept his opinions to himself for the most part. One of the first things his father taught him was how to walk the line. But when it came to Macie Regan, he had a hard time holding back.

He pulled the rose out from under the table and stared at the petals. Thoughts of Macie disappeared as he wondered what happened to his mystery girl. Every natural and unnatural possibility floated through his mind. There was one that he hated to admit, but it was the most likely scenario. She'd stood him up.

Zac dropped the rose on the table along with a twenty to pay for his drink and the waitress's time.

He'd give her until tomorrow to message him. Then he'd delete his profile and the app completely. He'd be done with her. Then he could move on with his life.

CHAPTER TWELVE

Macie's shirt stuck to her skin. Her hair dripped with sweat. It took her forty-five minutes to get home from Spoons. It would've taken her longer, but she walked as fast as she could in her heels. See if she'd wear those shoes again.

How could this happen? How could Guy be Zac fucking Sparks? She tore off her clothes, tossing them onto her futon instead of hanging them up. She felt like a fraud. Everything she'd done over the last few months had been to set herself up for her future, even chatting with Guy... Zac. But she didn't know it was Zac. She'd built her wardrobe to look professional, and she hated it. She put up these walls of cool confidence, but that wasn't Macie. Sitting in front of Zac tonight, knowing he had been on the other side of her screen for four months while she chatted without hiding who she was, staring into his eyes at his disappointment in seeing her, she wanted to crumble. She wanted to cry. She wanted to turn back the clock and never schedule that meeting.

She needed to paint. The question was what.

Macie pulled her supplies from the small closet near the bathroom. She threw down a drop cloth and set up her easel. Grabbing her brushes, she stood in front of her last blank 40x40 canvas in nothing but her birthday suit. Black and white, the colors blended in her mind. She filled her palette with both. Her brushed dug into the black. She didn't think about what she was painting. She let her anger, disappointment, heartache, and fear guide her. She swayed as the bristles swept across the canvas, black paint, white paint, flowing and smothering each other. An hour later, her arm ached, and the brush slipped from her hand, landing the clear plastic at her feet. The black and white swirled into a variety of grays, but still kept their own color. It was an abyss, circling wide then tightening in the center. She painted the rabbit hole she fell down. Everything in life always seemed so black and white to her, but she finally saw the grays.

She needed to climb out and face the music. It didn't matter that Guy was Zac or that Zac was Guy. What mattered was he got her. He understood the real Macie Regan. The one she didn't let many people see.

Grabbing her tablet off the table, she settled into her chair, paint and all. She didn't have a clue how to do this. How to tell Zac she had been there. That she was right in front of him the entire time. But she also knew she *couldn't*. She had to … she had to show him who she really was and not just Macie the anonymous person on the other side of the screen. She didn't want to give up the connection they had online, either.

Once the app opened, she went to their message stream and began to type.

I am so sorry about tonight. Work called me in.

She backspaced over all of it and started again.

Please forgive me. I know we agreed to meet tonight and I know how bad this looks that I wasn't there. I had every intention to be there, but something came up and it was unavoidable. If you don't, I understand. This isn't how I wanted our first meeting to go. I imagined a night of fantastic conversation face to face. I enjoy our chats. It should come as no surprise to you, but I constantly check my app to see if you've responded.

Or maybe it does in light of tonight. I hope not. I really do want to meet you, but my life is out of control at the moment. Just graduating from college, starting a very demanding job, living on my own for the first time. I'm overwhelmed. And the one thing I want to do, I keep screwing up. Story of my life right now. Screwing everything up.

Again, I understand if you don't want to talk to me again

She almost signed her name. Again. That would've been more of a disaster. To make things worse, her phone went off and it was a message from Lauren. Macie ignored it. She couldn't even tell her best friend that Guy was Zac. She had to deal with this on her own and she had to make things right with the Zac she'd butted heads with, so she could tell him the truth.

Maybe she wouldn't have to. Maybe she could get Zac to see the real her and forget the online her. Then she'd never have to tell him that she was the person he'd chatted with on Blind Friends. He'd never have to know. Smiling at her scheme, Macie put her tablet down and headed into the shower.

This plan could work. It would be perfect. And he'd never have to know the truth.

✐ ✐ ✐

Zac threw himself into work the next day. He met with new investors, ones he'd recruited from Lafayette. Most of his new clientele didn't have much to invest but he'd encouraged them to meet with him anyway. It was never to early to build a nest egg and plan for retirement. He also managed to get a few professors to move their portfolios to him. The work kept his mind off his mystery girl until the office quieted down in the late afternoon and she snuck into his thoughts.

Had she taken one look at him and bolted? Had she stood outside and laughed because she'd never intended meeting him to begin with? Had he scared her off somehow? He shook his head and focus on emails, stock options, news, anything to stop thinking about her.

It was getting close to five when his phone dinged a text. He glanced at the name. Chomper. He really needed to change that before Macie found out. But how would she ever know? It wasn't like he was going to hand her his phone and let her snoop through the contact list. And it wasn't like she'd ever see that when they were around each other. Nah, he'd keep it. If no other reason than the simple fact that it would upset her.

I'm supposed to be off work by five on Saturday, but probably won't get out of here until six. Come over after seven. Followed by her address and a brief set of directions.

Zac pressed one letter, *K*, but before he could hit send, Macie sent another.

I know the idea of talking to me disgusts you, but I'd also like to discuss investing. Maybe you can point me to someone who wouldn't mind working with me.

He stared at the screen. That didn't compute. He'd tried to have civil conversations with Macie about investing after college, but she was adamant her loans would make that impossible. It didn't make any sense. And did she really think he'd trust someone else with her money? Sparks Investments was about the personal, not the bottom line. His father had taught him that long ago. He'd trust his dad to do right by Macie but not many others. Despite years of antagonism, he knew she wouldn't invest in anything that went against her morals. He knew how she'd want to invest and what stocks she'd be most interested in. Anybody else would have to learn the quirks of Macie, of which there were many.

He hit send, still using the one letter response. His eye darted to the Blind Friends app. He hadn't checked it. The minute he got home the night before, he'd put his phone in the kitchen as far away from him as he could. He spent the rest of his night catching up on movies he'd queued on Netflix before falling asleep on the couch. It wasn't ideal, but it worked in the avoidance column. Thankfully, his stepmother had a flare for decorating and had picked out a nice couch for his apartment.

The app stared back at him. He shook his head and put his phone back onto his desk. It would have to wait until he was at home with a stiff drink. Disappointment was best accompanied by whiskey, straight.

"Mr. Sparks?" a voice called from the door to his small office. Zac glanced up from his computer to see his father's secretary. "Mr. Sparks would like to see you before you leave."

"Maureen, you've known me most of my life." Zac logged off his computer and stood. "It's Zac. Mr. Sparks is my father."

"You can be Zac when you're not here." Maureen smiled. Her warm eyes reminded him of his mother. She was old enough to be his grandmother. Maureen had started working for his father when Sparks Investments opened. She was already in her mid-forties then. "When you're here, you'll be Mr. Sparks and you *will* like it."

"Yes, ma'am." Zac knew better than to argue with her. He'd made that mistake before and wasn't about to do so again. "Do you know what the elder Mr. Sparks wants?" She raised her eyebrows.

"Just so I'm prepared."

"I believe he's meeting with several new staff members." Maureen didn't meet Zac's gaze as she led him down the hall. "Just a quick check in to see how it's going for everyone."

"Maureen," Zac said, drawing out her name. He leaned on her desk. "You hear everything around here. Is there something I should know?"

She smirked and continued typing. "I can assure you that if I heard anything, your father would know."

Zac nodded and straightened up. He slapped Maureen's desk a couple of times before turning toward the elevators.

His father's space was decked out in dark wood with a maroon couch that looked out the floor to ceiling windows of the corner office. It wasn't exactly his dad's style, but he'd let Amanda decorate the office. It was a contrast of light and dark, like the world of finance according to Amanda. The only thing his father refused to part with was the desk. Zac's mother had bought the antique as a present when he opened Sparks Investments. Amanda had it refinished, but she never asked him to replace it. Zac admired his stepmother for that.

Three of the new hires stood in front of the desk as Zac stepped into the office. His father leaned around the group and waved Zac forward. Zac wasn't comfortable discussing business in front of the newbies. He glanced at his competition. They weren't technically competition, but Zac thought of them that way. If they brought in more clients, and by default more money, then he'd look bad. In fact, he would look like a man riding his father's coattails. That was the last thing he wanted. Once that stigma set in, it never went away. Tyler was smart, but he had a one track mind. Zac didn't know Michael. Unlike Zac and Tyler, Michael didn't go to Lafayette.

"Glad you could join us, Zac," his father began from his throne behind the desk. "While it's only been a few weeks, I wanted to compliment you all on a job well done. You've started off well, but there's always room for improvement. Michael, you've too few investors. Work on that, please. Tyler, you've done well, but you should diversify more. It's all about balance. And Zac, you've brought in quite a few new clients, but nobody with any substantial funds. Go for some bigger fish. Now, I'm quite happy with your work and we'll meet again next month to see where you stand. Good evening, gentlemen."

The other two men shuffled out of the room, but Zac stayed behind. He waited for the door to click shut behind him.

"Bigger fish? My father always taught me that to build clientele meant to build from the ground up." Zac grinned, but he remained standing.

"Yeah, well, your father's a wise man." He motioned Zac into an empty chair. "But you do need to do more networking outside of the university and bring in more money. That's the bottom line here, son. It's all about the cold, hard cash."

"The board still wants to go public?" Zac knew the situation hadn't been settled, but not much had been said since it was first brought up.

"It's worse than that." His father leaned back in his chair and stared out the window. "They're trying to oust me."

"What?" Zac sat up faster than an arrow hits its target. "They can't do that. You built this company. How can they try to take it away from you?"

"They can. You and I both know the long-term goal is to sell to one of the big financial institutes." He shook his head and turned back toward Zac. "They're using my stint in the hospital as an excuse to say I'm unfit. Jackasses were the ones to put me in the hospital in the first place. Not that they care about that. Can I count on you?"

"Of course. What're you going to do?" Panic welled inside Zac's chest. This business was his father's, plain and simple. He'd do whatever it took to keep it that way.

"Well, we're going to war, son." His father stared him dead in the eye. "And you're my general. Rumors can be the deadliest. So make some happen. Make sure people know my health is fantastic. And make sure people remember why they are where they are. I made this place. It will either survive with me or die without me."

Zac nodded. This was exactly what they'd discussed before, but now was the time to enact it. "We've got this, Dad."

His father nodded and waved him out the door. Zac stood, leaving the office without another word. The situation was less than ideal and getting worse. He didn't want to play the role of corporate spy, but this was his father. This was his father's company. He'd sacrificed so much to build it. Zac sat back at his desk to gather his thoughts. Most of the office had left for the day. He glanced at his watch. It was almost five-thirty. Not that he had anywhere to be.

But he did. He needed to network. He picked up his phone and called Maureen. "Where does everyone go after work?"

"Besides home? Most of the younger employees head over to McKennon's for happy hour."

"Thanks, Maureen. You're the best." Zac hung up and grabbed his suit jacket off the back of his door. He'd head over to the bar, make nice, and show them he was their equal. His father had already started it by putting him in the same category as everyone else. He just needed to play that up.

CHAPTER THIRTEEN

He hadn't responded. She sent the message on Tuesday and nothing. By Thursday, Macie had stopped refreshing the app. The only bright spot in her week was the check from MatchInHeaven, LLC for the graphics on Blind Friends. There hadn't been any negotiations. They said here's the offer. She said okay. They also asked if she was available for freelance work. Again, she said okay. So far, no calls, but she had a little bit of hope. Her student loans would be coming due soon enough and every bit of cash she could bring in would help.

"Macie!" Nancy shouted as Macie hurried past the office. "Get in here."

Damn it. Macie had done a decent job at avoiding her boss in person. Emails and phone calls were still every two minutes. Macie stepped into Nancy's abnormally messy office. It looked like a hurricane rammed the room but left the rest of the station untouched. "What's up?"

"Alex." One word, that was all she needed to say for Macie to sink into a chair and wait for the rest of the shoe to drop. "He volunteered to host a trivia night for St. Raphael's. It's free promo for the station so make him look like the Hollywood movie star he thinks he is. Here." Nancy shoved the folder toward her. "There's a stack of emails in your inbox with more, but get that shit there done first and shoot it back to me."

"Will do, boss." Easy enough and no shoe dropping at all. Macie stood and walked to the door when the shoe found her back.

"How're your photography skills?" Nancy asked.

Macie closed her eyes for a moment before turning around. She'd almost made it to freedom. "Nonexistent."

"Grab a camera from Joe. And get existent." Nancy grimaced and massaged her temple. "He wants you to take photos of him for the social media pages. And a little video."

"Hire a cameraman. I'm not qualified to do any of that." Anger surged in Macie's gut as Nancy shook her head. "And I get a raise for all this extra work, right?"

"You get to keep your job. Isn't that enough?"

Macie walked over to Nancy's desk and dropped the folder on her calendar. "Nope."

She needed the job, more than Nancy realized, but she needed her dignity too. She'd been there almost a month, and until Alex decided she was to be his own personal bitch, she'd enjoyed it. But the minute Nancy bowed to Alex, Macie's life had been hell.

"You're a good designer," Nancy said. Each word was clipped with threat. "I'd hate to lose you over this."

It was a powerplay. One Macie would've made herself if she'd been in Nancy's position. But she had one last Hail Mary in her bag. "Found a replacement for Ian yet?"

Nancy jolted back as if someone had slapped her. "I've got a couple of people I'd like to hire, but there's only one spot, for now."

Macie smiled. If Nancy had anybody she wanted to hire, she would've pulled the trigger. A quick chat with Mark would confirm that. "Great. Just let me know when to clean out my desk."

The women stared each other down, but Macie knew she'd won. This time. There wouldn't be a next time. Taking this job had been a desperation move and there were other options out there. Macie promised herself then and there she'd get her resume back into circulation, even if it hadn't been that long and she'd applied to every design firm in the city. There was always more freelance work. And maybe she'd start selling her designs online.

"The trivia night is Saturday." Nancy dropped her gaze back to the scattered papers on her desk. "Be there by six-thirty."

"Oh, no can do, boss." Macie crossed her arms. "I'm not working ten hours then spending my free time with Alex this Saturday. I've got other plans that I cannot cancel."

"Fine. I'll get someone else." Nancy glanced up at her through her eyelashes. "This time. Next time you won't have an option."

Macie kept her mouth shut and simply nodded before stepping out of the office.

Wanna bet? she thought as she strolled toward her own cubicle closet and wondered how she was going to get out of this mess.

Happy hour wasn't so happy, but that was normally the case. Zac stood at the edge of the crowd, sipping a generic beer and eavesdropping the best he could. It wasn't easy. Most of his co-workers knew he was a Sparks. They were careful to keep their traps shut around him. He'd hoped the more booze the looser the lips, but they trickled out of the bar still too sober to talk. Except for one.

Tabitha Walton had been with Sparks Investments since January as the receptionist. She was gorgeous—long legs, tan skin, and flowing brown hair. Her doe eyes could entice any man into buying her a drink. Zac noticed she hadn't paid all night. She smiled at him and crossed her bare legs. Her skirt rode up to dangerous levels, and Zac knew a sign when he saw one. Tabitha didn't want to go home alone.

Zac signaled to the bartender for two more drinks even though he hadn't finished the one he'd been nursing for two hours. He slid onto the barstool next to her. "Hey, Tabby. How's it going?"

Tabitha shrugged and ran her finger around the rim of her glass. "Things are looking up."

Zac raised his eyebrows and downed the rest of his beer as the bartender set down another.

"So, Zac Sparks, prodigal son, heir apparent to the Sparks throne. Why are you here?" She rested her elbow against the bar and leaned her head on her fist. "Or do you like causing a stir?"

"I have no idea what you're talking about." Zac grinned, glancing down at her abundant cleavage. Maybe he could forget his mystery girl for one night.

"Oh, yes you do." Tabitha sipped her pink frou-frou drink. "Either you're here to get laid or you're here to make everyone else uncomfortable. I'm willing to bet it's the later, but I'm not opposed to the first."

"Maybe I just wanted to get to know my co-workers." He sipped his drink and kept his gaze on Tabitha.

"I'm not sure that's a smart move. Most of them feel threatened by you." Tabitha downed her drink and waved to the bartender for another. "You've got an advantage, you know."

"Not in the world of my father." He shrugged. "I've heard the board's threatened by him these days."

Tabitha raised an eyebrow. "Really? Hadn't heard that."

"Somehow I doubt that," Zac said. He knew she was lying by the way she avoided his gaze. "I'm sure you've heard everything."

"I *did* hear Walters mention something about a takeover. He mentioned it was already in full swing." Tabitha leaned forward putting her hand on his upper thigh. "Now that we got the information exchange out of the way, let's move on to more pleasant topics."

"As enticing as that sounds, I'm not sure it's a smart move," Zac said. He inhaled her smoky scent, a mix of bar and perfume.

"And all you make are smart moves, right?" Tabitha leaned closer until her lips brushed against his ear. "Smart moves aren't always fun moves, Zac Sparks."

"No strings," he said, needing to make it perfectly clear that if this happened, it happened once and never again.

"I don't like strings." Her hand slid up his thigh, her thumb flicking over his growing erection. "Unless you're tying me up tonight. Even then, I prefer handcuffs."

Zac slipped his hand under her skirt. He was never the type of guy to be so bold in a public place, but it was dark and her legs were between him and the bar. If anyone saw anything, they'd have superhuman vision. Her skin was soft, as he expected, and his fingers stretched toward her apex. He expected to find silk or satin, but all he discovered was more smooth skin.

"Jesus," he whispered in her ear. Zac rarely used such language. It was unbecoming, or so his grandfather had always said. Even now it made him feel wrong.

She nipped at his ear before drawing back. "If you'll just wait here, I'm just going to … freshen up."

Zac watched her hips sway as she walked away, one foot unnaturally in front of the other. He couldn't remember ever having a one-night stand. They usually ended up going out for at least a few months. Tabitha promised nothing more than a release, a way to forget *her*. That was exactly what he was going to do. It didn't matter why she stood him up. All that matter was that she had.

He pulled out his phone and swiped left to unlock it. The Blind Friends app had updated to a brighter white and a different font for the B and F. Shaking his head, he opened it up to delete his profile. His gaze darted to the messages as if on autopilot. One new message. It probably wasn't anything more than a new contact, but he opened the messages anyway.

It was from *her*.

Part of him didn't want to read it, he wanted to cut the whole thing out of his life. But the other half needed to know what she had to say for herself. He needed to know if she was the person he thought she was or if she was the exact opposite. He opened the message and read.

When he'd read through it twice, he leaned against the bar. He got it. Life wasn't exactly going smooth for him either. With his father's health issues, the takeover attempt of his dad's business, and just trying to figure out where he fit in, Zac understood more than she knew.

Tabitha's hand settled onto his thigh. He gazed up into her eyes and decided he wasn't going home with her. He wasn't going to have sex with her just to forget about his mystery girl. If he was brutally honest, he didn't even want to anymore. The moment was over.

"Sorry, Tabitha. Something's come up. I can't tonight." He stood and her hand fell away along with her seductive smile. "Raincheck?" he asked without meaning it.

"Raincheck." She rose on her tiptoes and whispered in his ear. "I guess my B.O.B. will do the job meant for you. And when we have that raincheck, we'll go all night."

Even though Zac had no doubt that she meant it, he had no intention of following through. Well, at least not until he figured out what was going on with his mystery girl.

The ten-minute drive to his apartment felt like an eternity. He wanted nothing more than to respond to her that they could meet this weekend or tomorrow or whenever worked for her. But he didn't want to scare her off, either. She was clearly going through a lot and needed time to figure it out. The most he could realistically do was listen via messages.

Before he stepped into his apartment, his phone rang. He glanced at the caller ID. Chomper. Why was Macie calling?

"Hello?" he asked, trying to keep the curiosity out of his voice. He let the irritation shine through.

"Sorry to bother you, but I... I thought since we're supposed to try this whole getting along thing that I'd make dinner for Saturday." Macie inhaled loudly into the receiver. Was the overly confident Macie nervous? Zac had a hard time believing that, but she sounded uncomfortable at a minimum. "It's going to take a while to go through everything and I figured it would be nice if I knew if you had any allergies."

Zac wasn't really sure how to respond. "No food allergies." Not that he had other plans on Saturday, but he hadn't expected it to take more than an hour. "How much stuff do we have to go over anyway?"

"Well, with the shower, there's the party supplies, the menu, the RSVPs, and we need to go through the guest list to make sure everyone has been notified. The invites went out already, but there's still time to contact anybody Ford wants to add. Sylvia's been leaning on me to get everything done. As if I don't have other things to do. Since Ford wants it joint, then I need you to give me some input."

"That's a ... quite a lot," he said.

"Then there's the bachelorette-slash-bachelor party. I've already made calls about a party bus, but in light of combining the parties, we'd probably need two. Or we'll have to do something else entirely. I had everything tentatively planned out, but nothing's been booked, thank God. The cost has to be a factor, too."

"I hadn't even thought about that." He just figured they'd all go to a club and get drunk. "Is there enough time to get everything done?"

"Barely, but if we work our asses off on Saturday, we'll have a solid plan to move forward with. Lauren's already ordered twenty more invitations for Ford's half of the shower, but I don't know if that's enough. Do you have his guest list?"

"Um... no."

"Okay, I'll get it." Someone shouted her name in the background. "Shit, that's Alex. I have to go. I'll see you Saturday."

She hung up and Zac pulled his phone away from his ear, staring

Lynn Stevens

at it as if it would tell him that wasn't Macie but someone pretending to be her. She was way too nice. Almost human.

He shook his head and sat on his couch with his tablet. Macie was a ball of energy welded together by confusion. He couldn't read her. And he wasn't sure he really wanted to either. He opened his app and reread mystery girl's message. Then he composed his own.

106

CHAPTER FOURTEEN

Glorious Friday. Even though Macie still had to go to work, the feeling of a Friday didn't disappear. She sat in her chair with her tablet, sipping coffee with enough sugar she should just own her own sugar plantation. The air conditioner kicked on, freezing the beads of water from the shower still on her bare skin. She'd get dressed before she left. There wasn't any reason to wear clothes in her own home.

The news was grim as per the norm. Even the celebrity gossip she secretly followed was depressing. Macie clicked on her Blind Friends app expecting nothing. He hadn't responded so far, why start now? The red one over the inbox surprised her. She opened it.

I read this and thought "yes, I do understand." Then I read it again and I found that even though I understand the situation, I don't understand the standing up. It's only fair that I'm honest. And honestly, I opened the app tonight to delete my profile and move on. I'd given up. And I'm not one to do so lightly. When I saw your message, though, I knew I wasn't ready to throw in the towel. (Where does that come from anyway? Clichés drive me crazy. After a quick Google, I found out it comes from boxing. When a fighter wants to end a fight, they literally throw in a towel. Now I know.)

Tonight I went to a happy hour with my co-workers. It was miserable and I didn't want to be there. I'm not welcome among the crowd for reasons that are obvious. Well, not to you but maybe one day they will be. So, I get it.

But life is always going to be overwhelming. Something is always going to come up. The key is to not let anything else get in the way of what you want. That's one lesson my father taught me that I know is true. Take my job, for example. I know why I'm unpopular, and I know it won't change overnight. I also know that I don't have to be friends with my co-workers, but it wouldn't hurt to be friendly. I have friends outside of work and they're all I really need. Having alliances inside the office, well... that never hurts. Work sometimes feels like war. You're constantly battling to prove yourself and get the leg up on your coworkers just to get ahead.

So here's what I propose going forward. We continue our conversations as we always have. If you want to meet me, then it's up to you. I won't suggest it again. You make that call.

Now that she knew it was Zac, Macie could hear his voice in his words. It was equal parts cringe-worthy and swoon-worthy. Macie had never denied Zac's hotness, but she'd always focused on his shitty attitude. Maybe it had really been *her* shitty attitude.

She sat up straight.

Oh my God. Did I do this to myself? The thought made her sick to her stomach. She'd never even considered it before. But it wasn't all her. Zac antagonized her and said things he knew would piss her off. Of course, if she hadn't been so damn defensive, she wouldn't have let him get to her so fast, so easily. He'd always seen her at her worst, and he'd always been quick to make a joke out of it. Maybe she'd just taken that all the wrong way to hide her embarrassment.

It didn't matter now. She had to let all of that go and move forward, because this Zac was not the Zac she'd known all these years. She had to try, at least. She owed it to herself.

Macie took her time responding, choosing her words carefully. Nothing she wrote to him could give away who she was. It took her longer than ever to compose the message. She'd never had writer's block before. Words wouldn't come to her. Macie typed out what she wanted to say, "It's me. It's Macie. I was there." Then she deleted it.

Her phone buzzed on the table beside her. The caller ID read "A$$hole" which meant Alex. He'd picked up her phone yesterday while it was unlocked and added his number. She changed the name.

Good morning. I emailed you some photos of a story I'm working on for the website. Please get them to me by eight this morning.

Macie deleted the text. He knew she'd get in at eight. Besides, this was her personal phone. If the station wanted her to be on-call, then they could provide her with a phone. She shook her head, putting Alex and Zac out of her mind. It was time to do something more important. She opened her web browser and started job hunting.

/ / /

Nobody would tell him anything. They all pledged fealty to his father as if he was an actual king. Not that Zac expected them to confess his father's potential downfall, but nobody would even talk about him. Nothing. Nada. Zilch.

Maybe it was just Zac. Maybe he wasn't meant to be a part of his father's war. Maybe he wasn't meant to be a part of Sparks Investments. That thought had crept into his mind over the last week. Was this what he wanted to do with his life? He would be financially secure. It would be smart. It would be easy. He was good at it. But was that what he wanted? He'd never asked himself that. It was a foregone conclusion that he'd take over the family business. But he'd never been the one to come to that conclusion.

Zac propped his tablet up in front of his monitor. He was sick of numbers for the day, it was time for a break. He opened Blind Friends, smiling at the new message before he even opened it.

I took this job because I needed it, not because I wanted it. The job I wanted never even called me in for an interview. Maybe I set the bar too high. Maybe desperation makes us do stupid things. I don't know. Regardless, it started out great. The first few weeks I thought I'd made the right choice. Then this past week something changed. Or rather someone changed it. A co-worker demanded all my time. To be blunt, the guy's an asshole. He's also the owner's son.

My boss gives him exactly what he wants at the expense of others. He's so bad that one guy quit, just walked out. And nobody does anything about it. Being down one in our department gives me a little power. I can push my boss, but only so far. I can't get fired or quit yet. I need this. Bills don't get paid on their own.

The first round of new resumes went out today. One month and I'm already looking for a new job. I'm terrified I won't find something else. I feel like I've already failed. But how is this my fault? How am I the one who failed? My boss failed me. I'm just doing what I can to remove myself from the situation. But then I ask myself, what if I don't find another job for a few months? Or even a year? Then what do I do?

I don't know. And that scares the shit out of me.

Zac sat back after reading. The owner's son? Was it possible that his mystery girl worked here? He stood and strolled down the hall, checking out each woman he saw in the rows of cubicles. None of the new investors qualified. They were all male. The clerical pool was small, and again, no new personnel that fit the description. He didn't even deal with them much as it was. The only person who might've fit was Tabitha, but she'd been with Sparks Investments for more than a month.

He reread the message.

No, he wasn't the asshole owner's son. Nobody had walked out or quit recently. He would've heard about it. His shoulders sagged in relief. If he'd offended anybody by his bloodline, he wanted to know. He wanted to fix it. Zac didn't want to be that guy, the one who took advantage of his situation, of his heritage.

He smiled at everyone as he headed back to his office. The phone on his desk rang.

"Zac Sparks," he answered as he plopped into his office chair.

"We need to talk," his father said before hanging up.

Zac set the receiver back in the cradle and shut down his computer for the day. He read through the message one last time before closing his tablet. It took him less than five minutes before he ended up in his father's office, and he regretted not getting there sooner.

"We're too late," his father said. His pale face and ruddy cheeks contradicted one another. His father sat slouched in his chair, a man defeated. "All the news that trickled down to me. All the information given to me by the board. All of everything about taking this company public had been in the works for longer than I was told. They called a board meeting today, one I found out about after it had started. They voted in favor. We lost the war before we could even fight a battle."

Zac collapsed into the chair in front of his father's desk. "What now?"

"Now," he said, standing to his full height, "we own forty percent of the company that I started. Now I'm on the verge of being tossed out. Now I decide if I stay or if I go. Now I stand tall in front of the others, because if I don't, I have failed."

"What about me?" Zac blurted almost without thinking. It had been on his mind since it first came up. "What do I do now?"

His father's face softened. "You do what you do, son. You'll be fine. You're bright and are more capable than most of the other guys here."

Zac nodded, his gaze dropped to the tablet in his hands. His mind drifted to his mystery girl. She was in a job she took only because she had to. He'd taken his job because it was expected of him. Maybe she wasn't the only one who needed a change. Zac stood, glancing at his father's slouched back as he stared out the window of his corner office. He'd lost, and he knew it, but his father would only let Zac see that brief moment of vulnerability. Not that too many people would've recognized it. Zac had seen it when his mother died. It wasn't something Zac thought he'd ever see again, yet here it was.

"It'll be okay, Dad," Zac said. He knew his father needed to hear that even if he didn't believe it. "Sparks men tend to land on their feet."

His father snorted and turned around. "That we do, son. That we do."

CHAPTER FIFTEEN

Macie wanted to strangle Alex before nine in the morning on Friday. By Saturday, she was noting places to hide his body. The dumpster behind the station was too obvious even if it was the most convenient. He made last minute demands and changes on perfectly good graphics. At one point he had the nerve to accuse her of photoshopping his face to make him look less attractive. Unfortunately for him, he'd done it in front of the entire newsroom.

"I didn't do anything to your face, Alex," Macie had said. "Blame that on your parents."

Snickers bounced around the newsroom. Once Alex stormed out, Macie even got a few high fives from the crew. She took great pleasure in knocking him down with well-placed sarcasm mixed with brutal honesty. Probably not the best idea since his father owned the station, but she was past the point of caring. And the stern email from Nancy was sent straight to the trash bin.

She had thirty minutes before she clocked out at six. Zac would be at her place at seven. She'd put a stew in the slow cooker for dinner before she left. Her small apartment was going to smell like a slice of meaty heaven. Her mouth watered just thinking about it. She worked her tail off the night before making the dough for fresh biscuits. The minute she walked into her place, she'd have to preheat the oven to bake them. Not to mention shower, change, and make herself look presentable without making herself look presentable. It was Zac, after all. He'd seen her throw up in the bushes outside more than one frat house. That was a bonus for her. He'd clearly seen her at her worst. He'd never seen her at her best. It was time she made him see her for who she really was—a compassionate, loyal human being. Not a raving bitch with permanent PMS.

The phone in her office shrilled, shocking her out of thoughts of Zac.

"Macie Regan," she answered.

"My office. Now." Nancy slammed the phone down without giving Macie a chance to breath.

This can't be good. Macie steeled herself before standing. She grabbed her tablet and her cell, knowing she'd need all the insurance she had against whatever tyranny Alex threw at her through her boss. What else could it be? She got along with everyone else, hit impossible deadlines, and did everything asked of her. On the short walk to Nancy's office, she changed his name back to Alex on her contacts list. She would revert it back to A$$hole later, or just block him all together.

The hallway was empty, and Macie couldn't stop the rock in her stomach from turning into a boulder. Her feet grew heavy, her steps slowed. The door to Nancy's office was closed, which was not like Nancy. The frosted window revealed nothing. Macie had no idea what she was walking into, but she knew without a doubt who made this happen. She took a deep breath and knocked on the door.

"Come in," Nancy said, her voice less angry than it had been over the phone.

Macie's heart kicked up a notch. She knew she wasn't getting fired. There was no way Nancy would let her graphics department be down by two. They were barely getting things done as it was. The department couldn't run with only three other people. Pulling up her metaphoric big-girl panties, Macie opened the door to the lion's den.

The man sitting at Nancy's desk had an eerie familiarity to him. His thinning blond hair bordered more toward a bright white tint. Piercing gray eyes lasered into hers. Even the heart shape to his face was familiar. Macie broke his gaze to find its biological match standing to her right. Shit. Nancy stood off to the side by one of her many filing cabinets. Macie turned toward her boss whose own steely gaze softened to graphite as it met Macie's.

Nancy wouldn't have been stupid enough to fire her, but the owner of the station would have no issue leaving the graphics department shorthanded. She had to act fast, be smart, and she had to be prepared to hear him deliver the final blow she knew was coming. Why else would she be there? The boulder in her stomach grew into a mountain. How was she going to survive?

"Ms. Regan?" Mr. Leffler asked. He leaned on Nancy's desk, his fingers steepled under his chin.

Macie swallowed and nodded. Let him think she was afraid. She wasn't. Sure, she was afraid of not having a paycheck, but she wasn't scared of this man. He was just a man. It didn't matter that he owned the station. It didn't matter that he was Alex's father. It did matter that he could fire her, but that was something she'd have to deal with. She made the decision then and there to be honest, and not to take any shit.

"Can you explain this?" he asked, turning the computer monitor toward her.

Macie leaned in to get a better look. It was one of the posters she'd made for an upcoming appearance featuring Alex at a charity 5k. Her eyes darted around the screen. There wasn't anything different. The colors were the same, the people, the city setting behind Alex, even the stupid grin on his face were all the same. There wasn't a single... then she noticed it. On the banner behind Alex's too big head someone had added "Fuck Off, Alex" in black.

"My patience is thin, Ms. Regan. Explain this or lose your job." Mr. Leffler tapped on the screen at the offensive writing.

"Clearly someone manipulated the image after I sent it," Macie said. She reached for the mouse and clicked over the words to enhance them. Leffler leaned away. It was like he was offended to share the air with her. Macie shook her head. "If I had to guess, I'd say someone with a touchscreen used their finger to add that to the banner."

"And you didn't do it," Leffler said, more as a statement than as a question. He glared at her to emphasize his point.

Macie stood and crossed her arms. If she was going out, which it looked more and more like it was going to happen, she might as well go out with a bang. "No. If I wanted to tell Alex to fuck off, I would say it to his face." Leffler sat back, his eyes wide and mouth open. "Besides, if I would do something so childish, don't you think someone with a degree in graphic design would be more creative and..." Macie snorted. "And would do that so much better? That's amateur and childish."

Leffler nodded.

"She has a point," Nancy said, stepping beside Macie. A sense of pride soared through Macie. Nancy was taking a stand and it was for her. "Just look at the rest of the piece for proof."

"I can prove it anyway," Macie added. She pulled her tablet out from under her arm and opened it. Within a few seconds, she'd accessed her desktop. "Here," Macie said, turning the tablet around, "this is my desktop in my office. She touched the file folder to open the documents and then tapped the file for the graphic. She opened each one and pointed out that none of them had the obscenity. "See?" Then she opened the email to the sent file and found the copy she emailed Alex. She opened that graphic, which clearly didn't have anything on the banner either. "I didn't do that."

"How do I know that's your desktop?" Leffler took her tablet and flipped through a few more files. Macie didn't really care. She wasn't stupid enough to keep anything personal on her work computer anyway. "And how did you access it?"

Macie smiled. Her remote access program was a secret Lauren gave her, and one she wasn't going to share. So she lied. "I backdoored my tablet to the PC."

Leffler nodded. "So you'd just tell Alex to fuck off?"

"Pretty much." She shrugged, knowing that statement might come back to bite her in the ass, but there was no reason to lie about it, either. She'd had no problem telling him off in the newsroom the other day. It was already documented. Macie didn't think she'd get fired over it, either, or anything else for that matter. She'd proven her innocence.

Leffler handed her the tablet. "Good. Somebody needs to, but don't make it a habit." He smirked, taking at least twenty years off his stern face. Macie could really see the family resemblance now. "If you have any issues with my son, don't take his shit. I like people who stand up for themselves and aren't afraid to say what's on their mind. That's the type of person that makes it in this industry. The other people who make it in this business are the ones who keep their friends close but their enemies closer. Remember that, too. Thank you for your time, Ms. Regan. You may go." Leffler turned his gaze to her boss. "Nancy, if you'd allow me use of your office for a bit, I'd like a word with my son."

"Yes, sir," Nancy replied. She took Macie's elbow and pulled her out of the room. Once the door clicked closed behind them, Nancy exhaled loud and long. "I thought you were a goner."

Macie laughed. "Me, too."

"Look, I know that putting you in that position was shitty of me. I ..." Nancy sighed, and defeat softened her body. She fell back against the wall, sinking down a few inches. "I need this job. I need this station." She smiled sadly and dropped her gaze to her feet. "I moved back here for it. If it goes south, I go with it. I wasn't willing to risk everything. If you went under the bus, I wasn't going to pull you out." She raised her head and stared at Macie. "I hope you can understand."

"I can." Macie bit her tongue for a moment, but Leffler's words came back to her like a sledgehammer to the temple. She needed to tell Nancy the truth, even if it hurt her boss while she was down. "And I can't." She faced Nancy head on. "I get it, Nancy. I get wanting... no, needing to protect yourself. But what about me? You're my boss. What about protecting me from his harassment? I do everything you ask me to do, even dealing with Alex."

"You do, and you did," Nancy replied. "And you're right. I was more concerned about my job than about the job I was hired to do."

Macie's chest swelled with victory.

"But you're wrong, too." Nancy stood straighter and pulled herself together. "I expect my employees to be adults and come to me with problems with coworkers. The situation with Alex is unique, but you still should've come to me once he started contacting you instead of me. The deal was you worked with him but only through me. Remember?"

Macie nodded. She did remember, but she didn't think Nancy wanted to be involved.

"So we both failed each other." Nancy crossed her arms, her defeat already forgotten. "Anything else you want to tell me now while I'm in a good mood."

"Yeah, actually," Macie said, fighting the blush rising to her cheeks. "Can you remind the reporters that we, meaning the entire department and not just me, work our butts off and when they drop off an assignment they can't demand it gets done in twenty minutes or less? Because that would be awesome."

"Now you're pushing it." Nancy grinned. "I'll send out a memo tomorrow." She reached out and clamped her hand on Macie's shoulder. "Thanks, Macie. Don't tell anyone I said this, but you're doing a great job here."

"That's nice to hear," Macie said letting her smile break through. She also knew that this was probably her only chance to be no holds barred with her boss. Everything would be back to normal after this.

"Get out of here." Nancy glanced at her watch. The band was old and worn in several places. It obviously had sentimental value, because Macie was positive Nancy could buy a new one. "You were supposed to be out of here twenty minutes ago."

Panic seized her chest. "Shit." She stared at Nancy. "Shit, shit, shit, shit. I'm going to be late."

"Then get the hell out of here."

"Right." Macie darted right toward Nancy's office before realizing she was going the wrong way. She was going to be so late. So very late. Late enough Zac might beat her to the apartment. She didn't want him to think she flaked. And he would totally think she flaked. That's what she was known for. On her way back to her office, she pulled out her phone and sent him a quick text that she was running late.

I swear I'm not going to blow this thing with Zac, she told herself as she logged off her computer and ran out into the Louisiana heat. *I hope like hell I have time to shower.*

Zac stood outside the door to Macie's building. He hated to admit it, but he was impressed she could afford to live in the converted school. A sign out front identified it as Franklin Elementary. The building itself shouted education. The city had shuttered several dying schools when he was a kid. They sold them off and a few were demolished, most were still vacant and deteriorating. A handful of them, including this one, were turned into apartments. With the resurrection of the BoHo district a few blocks away, Franklin School Lofts became prime real estate. He made a mental note of the developer to check out later.

He rang the buzzer to her apartment a second time. Impressed or not, he hated to be kept waiting. He bounced on his heels as a tenant pushed by him and unlocked the door. Zac grabbed it before it could close, timing it so the man wouldn't think he was a stalker. Fortunately for Zac it was a slow closing door. He slipped inside and stared at the foyer. Lights bounced off the marble floor, illuminating a maroon F with an interlinking E in the center. He could almost imagine kids strolling through with their books and backpacks, gossiping with their friends. It still felt like a school.

The foyer broke off into two hallways with a set of impressive stairs in front of him. Macie's apartment was 3E and there were only four floors to the building. He took them two at a time, winding himself as he reached the third floor. The exercise was exhilarating. He hadn't kept up his morning runs over the last couple of months and his body reacted. It was time to start again, maybe run a 5K at the end of the summer. He needed a goal.

Macie's apartment was across from the elevators. The doors were close together, so much so that Zac wondered how big the apartment could be. He raised his fist and hammered on her door, not really expecting her to answer. It would be just like Macie to blow him off in favor of something more exciting.

His breath caught and he stepped back from the door after she pulled it open. Macie stood before him in nothing but a thin black robe, drying her hair with a matching towel.

"Shit. I'm sorry, Zac," she said. Her robe opened further, dangerously close to exposing herself to him and anyone else who happened into the hallway. Macie didn't pull it together, either. She moved to her left and motioned for him to enter. "I got stuck late at work in a … meeting. I'm running a little behind. Didn't you get my text?"

"No, I didn't." He choked on the words, looking everywhere except her smooth skin. Macie had always been beautiful in a no-nonsense way. She hadn't cared what other people thought of her and that kind of confidence added to her sex appeal. Zac walked past her into the apartment. It was smaller than he'd anticipated. A tiny kitchenette lined the wall in front of him with a two-burner stove and small oven. The fridge wasn't anything more than he'd find in a hotel and fit under the cabinets. She didn't have a dishwasher or even a full-size sink. But that didn't stop her from cooking. A slow cooker sat on the counter, emitting the most glorious smell of roast and potatoes. He inhaled and grinned. "You really didn't have to."

Macie smiled and turned away from him toward what he assumed was the small bathroom. Over her shoulder she said, "Make yourself at home. I'll only be a few more minutes."

Zac watched her sashay away until she clicked the door closed behind her. He turned toward the living room. Or was it the bedroom? He hadn't seen any other doors so it must be both. Macie could probably live more efficiently if she moved into a complex like his. And probably cheaper than this place. He'd have to ask her how much her rent was. Could he? They were trying this whole friend thing so being concerned about her finances was natural and she'd mentioned discussing investments. Were they at that point? He didn't think so, but with Macie he never knew.

He sat on the futon and stared at the spread on the flat trunk in front of him. A large planner caught his eye. He knew he shouldn't, but he picked it up anyway. Inside was everything that had to do with Lauren and Ford's wedding. And he meant everything. Macie even had the measurements for the groomsmen, including his. Each day was a play by play leading up to the wedding. Zac had no idea Macie was this organized. It was impressive.

He put the planner back on the trunk and picked up a bulky portfolio. The first page was a mixed media art piece that took his breath away. Watercolors swirled an ocean wave behind a small wooden boat floating on the surface of the peaceful sea. The boat had been hand crafted with rough edges and no paint. He ran his finger over the waves, realizing there was crystalline element to it he hadn't noticed before. Whatever she'd used to make it stand out like this added to the 3D element of the boat. It was incredible. He'd known Macie had talent, but this was far beyond what he'd ever seen her do.

His gaze shifted around the small apartment, seeing things he hadn't noticed before. A small painting of autumn leaves, on an actual leaf, hung above a worn chair. A sculpture of a dancer covered in silver and gold foil sat on the desk under the window. His gaze settled on the easel he'd noticed when he first walked in. Black, white, and gray oil paints swirled on the large canvas, delving into light then darkness. Smaller swirls circled around the edge, as if being sucked into a vortex.

"That's not finished yet," Macie said.

Zac ripped his gaze from the art and turned it toward her. Her hair was still damp, falling down her shoulders in a cascade of chocolate.

The shoulders of her white shirt were also damp. Macie was dangerously close to winning a one person wet t-shirt contest. Her smooth legs drew his attention, but he knew that was even more dangerous territory. Why'd she have to put on shorts? Zac diverted his eyes back to the art. He wanted to stare at her longer, but that wasn't the best idea. Long term enemies trying to become civil didn't warrant sexual tension, but he felt it anyway. It wasn't the first time, either.

"It's still amazing," he said, not entirely sure if he was talking about the painting or her long legs. He motioned to the portfolio. "They all are. Why not show them in a gallery?"

"Not good enough." The mattress dipped beside him, but he kept his gaze on the boat. "And it's harder than you think to get a show at a gallery."

"Is that why you went into graphic design instead of art?" He glanced at her legs out of the corner of his eye.

"Graphic design is art, just a different form." She tucked her legs under her rear and pulled her t-shirt over her knees.

"Sorry, I didn't..." He closed his eyes and inhaled. It was just Macie. Smartass, annoying Macie. He opened his eyes and turned toward her. "This is weird."

Macie threw her head back and laughed, something he rarely saw or heard. Her normal expression toward him was a harsh scowl so this was a pleasant surprise. One he wasn't sure how to feel about, but he liked it nonetheless. "You have no idea." She pulled her legs out from underneath her and reached for the planner. "Let's get started. There's a lot to do and I've planned or pre-planned most of it."

"I noticed." He leaned forward as Macie opened the planner. "How much has Lauren actually done?"

Macie bristled beside him. "What's that supposed to mean?"

"I just meant that you've put a lot of work into this," he said, quickly backtracking to figure out how he could have offended her so damn fast. Zac motioned at the planner. "This isn't just the wedding. It's the shower, the bachelorette party, flight plans for both sides of the family. You've got everything here."

A buzzer sounded in the kitchen. Macie stared at Zac for a moment before getting up. She moved like a ballerina as she put something in the oven and set the timer. Zac watched, waiting for the Macie explosion. She strolled back into the living room and settled back onto the couch, albeit farther away than she had before. "The biscuits will be ready in ten minutes."

"Look, Chomper, I'm —" He froze when he realized what had come out of his mouth. They'd made a deal and he just blew it. Calling her Chomper was an automatic defense when he knew he'd set her off.

"Do you know why I hate it when you call me that?" she asked in a soft voice. Her head was down, and she picked at her cuticles. Zac wanted to take her hand and comfort her somehow, but how was more difficult than he realized. She lifted her head, tears rimming her eyes. "Never mind. It's stupid."

"It's not stupid." He swallowed hard. If they were going to be friends, this was one hurdle they needed to get over. "I … I only call you that when I know it'll piss you off or distract you from something I said."

Macie snorted. "Figures."

"Excuse me?" Zac sat back and stared at her. He should've known. The tears were gone. She'd pulled him in only to knock him down. Typical Macie. She was like a black widow waiting to bite his head off.

"I just…" Macie clenched then unclenched her hands. "Whenever you call me that, it reminds me of my most embarrassing moment. I'd seen these two hot guys across the room, and I strolled up to them to prove to my new roomie that I wasn't afraid of anything. Then I tripped. I fucking bit you." Her cheeks reddened. "And you remind of it every time we see each other, every time you call me that."

Zac laughed.

"Oh, fuck you, Zac. I don't need this —"

"Slow down, Mace." He held up his hands to stop the verbal onslaught. "I'm not laughing at you. Really. I'm laughing at the situation. We're both idiots."

"Well, I'm pretty sure one of us is." She crossed her arms and wrinkled her eyebrows.

"Fine. I'm an idiot." He shook his head. This could've been cleared up years ago if they'd only opened their mouths for good instead of evil. If they'd actually talked to one another instead of jumping to conclusions. "Tell me it's not a little bit funny."

Macie's glare softened, then she cracked a smile. "Maybe a bit."

"Ford and Lauren really want us to get along until the wedding." Zac held out his hand. "Truce? Like a real truce and not the bull we fed them earlier."

"I have a better idea." Macie took his hand and met his gaze. "Hi, I'm Macie Regan. I'm overly organized and a verbal tyrant. I also cuss like a sailor and give zero fucks who I offend. But I'm very loyal to my friends. Nice to meet you."

"Ah, I see," Zac said with a laugh. He could play this game. "It's nice to meet you. I'm Zac Sparks, former heir apparent to Sparks Investments. I love music, play guitar when I can, and am easily offended. I also have this thing about clichés."

"Wait, roll back there, buddy." Macie raised an artfully crafted eyebrow. "Former heir apparent?"

Zac shrugged. "It's a long story."

"Fair enough. But you play guitar?" Her eyes widened.

"I dabble."

"Dabble?" Macie crossed her legs and leaned an elbow against her knee. "Care to elaborate?"

Zac turned toward her easel, his ears heating. Why did he even bother to say anything? All Macie had said was the obvious. "Maybe some other time. I doubt you'd like it anyway."

"How do you know? It might be right up my alley."

Zac still couldn't look at her. The last thing he needed was to give her more ammunition for the moment the truce was over.

"Okay, fair enough." She stood and walked toward the easel, just out of his sight. "You know why I painted this? It was because I was going down a rabbit hole at work and I wasn't sure I'd make it out alive. It felt like my life was spiraling out of control." She motioned to the overall black, gray, and white spiral that covered the entire canvas. "Then I started to think about all the other times I felt like that. Like when Darren dumped me on Halloween. Or when my mom …" Macie's shoulders dropped. "When my mom told me who my father was. Or when I didn't get asked to prom. Those," she pointed to the smaller spirals, "are represented here. It's a never-ending problem. My life always has moments like this."

"What about the moments when you're not spiraling?" Zac asked softly. He didn't want to break the spell she'd fallen under. "Where are those?"

"That's just it, Zac. We're always spiraling toward the end. We're never in control." She turned toward him as the buzzer in the kitchen went off again. "Anyway, we should eat and get to work. There's a lot to go through."

Zac nodded, but he couldn't stop replaying her words. Was he spiraling? His entire life he'd been in control of everything. At least, he never felt like he wasn't. What would it feel like to let go? To just see what happened? Macie seemed to have a grasp of it. He stared at her as she explained what she'd already planned, but he didn't hear anything. How could she just accept that she had no control? How could she be so nonchalant about it? By the time they'd finished eating and gone over the parties, Zac had a newfound respect for Macie. Who knew, maybe their truce could end up being long term. Maybe.

✐ ✐ ✐

Zac was less enthusiastic about the bachelorette party Macie had planned. Instead of getting frustrated, she promised herself she'd listen and take his suggestions into consideration. It wasn't easy, but she managed. Every plan she had set into place needed to be scratched. That was the only headway they made. By the end of the evening, the only thing they agreed upon was starting over. At least he liked the biscuits.

This was going to be harder than she thought. Even though she knew he was Guy, it didn't make it any easier to get rid of past prejudices. Macie sat in her chair and stared out the window. Zac exited the building, stopping before the sidewalk. His jeans hugged in all the right places. Macie had never denied how attractive he was, but knowing the real Zac amplified it by a hundred. Getting past years of animosity would take time. And patience. More patience than she normally had.

Zac glanced back at her building before shaking his head and heading off down the sidewalk. He disappeared around the corner, and Macie finally relaxed. She wanted to confess everything to him the minute he stepped into her apartment. When his gaze trailed over her legs, she knew she at least had that on him. Macie stretched her legs out in front of her. They were her best assets.

Her phone vibrated on her desk. Macie was so lost in thoughts of Zac, she didn't look at the caller ID. "Hello?"

"Why is Zac leaving your place?" Lauren shrilled on the other end. Her flair for the dramatic sparked at the most unusual times. After all, it was Lauren and Ford who wanted joint parties.

Macie laughed. "Because we're planning the bachelorette/bachelor party. Why else would he be here?" *If only he was here for something else.* "Wait, how'd you know he was here?"

"Oh, that makes so much sense. And Ford told me Zac was there." Lauren sighed the kind of sigh that meant there was something else going on.

"So, one, are you stalking me? And two, why're you really calling?" Macie asked. Lauren never called unless she wanted something or needed something. It didn't matter if that something was information or notes for a class or for a recipe. Lauren was never one to call to chat. Macie liked that about her. It was one reason they got along.

"You know me so well." A door closed on Lauren's end. "It's Ford. He's stressing out like I've never seen. He got his first bill for his student loans earlier than we were told. And… it's higher than we expected. A lot higher."

"Like how a lot?" Fear squeezed Macie's chest. Ford had scholarship money. More than Macie had gotten. If he was panicking, what would her first payment look like?

"Like how-are-we-going-to-live a lot." She paused. Macie could almost see Lauren closing her eyes and covering her head with a pillow. Sure enough, Lauren's voice was muffled when she spoke again. "It's more than our rent. I'll have to get a job. Freelancing won't cut it. The money MatchInHeaven pays freelancers isn't enough long term. We could live off it for a while, but not for long. And we'll have to hold off starting a family. That alone is eating at him. It's eating at me, too."

"Ford's always been a traditionalist in a male chauvinist sort of way." Macie never approved of his desire to marry and start a family immediately, but Lauren wanted the same thing. Who was she to judge?

"Stop. You know I want a huge family. And it was in the plan. We planned out every aspect of this. How could we have miscalculated so … poorly? Even Zac thought we'd be in a good financial situation." Lauren's voice cracked. "What're we going to do, Mace?"

"Survive." Macie picked through her mail as she talked. A knot formed in her stomach. If Ford had gotten his, hers wasn't far behind. Most of it was junk mail but a white envelope with bright blue lettering caught her eye. There it was. Her first loan payment notice had come in. It wasn't supposed to start until six months after graduation, but there it was. She swallowed hard. If Ford's was more than their meager rent, how much was hers? She stared at the envelope for a moment before her gaze drifted toward the spiral painting. "That's all we can do."

CHAPTER SIXTEEN

For three days, Macie avoided her phone and her Blind Friends app. She went through the motions in zombie mode. Everything was done by the time she left work Sunday. That left Monday and Tuesday to curl up into a ball and hide from the looming bill on her counter. She couldn't pay it. She couldn't pay half of it. Hell, she couldn't pay a quarter of it. She could only pay the amount she'd budgeted for. She thought about calling the company and pleading her case, but it wouldn't do any good. So she did the only thing she could think of. She cried.

Then she wrote to Zac.

I'm ruined before my life even starts. I mean really starts. Not that life doesn't start the minute you're born, or conceived depending on your point of view, but you understand, right? I mean my adult life. Everything I've been working toward these last four years might as well have been a pipe dream.

My first bill for my student loan payment came in. It's far more than I expected. Like so much more I'd have to mortgage all my vital organs to pay half of it. I'm terrified. And I'm angry at myself for not realizing how much it would be. I even sat down with a financial advisor at school before graduation to help me figure out where I was and what I could reasonably afford. And we based that off the lowest salary I would take. I actually make more than what I expected. So how did I get it so wrong?

And what am I going to do?

I can go back to tending bar or waiting tables to make some extra money, but other than that I have no idea. And it wouldn't be enough. I suppose I could break my lease and find a cheaper apartment with a roommate, too. Even that feels like utter defeat.

I want to cry. I want to curl up in a ball and hide from the world. But what I want doesn't matter. If it did, I wouldn't be so damn broke.

Macie knew the minute she hit send that she shouldn't have sent the message. Up to this point, they'd been less emotional in their notes. To the point that she knew he was holding back because she'd hurt him. If he knew she hadn't really stood him up, he'd be less formal. But if he knew she hadn't really stood him up, he'd know it was Macie and then shit would've really hit the fan. She just needed someone to talk to. And he was the obvious choice.

A red one appeared on the inbox. Macie hadn't even realized she was staring at it.

I have a friend in a similar situation. He's devastated by the bill. It's hard to see him go through this, but that's the way loans like that work. You'll spend most of your time paying the interest without paying much on the principal. Once you've paid their interest rates, then you'll slowly pay down the amount you actually borrowed. It's like a mortgage, in a way.

It sounds like your financial planner was an idiot, too. Or he/she didn't know anything about student loans. I'd suggest paying what you can until you can meet with a professional advisor who can help you figure out where you need to be and what you can do to get there. You can always defer payment as underemployed, but that won't stop the interest from adding up. The short version now is to cut any expenses you can. I'd hate to see you take on another job, too. Getting ahead is hard enough with one job. I wish I could help more, but without having any details, it's hard to give advice. Just do what you can. And remember that you're not alone. A lot of other people are getting those bills, too.

Macie sighed. That definitely sounded like know-it-all Zac. It irritated her to no end. She wasn't about to let it go either.

127

You know what pisses me off. That nobody warned me. Go to college, they said. Get a degree, they said. That's the only way to get ahead, they said. You would think a damn high school guidance counselor would tell you about things like this. But, nope. Instead, it's the same bullshit. You have to have a degree to get ahead. But you have to pay out your ass for the rest of your life to get that degree. And you'll never get ahead.

My mom never went to college. She made her own way the only way she knew how. She wanted more for me. She's busted her ass her entire life waiting tables and catering to drunks. Now it looks like I'll get to do that along with my day job. Who's the fool here?

It makes me wonder if any of this was really worth it.

She hit send and stared at the message box, waiting for his reply. Her anger dissipated as she watched for the red one. She regretted how she wrote about her mom. It wasn't fair. Her mother did the best she could with what she had. She supported Macie and gave her everything she needed. Macie was happy even if she never had a new car or the most fashionable clothes. She encouraged Macie to be more than a waitress. Macie wanted to make her mom proud. Instead she felt like a complete failure. The message appeared and Macie didn't hesitate.

I wish I knew what to do to help you. Your mom sounds great. I'm willing to bet she's proud of you for working hard to get that degree. A friend of mine waited tables and tended bar through college. First at a diner, then at a local club. It wasn't so bad. At least, I don't think she hated it. She often bragged about the money she made on tips. There's no shame in it.

But maybe there's something else you can do? I don't know how to help since I have no idea what your degree is in or what you do for a living now. That makes it difficult since I'm pretty good with money. All I can do right now is listen. So, vent away. It won't help, but it will clear your head enough to think.

Macie clicked reply, but she didn't really know what to say. She did brag about the money she made working two nights a week.

What a fool she'd been. All of that cash and she didn't save enough of it. She'd stupidly listened to that school's financial advisor and saved a meager ten percent. She read the second paragraph again. *But maybe there's something else you can do?* What else was there? Most jobs in graphic design worked the same hours she already did. Anything she worked had to be outside of her regular hours. Nancy had given her the go-ahead to freelance, but Macie had no idea where to start.

The canvas caught her eye. It wasn't finished, but suddenly she knew what it needed, how to finish it. Macie set her tablet down and headed toward the closet by the kitchen. She pulled open the door, took out a larger canvas and a smaller one. They were the last of her art supplies. Time had been tight and so had the money. The first thing she'd cut out was art.

She stripped down and got to work. With each swipe of the brush, the tension left her body. Macie painted until her arms hurt, her back screamed, and she had no other choice but to fall asleep covered in white, black, and gray. As her mind drifted into oblivion, she remembered Zac's question and smiled. Why *not* sell her art?

✐ ✐ ✐

Zac didn't hear back from his mystery girl for a few days, but Macie sent him updates about the plans. She'd pressed forward with several of their ideas. The only problem she kept encountering was money. It became clear pretty fast that Macie was living paycheck to paycheck. It was also clear that her early plans had been budget friendly. Zac hadn't given two thoughts about how much money they'd need to put these parties together. He should've, but he didn't.

"Hey," Dave, one of his co-workers, said from Zac's open office door. "What's going on with your dad? Is he coming back?"

News had broken that Sparks Investments was going public. Zac's father had been famously missing from the press announcement and from the office since. His health hadn't been great since the gall bladder surgery and the heart attack scare. Instead of smiling and nodding like the yes man he'd need to become, he made himself disappear. Not even Zac had seen him.

"I really don't know," Zac said with a shrug. "He's been keeping to himself lately."

"Yeah, sure." Dave slapped the door frame twice and left.

But it was the truth. Zac had no idea if his father was done or not. He hadn't seen him in over a week and his father told Zac that time was needed. Zac knew what that meant—leave me alone until I'm ready to talk.

His phone buzzed on his desk. Zac glanced at the name first. Macie. He'd changed it after the dinner they had together. Now that he knew why she hated Chomper, he'd do his best not to use it at all. He almost smiled. Then he read her message and couldn't stop the grin.

Do you know anything about setting up an online store?

Zac typed back. *No, but I can figure it out pretty quick. What're you thinking?*

IDK. Thinking about the options. I hate to ask, but could you come over? Or I can come to your place? I think I want to sell my artwork. Or at least try to. And you know all this financial stuff. We never got around to talking about investing and I think I need to invest in myself first. Will you help me?

Zac sat up. Macie asking for his help? Did the universe flip on its head? Or was he in an alternate dimension? She'd mentioned discussing investments before, but he didn't bring it up when he went to her place. He'd figured she wasn't really interested.

You really want my help? he replied.

Yes.

One word, but it knocked Zac back in his chair. He would help her. But he knew he needed to be cautious. This was Macie Regan. There had to be another shoe that would drop on his head. Probably a worn out red Chuck.

When? He hit send.

Tonight? Or do you have a hot date? She added a winky emoji.

He actually had plans to meet with Ford for drinks. He wanted to help her, though. Ford would understand.

I'm free. Zac hoped Ford would understand. It wasn't like Ford hadn't cancelled drinks with Zac to rescue Lauren before. Zac smiled. Macie was far from a damsel in distress.

Great. When and where?

He thought about having her over, making dinner like she had done for him. Something stopped him cold. His apartment. It wasn't as warm as Macie's. Despite the small size, Macie's place felt like a home. His apartment felt temporary. *Seven? Your place?*

Sounds great. And, thanks.

Zac smiled at the kissing emoji. He knew it wasn't anything more than Macie being grateful, but it lifted him up for the rest of the day.

CHAPTER SEVENTEEN

Nancy didn't argue when Macie said she had to leave by six-thirty at the absolute latest. She didn't even bat an eye. Something was up. Macie sat in one of Nancy's uncomfortable chairs instead of leaving like a smart person would have done. She propped her feet on the edge of Nancy's desk, earning an evil eye. Macie shrugged and dropped her feet. Probably not her smartest move.

"What?" Nancy asked without looking up from the file on her desk.

"I should ask you the same question," Macie said.

"Everything's just peachy. Now get out of here before I change my mind." Nancy's red felt pen moved across the page.

"I call bullshit."

Nancy's head snapped up. They stared at one another for longer than necessary before Nancy's shoulders relaxed and she nodded toward the office door. Macie stood and closed it, settling back into the plastic chair.

"Your little stunt in front of the boss has given you a free pass for the time being." Nancy leaned back in her chair and steepled her fingers. "He said to make you happy. So that's what I'm doing."

Macie tried not to grin, and this really wasn't a grinning moment. Sure, she wanted to be happy, but she wanted to be treated fairly, too. A wiser person would run with it. "Good for me. What's in it for you?"

"Keeping my job." Nancy reached for a photo frame on her desk and turned it around. Two identical twins smiled at the camera. They weren't much younger than Macie and both were the spitting image of Nancy. "They graduate this year. And college isn't cheap."

"Ain't that the truth." Macie grimaced as the image of her payment came up.

"Yeah, so as much as I hate cowering to him, I need to keep my job." Nancy turned the frame back around, her face softening as she stared at her daughters. "For the time being, you're getting a free pass."

Macie nodded and stood. The conversation was over. "Thanks, boss." She stopped before she opened the door. "Nancy, can I ask you a question?"

Nancy waved her hand.

"Did I do something wrong?" Macie's fingers tightened around the doorknob.

"Your last two pieces were sloppy. They looked rushed." Nancy tapped her pen against her desk blotter. "You've done better with less time."

Macie grimaced, but she nodded. "Okay. Is there time to rework them?"

"I had Ethan fix them before he left this morning." Her lips pressed into a thin line. "Don't let it happen again."

"Yes, ma'am." A wave of disappointment crashed through her. Macie never wanted to turn in sloppy work, but Nancy was right. She'd rushed through the pieces and hadn't put enough effort into them. Her focus on how to pay her student loan bill had taken over her every thought. "I'm still good to freelance, right?" Macie blurted out.

"Yeah," Nancy said, staring at Macie. "There's nothing to say you can't. You have a non-compete that says you can't work for other stations, but nothing about freelancing. Why? What're you thinking?"

"Like you said, college isn't cheap," Macie said, pulling open the door. "Eventually you have to pay up."

Macie slammed into Alex's chest outside Nancy's office. He hadn't spoken to her since his father's verbal beat down a week ago and this was entirely too awkward. Everything had been through Nancy or email with Nancy cc'd. Not even a text message. Macie enjoyed the reprieve, but she had a feeling it was about to end.

"Regan," he said, planting his feet in the middle of the short hall.

Macie had no other choice but to engage. Her battle flags raised as she prepared for war.

"That last promo clip for my special feature was two seconds too long." Alex never tensed or crossed his arms. Nothing defensive.

"I hit all the parameters I was given. Nancy okayed it." Macie kept her arms down and her fists unclenched. If he wasn't going to get defensive, neither was she.

"Look, I don't want to argue. I'm in an awkward position here. I can't complain or even say I need something changed unless I want my father breathing down my neck." Alex sighed and his entire posture shifted from relaxed to defeated. "I want to do a good job. Sometimes that means being an asshole."

"Sometimes it means just asking like a decent human being and not screaming every cuss word on the planet at someone." Macie couldn't stop herself, she crossed her arms. "And I'm a fan of cuss words."

Alex smiled, and damn her if it wasn't actually genuine and attractive. "As a reporter, let me tell you one thing you need to remember."

"Oh, and what's that?"

Alex leaned down, shoving his hands in his pockets. "There's always more to the story."

Macie raised her eyebrows. Alex mimicked her, then turned on his heel and strolled away. There was something else going on with him. He all but told her. Curiosity nudged her forward, but she wasn't a reporter. She had no desire to be. She did want to be a good designer. In less than a minute she was in her office trimming the video by two seconds. It wasn't hard, but if that was what needed to be done for the job, she was damn well going to do it. She shot an email off to Alex, bcc'ing Nancy to keep her in the loop.

Ten seconds later her email chimed. It was Alex with a simple 'thanks'. Nancy didn't even get involved.

✦ ✦ ✦

Shit. She was late again. Although answering the door in just her robe again wasn't a bad idea, Macie didn't want to be too obvious. Besides, she knew Zac was attracted to her on a physical level. The way he took in every inch of her bare skin the last time was enough to know that wasn't an issue.

This, unlike last time, was a business meeting. She almost wished they'd met somewhere else. Her tiny apartment wasn't exactly visitor ready. Cleaning up came first, then maybe changing if she had time. Or maybe she'd change once he got there. The thought intrigued her. What would he think of her getting naked in her bathroom while he waited on the futon?

She shook it off. Not a time for seduction. She'd work on that later.

With ten minutes to spare, Macie put her dishes in the sink and ran water over them to soak. She threw her clothes in the armoire. That would have to be reorganized later. A quick feather dust over everything else and her apartment looked presentable. There wasn't enough time left to change so she freshened her mascara. Like her place, she was presentable. If in a messy professional sort of way.

Zac was notoriously punctual. Something Macie learned freshman year. Lauren and Ford had planned a sort of double date for them. Macie had no way out. Lauren knew Macie's schedule like she knew her own. She also knew Macie didn't have any plans since she'd sworn off guys after a disastrous date with a basketball player. Lauren had an appointment with her advisor, so she was meeting them at the restaurant and Ford had somehow managed to get out of picking Macie up, so that left Zac. Macie was late. She'd just gotten out of the shower and was hurrying down the hall toward in her room in nothing but her bra and undies under an over-sized towel. Zac waited outside her door. She noticed him as she tripped over the end of the towel and fell face first into the dirty tile floor.

"Hey, Chomper," Zac had said with his perfect smile. Giggles filled the hallway. "Have a nice… trip?"

If she hadn't hated him before, she hated him from that moment forward. She always claimed it was from the first time they'd met, but really, it was the fake date. His arrogance was on display full force. He was everybody's dream boat. Until he opened his mouth. Macie had been determined to let bygones be bygones. That moment was the true turning point.

Even the memory made her fume with untethered anger. What was she thinking? There was no way she could have a real relationship with Zac. He did whatever he could to goad her, to frustrate her, to piss her off in general. How could they move past that?

They had to move past it if there was any chance at a future.

Macie stared at her painting. She'd taken the bigger canvas and painted a larger spiral with the colors at an opposing line and the spiral churning in the opposite direction. Very carefully, she cut a square in the larger and inset the smaller canvas. She left a half an inch out, giving it more of a 3D appearance. Then she'd reinforced the backing. The effect was face-slapping. There was more work to be done, but Macie loved what she'd created. It was the first time she'd loved her art in a long time.

Everything she'd done in college felt forced. This was a piece of her.

She opened the portfolio on the table. The majority of her art was stored at her Mom's house. There wasn't a lot of it, either. Macie had destroyed most of her artwork. Not for any other reason than they weren't good enough. She'd kept the pieces she'd deemed okay. Looking at them now, they didn't speak to her. They were just there. Sellable, maybe, but not inspiring. Art should be inspiring.

Her phone lit up with a text from Lauren, but what really caught her attention was the time. It was ten after seven. Zac was late. That never happened. Macie's heart leapt into her throat, choking her on the intense beat. Where was he? A million things ran through her head, each disastrous thought cut off by the next then the next then the next. She watched another five minutes tick away until a soft knock pulled her from inside her head.

Macie ran to the door and threw it open, leaping into Zac's arms.

"Whoa, neighbor. It's nice to meet you, too. But, damn."

Macie jumped back and stared at the man standing in front of her. "Omigod." He grinned, and over his shoulder Zac did the same. Bastard. "I'm sorry. I thought you were…"

Her neighbor turned around, following Macie's pointed finger. "Lucky guy." He faced Macie, grin still intact. "Anyway, awkward as this has been, I just wanted to introduce myself." He held out his well-manicured hand. "I'm Barton Wilkes."

"Macie Regan." His hand was softer than hers. "Nice to meet you."

"Well, if you want to meet me again, I'm in 3C." He motioned to the door across the hall. "I make a mean chai latte."

Macie tried not to wrinkle her nose. "Thanks."

Barton brushed by Zac who raised his eyebrows. Once Barton was inside his apartment, Zac stepped forward. "What? No hug?"

"You're late." Macie crossed her arms. Yet again, Zac Sparks witnessed another embarrassing moment. And he made a fucking joke.

"Yeah, I lost track of time." He held out a manila file folder. "Research for starting a business."

Macie's eyebrows crashed together. "How did you know?"

He snorted a laugh. "You asked about setting up an online store, remember? What else would you want to talk about? Money, sure, but that didn't seem likely. And I have no idea how or where to sell artwork. I figured you might want to do something like this. Besides, Ford told me about his student loans coming due." He shrugged. "I know you had less scholarship money than he did. So…"

Macie stepped back, allowing him to enter her apartment. Logic. He'd just blindsided her with logic. She'd been prepared to tell him everything, basically pitch him the plan. He sat the file on her coffee table. The need to hug him overwhelmed her. He'd done all of that work for her. Without her asking. Without her begging, which she'd been fully prepared to do. He really was the guy she'd 'met' online. She just needed to show him she was that girl.

"Zac…" she whispered. He turned toward her. Nerves racked her body as she stepped forward and wrapped her arms around his waist. Her head fitted perfectly against his shoulder. She relaxed against him as his hands touched her waist. "I was … You're never late."

He squeezed her gently. "Not usually, but it's been known to happen."

"Don't let it happen again." She let go, realizing how that sounded. It sounded way too… girlfriendy? Needy?

Zac's mouth twisted into a knot. "You were… worried about me?"

"You're never late." Macie sat on the futon, hoping that would be the end of it. She wanted to say more, to tell him she was his mystery girl. God, she hated how she lied. "Show me what you brought?"

Zac settled in next to her, but Macie could feel the tension rolling off him. She closed her eyes. She'd royally fucked this up already. It was time to get back on track. Refocus on the plan to start her own business, and not on the plan to get Zac to see her for who she really was.

/ / /

Bipolar? No, that was not how bipolar people act. Macie didn't suddenly worry about him after years of animosity. Something else was going on. What would Ford call it? Transference. Yes, that was it. Macie transferred her emotions onto Zac's tardiness. That made more sense. Focusing would be a better idea.

"So, it's not that hard. I can set you up as a corporation, but the fees can be high once you take in the city and state requirements." Zac rubbed his hand over his face. "You could probably get away with no business license for a month or so if we don't incorporate right away, but that leaves you at risk for liability. Personally, I mean."

"A corporation would protect all this?" Macie deadpanned as she motioned around her small apartment. "I think I'll be fine."

Zac shook his head but hid his growing smile. "Fair enough. Other than selling your art, you didn't tell me what this business was for."

Macie stood and paced the short room. She kept her head down as she rubbed her chin. Zac wondered what was going on in her head, but he had feeling he was about to find out.

"You know the invitations I made for Lauren and Ford?" she asked, stopping dead in front of him. After he nodded, the pacing continued. "Graphics. People want their weddings, birthday parties, or whatever, to be unique. I'll customize invitations, programs, thank you cards, stuff like that. But I'll also make some pre-made designs too. At a cheaper price than my custom jobs. I figure it would take about a month to get those done and up on a site. Then I can start advertising."

"You could make book covers. There's a big need for those, too."

Macie jumped. "Great idea. That's something I can add down the line, like in six months or so."

"Mace, you need a solid business plan." Zac leaned forward and rested his elbows on his knees. "And you'll probably lose money the first few years."

"No, I won't. I mean, I probably won't make enough to get me out of debt, but I have a second plan for that. I just…" Macie plopped beside him. "I've been thinking about what you said. About Mom being proud of me and about getting my degree and all that. I … I want to be my own person. My own boss. Working at the station was temporary when I took the job, but even more so now. I can make this work. I'm willing and able." Her eyes softened. "Aren't I?"

She wanted his validation. *His.* What was going on with this girl? "How much debt, Mace?"

Her eyes darkened. "Enough."

"I did some research on student loans." He pulled a page of notes out of the back of his folder. "You can defer if you're underemployed. Based on what I think you make, that will never fly so deferment is out. I did learn that you can make the minimum required payment until you're on your feet better. That's different from what your bill says."

"Seriously?" She took the information from him, skimming over the facts. "Thank you."

"You're welcome."

"Zac, you've given me a lot of heartache over the years, but you've never lied to me." She sat up and stared straight into his eyes. "Do you think I can do this? Do you think I can be successful?"

"I know you can do it, Mace." Zac felt his chest balloon with pride. She really did value his opinion. "And I'm going to help."

"I can't pay you." Horror sketched her face.

Zac shrugged. "Can't a friend help out another friend?"

"So we're friends, now?" Macie's lips quirked into a grin.

"It's weird, but I think we're getting there."

Macie's laugh filled the room. "Lauren and Ford can never know. They'll act all triumphant and superior."

"We'll keep it our secret." Zac nudged Macie's shoulder. "Ready to get started on this?"

Macie held out her hand. "Yep. I'm ready, partner. Are you?"

"Partner?"

"I figured maybe if you wanted to be my partner instead. I do the creative stuff. You manage the money and shit." Macie shrunk back. "I mean if you want to. I've never been great with money. If I had, my savings account would be full of my tips instead of pennies."

Zac smiled. "Let's get this started first and see where it goes. Then we can talk about that later."

"Right. It may be an epic failure."

"Or a massive success."

"I'm going with that one."

"Me too." Zac shook her hand. *Partners. Huh.*

CHAPTER EIGHTEEN

Zac left late. As tempting as it was, Macie didn't ask him to stay. She'd wanted to, especially after things started to get playful. He'd bumped her shoulder. She'd swatted at his arm, letting her fingers linger longer than necessary.

The last time she'd written him through Blind Friends, she'd mentioned how crazy her job had been. That was a few days ago. She hadn't checked in since last night when there'd been no response. He was busy, too, she reminded herself as she opened the app. The magical one appeared in the inbox. She tapped his message and read.

> *Things have been a roller coaster for me, too. I'm beginning to wonder if my chosen profession was the wrong choice. Not because of the company but because of me. The job offers me no challenges. It doesn't set my heart on fire. It doesn't even wake it up. A friend recently told me that I should do work I'm proud of. I thought I was going to, but not anymore. Maybe I'm just doubting myself.*
>
> *That same friend, who I'd never thought I would call a friend, is so alive with energy and... well, life. And not afraid to say what needs to be said or to do what needs to be done. I don't think I've ever had that freedom.*
>
> *It's scary.*

Macie read it again. Zac didn't want to be in finance? Was that why he was so willing to help her? She thought back over her last few get-togethers. He hadn't said anything about his job. Nor had she asked. She was too busy being self-involved. If she wanted this to work, and she did the more she got to know Zac, then she needed to be less selfish. Starting now. She began to type.

I feel like I've been too busy venting about myself and not asking enough about you. I'm sorry that you're unhappy. That's the last thing I want to hear. Happiness isn't just about finding your career. It's about making the most out of what you have. I don't have much of anything, right now. But I'm working on a way to fix that. And that itself makes me happy. I don't remember where I heard this: Life is about the journey, not the destination. So, what can we do to make your journey the best?

Macie hit send. Then she realized her mistake. *What can WE do?* She didn't want him to think she wanted to meet just yet. After the wedding. After she got Zac to see the real Macie Regan. That sounded so terrible. Like she was some harlot bent on making him fall in love with her. She knew he cared about her. He just didn't know it was *her*.

The next few days flew by. Nancy hired a new designer, taking some workload off Macie. But she was still stuck with Alex, who had become Dr. Jekyll more than Mr. Hyde. He was polite, professional, and not a prick. She wasn't sure how to take that.

She also took a step back from her 'new' image. Since joining the station, Macie had done whatever it took to look the part of business woman, or what she thought was professional. The rest of the crew wore jeans. She wasn't on-air talent, so there was no need for her stuffy clothes. She dressed like herself—jeans, black shirts, and black biker boots. She put her silver hoop back in her nose and the silver bar back into her eyebrow. The final touch was her hair. She streaked it electric blue. Just a touch of color, but enough to make her feel normal again. Apparently, it stood out.

"That's a new look for you," Alex said from behind her.

Macie jumped in her chair. She'd been focused on the image on her screen and the music coming out of her phone. Turning around, she smiled. "Not new. Old. Don't you like it?"

A crooked smirk lifted his lips. "Without offending you, it's hot."

"No offense taken." Macie turned back to the screen. If she was totally honest, she appreciated the compliment. Most people didn't notice her new-old look around the station. "What's up?"

"Did you get that promo I sent?"

Macie felt his hand push down the back of her chair. His breath drifted past her cheek. "Yeah. Next on my list."

"Okay. I hadn't heard anything and you're usually pretty fast." He leaned forward until his face was even with hers and his focus stayed on her screen. "Is that for Mandey? The lead in for her six o'clock?"

"Yeah, it's not done yet. She likes this font, but I don't think it fits the story." A wail interrupted the music on her phone. Macie glanced down at the screen at the same time Alex did.

"Who's Zac? And why does he need to meet?" Alex asked.

Macie reached for her phone and swiped the message clear. It was none of Alex's business, but Macie knew he wouldn't let it drop. "He's helping me plan a bachelorette-slash-bachelor party. Our friends are getting married soon."

"Ah, so he texts you in the middle of the work day with an urgent need to meet? Sounds like more than that to me." Alex leaned back, clearly satisfied with his conclusion.

Macie wasn't taking the bait. She kept working on the promo, finally finding a font that worked better and that Mandey wouldn't realize wasn't the one she'd wanted. It was subtle, but it made all the difference. "Well, that's Zac. He thinks of something and has to share it right away." Macie smiled and tapped her mouse. "It's nice, though. He says what he wants, when he wants it. If he thinks we need to meet, then we have something to talk about. There aren't any games with him."

"Now that definitely sounds like more." Alex sighed. "How long have you two been seeing each other?"

A loaded question. One Macie didn't want to answer. Instead, Zac did it for her. "About three months."

Macie's eyes widened. She picked up her phone and, sure enough, there was Zac's face showing a connected call on speaker.

"So I'd appreciate it if you'd stop hitting on my girlfriend," Zac said. The hint of irritation in his voice was a nice touch.

"Whoa," Alex said with his hands up in defense. He backed toward the door. "Not hitting on anybody. Just asking about work and making polite conversation." His gaze met Macie's. "Let me know when you're done with that piece."

Macie threw him a generic salute as she fought to keep the giggles at bay. The minute Alex had cleared the door, Macie let her laughter fly. She took Zac off speaker and put the phone to her ear.

"Guessing that's Alex the Evil."

"He really wasn't hitting on me," Macie said.

Zac snorted. "Yes, he was."

"Whatever. Thanks for the save regardless. Alex isn't someone I'd be interested in."

"Probably a good idea. Did you mean what you said? About me?" Zac's voice dropped to a soft tenor. Macie's insides heated instantly. "That I don't play games?"

"Well, yeah. Even when we were fighting like middle schoolers, you never held back. I always liked that about you." A blush covered her cheeks, but Macie didn't care. It wasn't like Zac could see it. "It's nice to be open with someone."

Zac laughed. "Yeah, but you have to admit, it's a little weird, too. I mean, of all people I could be totally honest with, it would be my sworn enemy."

A pit formed in Macie's stomach. She hadn't been totally honest with him though. Tears rimmed her eyes as she realized she could lose him over one tiny thing. Okay, it was a huge thing. "Zac…"

"Mace…"

"I…" She couldn't do it. She wanted to tell him she was on the other side of the app. She needed to tell him. But not yet. It wasn't that she wanted to be deceitful, but she wanted to make sure he wouldn't run when he learned the truth. "I should go. I've got a lot to do."

"Yeah, okay." He huffed into the phone. "Let me know when you want to meet."

He ended the call. Macie put her head on her desk and composed herself. *Not yet.*

✐ ✐ ✐

Zac knew he shouldn't give a second thought to this Alex guy hitting on Macie. It wasn't any of his business. He set his phone down and settled back into work, but his heart wasn't in it. The job he'd been working toward wasn't what he wanted anymore. In two short months, he'd realized this his dad's dream wasn't his. Actually, it had taken longer than that. Since Zac could remember he'd been groomed to take over Sparks Investments. Now that the company was going public, it would never happen. It left Zac in a lurch. He wasn't sure if it was a bad thing or a good thing. Helping Macie, researching what she needed to do to start an online business, that felt right.

He picked up his phone and clicked on her contact information. Yeah, they'd just talked, but he wanted to ask her what she thought. His thumb hovered over the video chat. He wanted to see her expressions when he asked her opinion. Macie's face never hid anything. He liked that about her.

"Mr. Sparks," one of the new assistants said from his door. He flipped his phone over and smiled. "There's a gentleman here to see you. He wouldn't give me his name but told me to tell you 'domestic beer sucks'."

Zac bit back a laugh. "Send him in."

Ford strolled through Zac's door, closing it behind him. "Nice digs, buddy."

"Thanks. What brings you by?" Zac leaned back in his chair and put his hands behind his head.

Ford's normal jovial smile disappeared. "Am I making a mistake?"

"That shirt's a mistake." Zac pointed to the 'Vote for Me' t-shirt. The shirt was yellow, the lettering rainbow. Ford made it for a campus rally for the election last year. It was his mild-mannered way to protest all the candidates. He actually got four votes. "Other than that, I don't know what you're talking about."

"Marrying Lauren. Am I making a mistake?" Ford stared straight at his friend. He slouched in his chair. That was unusual, but Zac was more concerned about Ford's pale skin and bloodshot eyes. "Am I?"

Zac's arms fell to his side. He wanted to say yes. It was too soon to get married. They'd just graduated and had plenty of time. But Ford had been talking about marrying Lauren since the night they met. He'd saved for the perfect ring for two years, even working extra jobs Lauren didn't know about. Besides, Zac had shared his concerns before and they'd fallen on deaf ears. Now wasn't the time to bring it up. "Why would you even think that?"

Ford turned away from Zac, settling his gaze on the generic painting on the wall. "I … All my planning, I never expected to be in this much debt. I knew I'd have student loans to pay off, but … It's too much. Way more than I ever thought. I don't want to bring her down to my level."

"What did Lauren say?" Zac asked, knowing good and well what Lauren would say. If Ford bothered to talk to her at all.

Ford's head snapped back. "What does she say about me doubting whether or not to marry her? Do you really think I'm that stupid? Lauren would kick my ass out and tell me where to go."

"I meant about the debt. The loans."

"She said we'd get through it." Ford shrugged. "We'll just have to put off having kids for a while." He moved to the edge of his seat, resting his elbows on the corner of Zac's desk. "But she doesn't want to. You know we've been planning this wedding for well over a year, even before I officially proposed. And we've been planning the family, too. It's what she wants. I'm destroying her dream."

"Altering, Ford. Not destroying." Zac reached out and put his hand on Ford's shoulder. "Sometimes we spiral out of control in life and all we can do is survive."

Ford wrinkled his eyebrows. "That sounds like something Macie would say." His frown deepened as his gaze settled on Zac's desk. "Speaking of Macie, how're things going? You haven't called me for bail yet."

Zac turned and glanced at the back of his phone. "Good. She already had most of the work done on the party. We've got more work to do tonight."

"Over the phone?" Ford's voice buried his amusement.

"No, we'll probably meet at her place." Zac picked up his phone but put it back down. Anything to avoid Ford's psychological scrutiny.

"Her place? How many times have you been there?" Ford narrowed his eyes, psychoanalyzing Zac as expected.

"A few. Why?" Zac diverted his gaze to the computer. He couldn't let Ford see that the line of questioning was getting under his skin. Another cliché. He typed himself an email to look that one up too. Although a memory tickled the back of his brain about it.

Something about actual torture. Or maybe it was this conversation that was actual torture.

"I've never been there. And Lauren's been there once, for wedding stuff. Macie's rarely home as it is. Is something going on?"

Zac's head snapped toward his friend. He'd never lied to Ford about anything significant. Was this significant? It felt like it was. Either way, he'd tell Ford white lies here and there, but when it came down to the big stuff, Zac preferred honesty. But this, whatever this was, wasn't something he wanted to share. "Like I said. Party planning."

"At Macie's?" The skepticism overflowed in Ford's voice. "Why not over the phone?"

Zac laughed at that. "Obviously you've never seen Macie's wedding planner. It's huge. She has this incredible system that has to be seen to be believed. Every tiny detail is penciled in, even contingency plans if something falls through. It amazed me." He shrugged, not bothering to wipe the stupid grin off his face. "Seeing what she's got planned and hearing it are two different things. Once I saw everything laid out, it was easier for us to work together."

"Nothing else?" Ford asked.

"Fuck, Ford. What's with the fifth degree?" Macie's voice shot from Zac's phone. Ford's and Zac's heads twisted at a dangerous speed. "You're the one who insisted on the joint bachelor party. How the fuck else are we going to work on it?"

Blotches of red splattered across Ford's face. "Do you always have to be so vulgar?"

"Someone has to." Zac could almost see Macie shrug her shoulder and grin. He leaned his chin on his hand, using his fingers to cover up his own smirk. "And it might as well be me."

"What else did you hear?" Ford asked, panic raising his voice until he cleared it. Macie was silent for far too long. Ford's freak out went nuclear. "Dammit, Macie, what else did you hear?"

"Wow. Bradford Coleman said *dammit*. The world's coming to an end." She sighed, loudly and, more than likely, deliberately. "I only heard you give Zac shit about coming to my place. Yes, he's been there more than Lauren, but Lauren's been busy with last minute wedding changes and her mother. So we catch up when we can, wherever we can. And there's more going on between me and Zac."

That got Zac's attention. "Wait—"

"What?" Ford snapped. His concern about Macie overhearing his cold feet all but disappeared with Macie's bold statement.

"We're getting along. Like you and Lauren asked us to. Dare I say it, but we might even be friends."

Ford smiled, but Zac's entire body deflated. When Macie had said there was something more going on, he'd thought about how he'd stared at her long legs or caught himself gazing at her lips, wondering how they'd feel against his. He hadn't realized how much he'd wanted her to call him out on it. For Ford's sake, he nodded.

"That's actually great." Ford pushed himself up using the arms of the office chair. "I need to go, Zac. We'll talk more later."

"See ya, buddy." Zac stood and held out his hand. Ford gave it a firm handshake.

"Bye," Macie shouted through the phone. She waited three beats. "Is he gone?"

Zac picked up the phone and flipped it over. Macie's smiling face stared back at him. "Yeah, he's gone. So I guess it's pocket dial day."

"I always preferred butt dial. Although I've never been video butt dialed before." She shrugged but the concerned expression told him she'd heard more than she'd let on. "What was Ford so worried about? What did I miss?" Macie's tone softened with each word. "Not the wedding?"

He didn't want to lie to her, but he didn't want her to know that Ford's cold feet were icy. It was a fine line to walk. "He's just being a typical man. Nothing to worry about. He's not going to leave her at the altar."

"I'll cut his nuts off if he tries."

Zac laughed. "I have no doubt that you would. I like the hair, by the way. It suits you."

Macie tugged on the blue stripe. "Thanks. So tonight?"

"Chinese?" Zac asked. "I'll pick some up on my way over."

"I haven't had Chinese in months. That sounds so good. It's been back to ramen and dollar frozen meals for me lately." Macie let out a frustrated growl. "I can't—"

"My treat. We've got a lot of information to go over. I need you well-fed to focus."

"Valid point. You know my focus disappears when I'm starving?"

Zac smiled. *I know more than you realize.* "Pork fried rice, no onions?"

"Yes." Her voice took on a breathy, seductive tone. Zac wanted to hear her whisper that in his ear. "You remembered my Chinese order?"

"Did you forget the once a month Chinese meals when Ford and I still lived in the dorms? Lauren dragged you over to our room and we'd stuff ourselves while we studied." He knew she remembered. It was one of the few times they'd get along. At one point, Zac had even helped Macie get through a math course. Macie only ever ate the pork fried rice.

"Good times," Macie said. "I've got to go. I... I'll see you around seven."

She disappeared before Zac could respond. It was just as well. He was about to say 'it's a date', which it wasn't.

But he wanted it to be.

CHAPTER NINETEEN

Things had been weird. The universe aligned in a way that made Macie nervous. She waited for the bottom to drop out. Since Zac had come over to help her set up her online business, they'd talked almost every day. Both online and on the phone. He'd been amazing, and he'd seemed happier. She had noticed his lack of enthusiasm for his job over the last month but helping her rejuvenated him. That made her happy. A lot about Zac made her happy, lately. Just being in his presence lifted her out of any funk.

It also helped that she'd gotten her first freelance job through her website. It wasn't much, but it was a start. The next step was to sell her artwork. That was a much harder road to walk, and she needed to build her inventory. That would take time, especially since she hadn't finished *Spiral*. She stared at the painting. It was still missing something important. She glanced at the time on her phone. It was early, and the bachelorette party wouldn't start until three. Zac had offered to meet her at her place. He wanted them to show up together to make sure everything went as smooth as silk. The first part of the party wasn't one Ford, or any of the other guys, would appreciate.

Macie stripped off her clothes and grabbed her brushes. The edge of the inner canvas needed covered. With what, she didn't know. She only knew it needed to be dark. The paints sat unopened beside her palette. Instinct had gotten her this far, so she reached the tube that spoke to her, Payne's gray. Seemed appropriate. A tube of Crimson Alizarin hid behind a tube of Cadmium Red. The crimson was darker, and it would do better against the gray. Especially after she mixed the gray with Zinc White. Macie loaded her palette. Leaving globs of gray and white along the edges and pulling small portions toward the center to mix. A small amount of crimson sat alone. She put on her headphones, blocking out the world and letting the sound of a thunderstorm fill her head and take her to a place where her mind focused only on the task at hand. With a small brush, smaller than the one she used for her eyeliner, Macie began to paint the vision forming in her mind.

The brush moved slowly over the canvas, creating lines of dark gray, light gray, and white. The lines swayed in and out, up and down. The motion mesmerized her until the paint told her where it needed to go. Macie didn't see anything except where to go next. She added lines and dots of crimson sporadically. Dabs of white also filled space she felt were empty. She stepped back, viewing the small portion of canvas she'd covered. Haunted faces gazed back at her, *into* her. She took another step away from the painting and their gazes only intensified. Frozen. In hell. Unable to move. Their mouths were open, screaming in a silence so powerful Macie felt it in her stomach. She stepped back again, her bare back hitting the door.

Violent pounding vibrated the wood at her back and Macie jumped, pulling her headphones free from her ears.

"Macie," Zac shouted through the thin wood. "Macie, are you okay?"

"I'm fine," Macie shouted back. She reached for the door, only remembering her lack of clothes a second before she opened it. "Just..." She glanced around her messy apartment for something to throw on. "Give me a second." *Or two. Why is he so damn early?* She found an old Saints football jersey and a pair of black shorts. "Hold on," she added as she brushed her hair back with her fingers. *Good enough. I'll take a shower after he leaves.* She opened the door to a very irritated Zac.

"You're not ready?" He stepped into the apartment without waiting for an invitation. Very un-Zac-like. "What happened here?"

"I've got plenty of time to get ready," Macie snapped. She wasn't in the mood for Zac to bring back the bully he harbored inside. "What're you doing here already?"

"It's two-fifteen." He turned to face her, his gaze drifting down her body.

She opened her mouth to call him out on his obvious gawking when what he said registered. "Two-fifteen? Shit." She grabbed her phone, seeing several missed calls from Zac and a few not-so-nice texts. "Shit. Shit. Shit." He'd been outside for fifteen minutes. "I… Fuck. I need to take a quick shower."

"Hurry up." Zac stared at the painting, at the faces she'd painted. "I'll wait," he said in a much softer tone.

Macie didn't hesitate. She rushed into the bathroom and scrubbed the paint from her body. Hurrying as fast as she could, she braided her long hair while it was still wet and lined her eyes in black. There wasn't enough time for full makeup. There was barely enough time for her to get… Shit. Her clothes were in the armoire in the front. She reached for her thin satin robe, a stupid buy when she was drunk one night. Robes had never been necessary, even in the dorm. Macie preferred throwing on a tank and shorts after a shower. But she didn't have those, either. She tied it around her waist, aware that the thin material would show her nipples the minute the colder air of the apartment hit her. She sucked in her stomach and opened the door, walking toward her armoire like a runway model.

"Wha—" Zac began, cutting himself off.

Macie glanced at him with a raised brow. Zac's mouth stayed opened and Macie pursed her lips to keep from smiling. Her stomach flipped from the way his eyes traveled to her bare legs. Macie had never been ashamed of her body, never tried to hide it, but she never pranced around half naked, either. Well, not unless she was painting, but that was more about saving her clothes than anything else. Exhibitionism wasn't normally in her nature. At least not until she saw the way Zac's gaze caressed her. She stopped beside the armoire, bending at the waist to reach the drawer where she kept her bra and panties. With careful deliberation, she pulled out a black lace thong and matching bra, not bothering to hide them from Zac's prying eyes. His sharp inhale told her she'd made the right choice.

She opened the top door, reaching for her favorite jeans until her gaze spotted a purple galaxy skater skirt hanging in the corner. The matching elbow length gloves were in another drawer. It was something she'd worn a few months ago, but a style she'd all but abandoned once she started at the station. Not that it was work appropriate even on the most casual dress day. This night was about celebrating Ford and Lauren. She didn't want to pretend to be someone she wasn't. Not tonight. Not ever. She grabbed the skirt and a black tank, rushing to the bathroom to change. When she stepped back into the living room, she felt more like herself than she had in a long time.

"You look great," Zac said as he stood. "And normal."

"I didn't look normal before?" Macie stalked passed him, not entirely sure she liked his comment. Yeah, he said she looked good, but what the hell did normal mean? She opened the drawer in her computer desk and slipped on the gloves.

"You looked … different." Zac shoved his hands in his pockets, rocking back on his heels. "Not like the Macie I've known for four years."

"Is that a bad thing?" She turned to face him.

"No, but it…" He pulled one hand free and ran his hand through his hair. She took a moment to check him out. In her rush to get ready, she hadn't noticed that his standard polo shirt had been replaced by a black button-down shirt covered with a tight-fitting vest. A black tie rounded out his new look. "I don't want to fight."

Macie smiled. "I don't want to, either. I just…" She sighed and closed the distance between them. Gazing into his eyes, she opened her heart and her mouth. "I just really wanted to know what you're thinking."

"That's dangerous ground for us." A corner of his mouth lifted.

"True." Macie stepped back. "I like this." She motioned up and down his body, her fingers skimming over the fabric of the vest. "It's different, but it suits you."

"And this," Zac imitated her motions, brushing his finger over the gloves, "suits you."

"Change is good," she whispered.

"Not always."

Macie lost herself in his eyes, imagining what could've been, what still could be. The room heated around them. She felt it. She knew he felt it, too. His eyes darkened as they drifted toward hers. Macie angled her head, giving him full access to her lips, her neck, wherever he wanted to go. Zac's head tilted until their mouths were aligned.

Then he stepped back. His face flushed with either heat or

embarrassment, Macie wasn't sure which, but she really hoped it was the sexual tension that exploded between them.

"We're going to be late." He opened the door, holding it for her.

Macie nodded. She moved into the hallway, carefully brushing by him with a breezy touch. He inhaled fast and hard. She kept the excitement to herself but noted that it was time for Zac to meet his mystery girl.

✎ ✎ ✎

The mani-pedi was different. Zac hated to admit it, but having his feet massaged felt pretty good. No wonder Amanda and his sisters enjoyed it so much. He'd stolen glances at Macie during the process. She looked more uncomfortable than Ford. Then the small wedding party moved on to the 'guy' portion of the afternoon, and as much as Zac hated golfing, Ford loved it. They headed toward the driving range. A round of golf was out of the question with the time constraints. Macie had a surprise dinner arranged for Ford and Lauren at the diner where they had their first date. While they ate, the rest of the wedding party would head over to the final destination: Hoof.

Macie stepped up to the tee next to Zac's. Her hands were all wrong, her feet too close together, and her head too far down. He watched her take a pitiful swing, cursing like a sailor on leave. Zac couldn't stop the grin plastered across his face.

"Why don't you help her?" Ford said beside him. He lifted a cold water bottle to his lips, eyeing Zac as he took a sip. "You may hate this game, but you're good at it." Ford's gaze shifted to Macie for a moment before settling on Zac. "Besides, you haven't taken your eyes off her all day."

"That's not true." Zac dropped his head and readjusted the strap on his glove. He'd been stealing glances at Macie way too much, but he never thought anybody would notice. Ford noticed everything. He knew that, but it hadn't crossed his mind. Not much else had crossed his mind, except Macie. Her smooth skin, wicked smile, and legs that went on for days. Yeah, Zac had definitely been preoccupied.

"Keep telling yourself that, buddy." Ford slapped Zac's shoulder.

He pointed toward Macie's tense back as she teed up for another go. "Help her out, at least. She's going to end up throwing that club or worse, sticking it up some guy's ass. My money would be on yours since you planned this little excursion."

Zac laughed. "Bad bet, Ford. You and Lauren are the ones who wanted a joint party. Macie wouldn't forget that little detail."

Ford snorted and stepped up to a tee. His smooth swing sent the ball sailing in a straight line for two-hundred yards. Nice. Ford had come a long way since they were freshman. He'd jumped at the chance to play golf with Zac and his father. Ford had become part of the family, and Zac hoped that didn't change any time soon, either. A slew of F-bombs drew his attention back toward Macie. Lauren tried to calm her down, but a sharp glare by Macie sent Lauren back to her own tee. Zac chuckled under his breath.

"Mace, want some help?" he asked as he stepped closer. She spun around, frustrated and angry. He knew she was more pissed at herself than him, but he also knew to tread lightly. "I'm a great teacher. Ask Ford."

"Fine." She crossed her arms over her chest. "I don't get why people think this is fun."

"Not everybody does." He stepped onto the green Astroturf and placed a ball on the tee. "Personally, it bores me."

"Why bother, then?" she asked, letting her arms fall to her sides.

"Because my dad likes it." Zac shrugged. "We golf once a month, sometimes more if he's in the mood. It makes him happy. And I get to spend time with him, so it's worth it."

Macie's body relaxed. "That's actually sweet."

"I'm not a jerk all the time," Zac said. He moved behind her and wrapped his arms around her. Macie tensed up for a moment before relaxing into his embrace. "Letting go of the tension is the first step." He slid his hands down her arms, too slowly. He didn't even need to do all of this, but the opportunity presented itself and it was too good to resist. Besides, he wasn't going to let it go any further. His mystery girl was still there, waiting. He cleared his throat and covered Macie's hands with his own. "Let me guide you through a swing."

"Mm hmm," Macie replied.

Zac's body melded around hers. Every curve, every line fell into place with him. He slipped his foot in between her legs, separating her feet so she was standing shoulder width apart. Macie's sharp intake of breath set him on fire, and he pulled back so she wouldn't notice the tightness in his pants. After repositioning himself in more ways than one, Zac guided her arms back in a slow smooth arc. His heart hammered in his chest. He let out a rush of energy as they brought the club down together, smacking the golf ball out onto the range.

"Whoa." Macie leaned back against Zac, setting every nerve in his body on high alert. "That was intense."

"Yeah." He resisted the need to tighten his arms around her. "Wanna try it on your own?"

"I'm..." Macie sighed. "Sure. Why not."

Zac let go of her hands, sliding his up her arms before stepping back completely. He missed the heat of her body, the feel of her against him. But he did enjoy the view of her ass as she placed a ball on the tee. Her back rounded too much and her legs were too far apart. Zac waited, only managing to get his hand up in time as she pulled back too fast, too hard, and too far. The club hit his palm, stinging it more than he expected. Macie didn't even notice as she started to follow through, leaving the club behind in Zac's hand. She spun around completely. Zac caught her around the waist before she fell, and her hand slapped against his chest. With a blush covering her cheeks, she lifted her head and stared into his eyes. Zac wanted to smile, to comfort her, but he was paralyzed. Tears rimmed her eyes. He knew why. She'd told him that he'd always seen her at her worst and here they were again. He didn't understand it. Every time she'd been beautiful, perfect in her imperfections because she owned them. She'd always been Macie, even when they hated each other.

"You're trying too hard," he whispered.

Macie's lips parted then lifted into a smile. "That's it? No witty comeback. No new nickname?"

"Well," Zac grinned, "I could call you Spin, but I don't think that would go over so well."

To his surprise, Macie laughed. "I think maybe we should try that again. Together?"

Zac nodded, unable to actually form words. He wanted to put his arms around her again. He shouldn't want that, but he did. She sighed as his hands skimmed down her gloves. He buried his nose in her hair, inhaling the vanilla and lavender. Macie shuddered. He really needed to get it together.

"Ready?" he whispered in her ear.

"You have no idea," she said.

They pulled the club back and smacked the ball dead ahead. He didn't let go. Macie leaned against him. It was nice, perfect. And not in the cards. He needed to stay off this road.

"You should be good now," Zac said, dropping his hands and stepping back.

Macie nodded and stepped back up to the tee. She shanked it to the left, but she did so with a smoother swing. After a few more swings on her own, she made adjustments based on Zac's suggestions and set the ball on a straight course. Zac watched it sail about a hundred yards with a smile. She'd done it. Macie never had been one to give up easily, but she'd always been more of a 'I'll do it on my own' type. Over the last few weeks, that had changed.

Lips pressed against his cheek. He closed his eyes, savoring the feeling. She left them there longer than a quick peck.

"Thank you," Macie said. "I mean it. Thank you for everything."

He turned toward her, but she'd already stepped away from the tee.

✏ ✏ ✏

The real party started at the club. Macie arranged for the VIP section with her former boss, which was just a cordoned off area for the party. Two years of bartending at Hoof had its perks. He didn't charge her for the space or the cover. Of course, she'd also talked to him about picking up a shift here and there after the wedding. Freelancing would help once she got some gigs, but she needed money sooner rather than later.

Hoof's large dance floor spilled over with students from Lafayette and a nearby community college. They danced like tomorrow would never come. She'd done the same, once. Tomorrow came like always. It had only been six weeks since she completed her degree and she felt middle aged.

"Whatcha thinking?" Lauren asked in her ear.

Macie smiled, lifting her bottle to her lips. She took a long pull from her beer. "Not much."

"Liar." Lauren nudged Macie with her shoulder. Her long hair spilled down her shoulders. Lauren flipped it back, laughing at nothing. Typical Lauren.

"Not lying." Macie turned away from the dance floor. The VIP room was roped off by black velvet and a half wall of wrought iron fencing between two large brick beams. Macie leaned against one. Lauren and Ford's friends crowded the tight space. Strobe lights bounced off their skin and clothes. It gave Macie a headache, or maybe that was just the beer.

"I wanted to thank you again for helping Mom with the shower." Lauren shook her head. "There was no way she could've done it without you."

"I'm sorry I missed it," Macie said. According to Zac, Sylvia had sent all the men into the basement to play pool while the women chatted. Her gaze settled on Zac. He smiled at something Ford said, then laughed. A five o'clock shadow covered his chin. Another button had come undone near the top of his black shirt.

"Why are you staring at Zac like he's cheesecake?" Lauren leaned against the beam beside her.

Macie rolled her eyes.

"Fine, don't tell me, but everyone's seen it." Lauren leaned in as if anyone could possibly hear them with the music at Deaf-Con two, added emphasis on *deaf*. "People keep asking me when you guys hooked up. I was dumbfounded at first, but now… well, now I need to know if you have actually hooked up. You have, haven't you?"

"No," Macie snapped, turning toward Lauren. "We have not hooked up. Just … friends."

"Friends?" Lauren snorted and sipped her gin and tonic. "Sure, Zac gives you a sexual golf lesson and you two are just friends. You might as well have dry humped each other on the tee."

"Lauren!" Macie's shock reverberated down her spine.

"It's true." Lauren tipped her glass toward Macie. "And you know it. So what's the deal?"

"There's no deal." Macie turned away from her friend. "And you're delusional."

"Sure," Lauren said. "So what's the deal with the guy on the app? You still talking to him?"

Macie's smile spread so fast it hurt. "Yep."

"Ah, now I get it." Lauren nodded. "That's the hold up. Why don't you meet him and get it over with so you can bone Zac?"

"Jesus, Lauren. You have one drink and you're spewing innuendos. That's *my* job." Macie smiled and drained the rest of her beer. "I'm going to get another. Want one?"

"Nah, I'm good. Threes my limit anyway." Macie turned toward the bar, but Lauren stopped her with a hand on Macie's elbow. "Seriously, Mace, don't keep waiting for the right moment. It might just disappear before you know it."

Macie smirked, but Lauren wasn't wrong. This fine line Macie walked with Zac got thinner by the minute. She stopped at the bar and raised her bottle, shaking to indicate she wanted another. No, she needed another. It felt like an eternity since she let loose and with a rare Sunday off work, she was determined to have fun and act like any other twenty-two-year-old. She glanced over her shoulder to where Zac stood with a bottle blonde. He smiled at the petite girl who clearly wanted to see what was under his Dockers. She ran her hand along the buttons of his shirt. Macie noted that Zac didn't bother to step back. Anger surged through her. When the bartender dropped off her bottle, she downed it and signaled for another. All while staring at Zac as he let some bimbo hit on him.

She took the second bottle, grabbed the first guy within reach, and pulled him out to the dance floor. Jealousy wasn't her game. It wasn't her usual reaction and trying to make the guy she'd spent the better part of her college years hating jealous, seemed like a stupid play. It didn't seem like it, it *was* stupid. Zac wasn't interested in her. He wanted the digital version of Macie Regan, and he'd probably flip his lid if he knew the truth. She tried to get him to know the real her, and obviously that failed. It was time to cut her losses and move on. A one night stand with a complete stranger was just what the doctor ordered. Macie led the guy into the center of the crush of bodies. She turned to face the randomness her hand found and just about shit a brick.

Alex fucking Leffler.

"This is … unexpected," Alex said.

"Shit, I'm sorry. I just wanted to—"

"Make the boyfriend green?" Alex nodded over Macie's shoulder. Zac glared at them. "It's working, but I don't think he's going to storm onto the floor to rescue you, yet. Wanna make him?"

Macie laughed and leaned in so Alex could hear her. "With you? You're kidding, right?"

"Just for fun, Macie." He glanced over her shoulder. "He's already getting pissed off."

"I doubt that," Macie replied, adding an eye roll for good measure. "He's not exactly who you think he is."

Alex raised an eyebrow. "Maybe not officially, but he's into you. I'll prove it. Dance with me and you'll see how fast he cuts in."

"If you're game?" Macie grinned. "And if you think this means anything other than that, you're an idiot."

Alex leaned down so they were eye to eye. "We've already established I'm an idiot."

"Wait, what're you doing here anyway?" she asked, curious why Alex just happened to be at Hoof.

He shrugged. "My cousin suggested I get out of my comfort zone and meet new people. Apparently, he just wanted a wingman" He pointed to a couple who were dancing like they were intent on the night leading to a bed.

He held out his hand. "Let's get this party started, shall we?"

Macie's grin widened as she put her hand in his. Alex smiled and spun her around, pulling her back against his front, and his hot breath found her ear. Macie hated to admit it, but damned if that wasn't a turn on. Macie raised her arm, putting her hand around Alex's neck as they moved together from side to side. His hands wrapped around her waist, his chin settled on her shoulder. Macie glanced toward the last place she'd seen Zac, but he wasn't there. He stood right in front of her, pissed off and hotter than the sun.

"Mind if I cut in?" Zac asked through gritted teeth.

Alex's hands disappeared from her waist and landed on her shoulders. Macie wasn't expecting what happened next. Alex spun her around, shoving her into Zac's arms. "She's all yours, buddy. Just treat her right. She knows where to find me."

Macie mouthed "thank you" and Alex did the creepy winking thing. She hated guys who winked.

Zac's hands settled on the side of her hips. His lips brushed against her ear as he said, "If you wanted to dance, you could've picked a better partner."

"The partner I wanted was busy with a blonde bimbo." Macie pressed back against him.

Zac responded by sliding his hands across her stomach. "Plenty of guys with blonde bimbos on their arms, Mace. You need to be more specific."

The music turned to a faster beat. Macie's hips moved with Zac's, following along. His fingers spread across her stomach, flattening her against him until there was nothing but fabric separating their bodies. Her heart hammered in her chest. She snaked her arm around his neck, curling her fingers into his thick blond hair.

His breath drifted over the skin of her neck and she tilted her head.

"There's a guy over there, for example, with a gorgeous blonde with a huge rack. Is that who your talking about?" Zac asked into her ear.

Macie's knees weakened as the desire melted her from the inside out. "You know who I meant."

"No, I don't." He spun her around until they were eye-to-eye. "I'm an idiot sometimes. I need things spelled out in black and white."

Her breath hitched in her throat. No amount of alcohol could've prepared her for this moment, and she was well past her normal limit. Words were what he wanted, but she couldn't say anything. Besides, she'd always lived by the actions-speak-louder rule. Why change? She didn't smile, didn't even crack a grin. Her hands slid up his arms, over his thick shoulders, and around his neck. She teased him with her fingers in his hair and pulled his head toward hers. Zac's arms tightened around her waist. Macie needed the anticipation, the seduction. She brought her forehead to his and let her body move to the music.

"Macie?" Her name wasn't more than a whisper on his lips, but she felt it in her core.

"Dance with me, Zac," she said. "Nobody else but me."

His body moved with hers, through each song, each beat, they danced. Somebody offered them drinks, but neither one saw who. They didn't care, either. They only had eyes for each other.

CHAPTER TWENTY

Macie knew she was tipsy, but she didn't give two shits. Besides, tipsy didn't mean too-drunk-to-remember. Zac held her hand as they walked toward her apartment building. He didn't sway like he was drunk, or even on the way to drunk. The heat of summer helped sober her up, so did the dancing. She knew this was the epitome of a bad idea. She knew it wasn't the right time, but she didn't care. She wanted Zac. He wanted her. At least, based on the bulge in his pants. Macie keyed in her code to the building and practically pulled him up the stairs to her floor.

She didn't look at him as she unlocked the door and stepped inside. Only when the latched click did she turn around. She half expected him to be gone. He stood in front of her with his hands in his pockets and confusion covering his flushed face.

"What're we doing, Mace?" he asked.

She closed the short distance between them and put her hands on his chest. "This."

Then she raised onto her tip toes and kissed him softly.

Macie fell back on her heels and waited. He didn't move. He hadn't even kissed her back. What had she done? It was too soon. She knew it, but in her damn impatience, she did what she wanted anyway. He stared at her as if she'd grown another head. Her leg dropped back, prepared to step away, but she held out because she hoped for some reaction from him. Maybe they were both drunker than she thought. Alcohol normally killed inhibitions. She let her hands fall from his chest.

"Sorry," she whispered. Her eyes closed, because God knew she couldn't look at him anymore. Another embarrassing moment witnessed by Zac Sparks. Tears welled, but damned if he was going to see her cry.

His fingers skimmed along her jawline. Macie's eyes snapped open. He tilted his head and slowly closed the distance, pressing a gentle kiss on her lips. "This?"

She swallowed the knot in her throat and nodded.

Whatever caused him to hesitate disappeared. Zac pulled her against him, kissing her with a gentle rush. Every cell in her body exploded. She needed to free him of his oppressive clothing, free his body to take hers. Never had she wanted anyone as much as she wanted Zac. No she needed to feel him inside her. Needed to feel him take her. Macie let Zac guide them with his tongue. She let him lift her and press her against the wall. Her legs wrapped around his waist. His erection pressed against his zipper, pressed against her.

"Zac," she whispered as his lips moved down her jaw, over her neck. "Now. Please."

Begging wasn't her normal cup of tea, but if she didn't feel him soon, she was going to combust. He didn't stop his assault on her neck. If anything he slowed down.

"Zac?" she asked.

He stepped back, breaking the seal of their bodies. His gaze drifted down her body, only serving to make her hotter. She waited and tried to remember to breathe. Never had she wanted a man like this before. Sure, she'd had some amazing sex, but there wasn't this all-consuming need that overpowered her. And she'd never wanted anybody else to take charge, to put her first. Most guys didn't do that and she prayed Zac would be the first.

She opened her mouth, ready to beg if she had to, when he reached out. His fingers skimmed along her bare arm from her shoulder to her elbow, hooking inside the glove. He slid it down her arm with achingly slow progress and tossed it on the coffee table. With the same process, he removed the second glove. Macie had never felt more exposed in her life.

Zac stepped closer, tugging her black tank free from her skirt and lifting it over her head. His hands trapped her arms above her head and against the door. He kissed the top of each breast. Her body screamed for more, but he wasn't going to deviate from whatever plan he had. Macie wished she knew what was going on in his head. The anticipation was eating away at her. His hands left her wrists and barely caressed her skin as they drifted down to her waist. Macie threw her tank across the room, not caring where it landed. He slipped his fingers under her waistband, dropping to his knees as he lowered her skirt to the floor and leaving her only in her matching bra and panties.

Macie's eyes watered over as he sat back on his heels and stared up at her. Their gazes collided and the spark that started this only intensified. Zac slid his hand up her calf, lifting her leg onto his shoulder. His lips skimmed along her inner thigh. He never broke their heated gaze as he slipped his fingers under the thin material still covering her.

"Zac," she pleaded.

He teased her, circling the edges of her nerves until sliding a finger inside her. Macie's breath hitched in her throat, but it wasn't enough. She needed more. She wanted more. All of him. Not just one little digit. Macie sighed in frustration when he removed the lone finger. She kept his gaze as he grinned.

"Damn you," she whispered.

Zac chuckled. He reached up and pulled her panties down, fully exposing her to him. "You don't like this."

"I think I like it too much," she said.

Zac kissed along her thigh again until coming to her sweet spot. His tongue licked her to the edge, then buried itself inside her. Macie cried out quietly as he pleasured her with his mouth and her body rode the orgasm that shocked her into submission. Zac Sparks could do anything he wanted to her, anytime he wanted, as long as he made her feel like she did in this moment.

"Jesus, Macie. You're gorgeous." He kissed his way up her stomach, standing to his full height. With one swift move, he unlatched her bra. There was nothing slow about the way he took her breasts into his mouth, rising the peaks of her nipples until they hurt then nibbling at them. Macie was ready to explode again. "Where?"

"Here. Right fucking here," she ordered.

Zac pulled off his shirt and let his pants fall to the floor. He didn't hesitate after rolling on the condom then burying himself inside her. Macie wasn't quiet as he moved inside her, crying out with the pleasure of each thrust. He pressed against, pushing himself to the hilt and filling her completely. Macie's heart raced against her breath. She needed this. She needed him. This wasn't sloppy drunk sex. She was completely sober. It was so emotionally powerful, so much *more*.

She exploded around him again, her body weakening to the point he had to hold her up. Once the first wave was over, another crashed through her riding along with Zac's own orgasm. She couldn't think. Her mind only registered how she felt, and it was overwhelming. They didn't move for a long time. The weight of Zac's body holding them both against the wall. Without a word, he pulled her into his arms and carried her to the futon. He held her against his flushed body as he tugged the frame into a bed then helped her down. Macie's brain was mush. She wanted nothing more than to sleep. But only if Zac stayed. She held out her hand, inviting him to join her.

He settled in behind her, wrapping his strong arms around her in a protective cocoon. He brushed her hair back from her neck, kissing her gently and Macie fell into the best sleep of her life.

🖉 🖉 🖉

The sun shattered his sleep. Zac didn't want to wake up. He was too comfortable, too warm, too happy. The sun was bright for a Sunday, and since when did he forget to close the blinds? He squeezed his eyes tight and squeezed the warm body lying next to him. Comprehension slapped him in the face and his eyes shot open. Dark hair cascading over a bare shoulder. He knew that shoulder.

Zac slowly lifted his arm from around Macie's waist. With each movement, the night before rushed back at him. The dancing. The want. The need. The taking. This connection with Macie had been intensifying for weeks, but he never saw it going down this path. Even in hindsight as it happened, he hadn't expected it. Nothing in their relationship had ever led to this. How did it happen?

Idiot. He knew *how* it happened, just not the why. Alcohol. Blame it on the whiskey from the party. It had gone down smoothly. Except, he wasn't that drunk. A little drunk when they left Hoof, sure, but not drunk enough to lose all sense of propriety. Not drunk enough to forget who he was with or what they were doing.

He had to get out of there.

Leaning up on his elbow, he glanced around the room. His pants were by the door. His shirt was on the stove. He shook his head. That was just where it landed. His shoes were a mystery, and if he was a betting man, he'd bet they were under his crumpled pants. He glanced down to figure out how to untangle himself from her smoking hot body.

Macie slept with her hands tucked under her head. A small smile softened her face. She was beautiful. So damn beautiful it made him ache for more. He reached down and moved a lock of her hair from her cheek. She shifted toward him, snuggling her body closer. The blanket fell away from her chest, revealing her perfect breasts.

The memory of those in his mouth set him on fire.

He had to get out of there.

This wasn't supposed to happen. He needed to remind himself that this was Macie the great antagonizer. It didn't matter if they'd been getting along for Ford and Lauren's sake. Once the wedding was over, they'd never have to see each other again. That was the deal.

Sex, no matter how good it was, was not part of the deal.

Besides, he had his mystery girl. Guilt stabbed him in the center of his chest. He cheated. Yeah, technically he wasn't *with* the mystery girl, but he'd committed himself to her until they met. If they met and stayed friends, then fine. He'd move on. But that girl, she was so perfect for him, and sleeping with Macie had not been part of the equation. Sleeping with Macie was a huge mistake. Sleeping with Macie was the best night of his life.

Zac slipped off the futon and headed straight for his pants. As he suspected, his shoes were hidden underneath. He shook his head as the rush of memory tore through him. They hadn't even made it to the futon. He taken her right there, right against the front door. There was no slow and steady move about it. And it was incredible. He was pretty sure slow and steady would've been just as amazing. Completely sober probably would've been beyond all of it. He shook his head. It didn't matter. This was a mistake.

Dressing as quickly as he could, he moved around her tiny apartment in stealth mode. Dick move, sure, but he didn't want the morning after confrontation if he could avoid it. He didn't even know what to say to her. 'Thanks for the sex. See you at the wedding,' wasn't going to cut it with Macie. No, he couldn't have any kind of conversation until his head was on straight.

He moved toward the door, glancing over his shoulder one more time to take in the beauty of a sleeping Macie. Only she wasn't sleeping. She was wide awake with her hurt feelings on rare display over her face. Zac's hand fell from the doorknob as he turned to face her. She didn't say a word. She didn't have to, he could read it on her face. She knew he was bolting on her. He never in his life would've thought she'd be hurt by it.

Macie stood, letting the sheet fall from her naked body. Zac's gaze took in every inch of her in the morning sun. How could he just walk out on this beautiful woman without an explanation? He loathed himself for it and despised himself more for still wanting to leave. Macie didn't say anything as she strolled toward him, completely unashamed of her exposed skin. Even that was a turn on. A woman confident in who she was and how she looked had been on his checklist for a very long time. And here she was in front of him as he was ready to run out the door. Macie didn't stop until they were toe-to-toe. Her head tilted back and her eyebrows crinkled together. Zac swallowed hard.

"Mace." His voice burned through his dry throat.

Macie didn't answer with words but with her mouth on his neck.

Zac weakened under her gentle touch, but he fisted his hands together and forced his arms to stay locked at his sides. "Macie, stop."

She pulled back and stared up at him. Tears filled her eyes before falling down her heated cheeks. She pursed her lips and nodded. Her voice cracked around each word. "It meant nothing to you?"

He never thought Macie would show any emotion other than disgust or anger, but she laid it out in front of him with five little words. "That's …. Yes, it meant something."

"But not enough for you to face me this morning," she said, nodding again and stepping back until he could see her entire body. "Just another notch in your bedpost."

"Jesus, Macie, that's not true. I'm not like that." Zac wanted to fall to his knees and beg for forgiveness, but he had no reason to. Macie wasn't more than a friend at best. This was just a colossal mistake. Why couldn't she see that?

"Then what was it, Zac?" She put her hands on her hips, her fiery attitude returning on full blaze. "If that wasn't another fuck for you, what was it?"

He didn't know what to say to that. Macie had always been brutal in her honesty, but this hit him in the gut. "I don't know," he answered, because he didn't.

"Seriously?" She threw her hands above her head. "Well, I'll tell you what it was. It was perfect. It was fantastic. And it clearly meant more to me than to you. I thought... It doesn't fucking matter what I thought. You're still the selfish asshole I met freshman year."

"That's not fair," Zac snapped.

"It's not?" Macie closed the distance again. Her anger shook her entire body. "Then why are you leaving? Why were you going to take off without saying a word?"

"Because I'm in love with somebody else," he said.

CHAPTER TWENTY-ONE

She wanted to know who. In her head, she demanded to know. But there wasn't any point. The only person she'd fooled was herself, and poorly at that.

"I'm sorry," Zac said. He had enough shame to duck his head, but she didn't want that.

"Look at me," she said. When he didn't, her anger exploded. "Grow some fucking balls and look at me."

Zac's head snapped up and he met her gaze.

"Does she know?" Macie asked. She fought every urge to cry, to be that stereotypical girl that the media loved to play up.

Zac averted his gaze once again. "Can you put some clothes on? This is a little distracting."

Macie rolled her eyes. Her body was good enough for him last night. She reached into a drawer and pulled out a t-shirt that hung to the top of her thighs. "Better?"

Zac glanced toward her and winced. "Not really."

"Whatever. Just answer my question. Does she know?" Macie resisted the urge to cross her arms over her chest.

"Is this really appropriate conversation?" Zac rubbed the back of his neck. "Considering."

"Considering what? The fact that we fucked?" Macie smiled as he winced again. He was such a prude sometimes. "What else do you want me to call it, Zac? It wasn't *making love*. Obviously."

"I don't know." He reached for the door again. "I should really go."

"Running away? That's so like you." Macie knew she was being a bitch, but she couldn't stop herself.

"Stop it, Chomper," Zac said with the same poisonous tone.

"Look, you regret something that I don't. We've established that." Macie backed away from him and sat in her wingback in the most unladylike position possible. She threw one leg over the arm of the chair, completely exposing herself. "You've seen me at my best and my worst. Just answer the damn question."

"No," he said. Zac shook his head and leaned against the door.

"No, you won't answer me? Or no, she doesn't know?" Macie's hope soared.

"She doesn't know," Zac muttered.

"Why?" Macie fought the smile building inside her.

"I haven't exactly met her yet." Zac's cheeks blazed a brilliant red.

It was her. Internet her, but her nonetheless. She wasn't sure until he admitted it. Telling him now was out of the question. The timing couldn't be worse. So she'd have to do this a little differently. "Excuse me?"

He closed his eyes. "You know that app Lauren and Ford created?"

"Lauren created. Not Ford. And yes, I did the graphics remember?"

"I met her on there."

"But you haven't actually met her."

"No."

"Again I ask why?" Macie closed her legs and leaned forward, resting her elbows on her knees. "Maybe this whole one-night stand could've been avoided."

"I thought you didn't regret it." Zac glanced anywhere but at Macie.

"I don't. And I'd be more than willing to prove that to you."

"Mace—"

"But clearly you regret it. So you need to get this whole mythical girlfriend out of your head so you can see what's standing right in front of you."

He couldn't avoid her after that declaration. His head swiveled toward her, his eyes wide enough to be cartoonish. "What?"

"Did you ever think the person on the other end could be a guy?

Or a lunatic? Or an axe murderer?" *The woman standing in front you? You're arch rival? The person you just had a fantastic one-night stand with?* She really wanted to tell him.

"She's not."

"Then why haven't you met?"

He didn't answer, so Macie played the game out for him. It bothered her that he didn't own up to it, and that she'd played him. She couldn't think about that now.

"Wait, you tried to meet and she stood you up?"

He nodded once.

"Zac, let her go." She softened her voice, letting the emotion she'd held back flood through. She stood and walked to him, resting her hand on his chest. His heart beat against her palm. "Let her go and come to me. We're good together. We challenge each other. Life will never be boring. Let this happen."

He put his hand over Macie's. "If only I could. But I have to see this through, Macie. And I don't regret what happened last night. Just the timing."

Macie raised onto her toes and kissed him softly. "Our timing has always sucked. Since day one."

Zac smiled. "I should go."

Macie nodded, settling back onto her heels. She stepped away from him again. Zac opened the door. Her emotions waged inside her. She was hurt and elated at the same time. He loved her. But only the her online. He wouldn't let himself love the real life Macie because of the digital Macie. She was fighting a losing battle with herself. It was a weird sensation. If she hadn't suspected that Zac was talking about the digital version of herself, Macie probably would've kicked him in the nuts for trying to sneak out on her.

There was only one solution. It was time to let him know the truth. She grabbed her tablet and opened the Blind Friends app.

I've been thinking. Life is always going to get in the way, but we have to take control. I'm ready to take control. Meet me at Shaw's Park in the big gazebo at 8pm tonight. If you'd still like to meet that is. Bring cracked corn to feed the ducks so I'll know it's you.

She pressed send and waited. Within a minute, Zac responded,

I'll be there.

🖊 🖊 🖊

Zac paced his apartment. All he could think about was Macie. Her soft body, her perky nipples, her perfect mouth. Just the thought of her sent him into overdrive. When the message came in, it was as if his mystery girl knew what he'd done and wanted to call him out on it in person. The worst part was he didn't feel guilty about sleeping with Macie. He felt guilty that he'd ran like a coward. And that he agreed to meet this mystery girl. And that he claimed to be in love with this mystery girl.

Was it a claim or truth? Zac wasn't sure. Without meeting her, without seeing her in person to know if there was that spark of tension between them, he just didn't know.

The day dragged like a stretching cat. He cleaned his already spotless place, did his laundry, took his tiny bag of trash out to the dumpster, and still had six hours to burn before he went to the park. Around noon his phone rang with Ford's smiling mug on the screen. Zac ignored the call. The last thing he needed was the third degree from his best friend.

Then the text came in.

What happened last night? Ford added a winking emoji. Zac hated emojis.

He didn't want to answer, but a pure lack of answering was itself an answer. So he lied. *Nothing. Why?* Before he hit send, another message came in.

I regret nothing. Macie's text slapped him back to reality. He'd hurt her.

Me either. He responded. *Except this morning. I regret the way I left this morning.*

Don't.

He didn't know how to react to that. And Macie didn't give him a chance to.

You should never regret saying how you feel or what's on your mind.

What's on your mind? He thumbed in, hitting send before he realized it was probably something he didn't want to know the answer to.

You.

Zac froze. She'd surprised him more and more every day. If he'd known this version of Macie the last few years, things might have been very different.

I have to go. She texted. *Working a half day. Talk to you later.*

Ok. He was such a jerk.

Another text came in from Ford. *Bro? Come on. Lauren and I are dying here and Macie's not answering. Did you guys hook up last night?*

If Macie wasn't telling Lauren, Zac wasn't going to tell Ford. They'd have to just not be in the know. Zac picked up his laptop and opened the business plan he'd started. Helping Macie start her own company had given him an idea on his future. He didn't want to just help people prepare financially for old age. He wanted to help people make things happen in the present, to help them follow their dreams. Zac's plan was in the early stages and there was a lot he needed to figure out before jumping in feet first, but it was solid. He just needed a backer. Fortunately, he knew a man with deep pockets who would do anything for him.

Everything was in the details. Like Macie's online business, this would have to start off as a part-time endeavor. Digging into the details distracted him enough to pass the time. It was almost six when he stopped. There was still two hours to kill before he left to meet her.

Meet her.

The idea of seeing this perfect creature in the flesh sent his heart racing. He'd been able to open up to her in a way he never had before. The anonymity made it easier, but that didn't explain the pure connection he felt with this woman. All the warning bells shot off in his head. What if she was taller than him? What if she was fifty years old? What if she was crazy? He didn't care if she wasn't as beautiful as Macie. He didn't care if she was older. And she had to be a little crazy to meet some random guy in person. No, focusing on the positive served him better than focusing on the negative.

Dinner. He needed to eat. Zac turned his attention to cutting up vegetables and chicken then stir-frying them in a sweet teriyaki. He spooned the chicken over rice, savoring the smell. Sitting at the table, he realized it was quiet. Too quiet. The silence left him room to think and that was not what he wanted to do. His mind kept replaying the night before. As much as he wanted to focus on the upcoming meeting with his mystery girl, he couldn't stop thinking about Macie. Her hands over his skin, her tongue dancing with his. The way her body fit against him. The way she moaned his name. It had been more than sex for her, and if he was honest, it meant more to him, too.

He just couldn't let go of the girl who'd captured his mind over the last several months. It wasn't fair to Macie. It wasn't fair to the mystery girl. It wasn't fair to him, either. He kept going through the vicious circle, trying and failing to find a solution. There wasn't one. The only thing he did achieve was killing enough time. He showered quickly, then selected his clothes as slow as a teenage girl on a first date, finally settling on a navy blue button down and khakis. Not too casual, not too formal. It was too business, but that was who Zac was.

The drive to Shaw's Park took less time than he expected, or maybe that was just nervous energy. He parked with fifteen minutes to spare. Shaw's Park was north of Lafayette's sprawling campus and a favorite hangout of students. People could be found jogging on the paths, kayaking in the large man-made lake, or playing a spirited game of disc golf. The gazebo overlooked the lake to the west, giving a perfect view of the sunset. It was where Ford proposed to Lauren last summer during the solstice. That wasn't lost on him when mystery girl mentioned it, but a lot of people came to the park and the gazebo was a prime spot for romance.

Nobody else was there, fortunately. Zac leaned against the railing, tossing the corn into the lake, and watched the sun drift toward the horizon. Sweat built between his shoulder blades. A hot breeze brought the sweet scent of the nearby rose garden. Zac closed his eyes, enjoying the fresh air and the heat of the sun on his face. Spending sixty hours a week in the office made moments like this more precious.

"You're early," an eerily familiar voice said. "I'd wanted to get here first."

Zac spun around to face the answer to his mystery. When his gaze settled on her perfect features, he fell back against the railing. "You?"

Macie shrugged with a nervous smile on her face. "Me."

"You," he said again, trying to grasp this. His heart sped up as he stared at her in an innocent white sundress. She was almost angelic. But this was Macie, not some ethereal being. "You're her."

"Or she's me. Depends on how you want to look at it." Macie kept her distance, staying at the entrance of the gazebo. "Are you..."

Zac turned away from her. Macie. Fucking Macie. This wasn't right. This wasn't how everything played out. Then a thought struck him like lightning. She played him. She played him so easily, so effortlessly. All this time he thought he had fallen in love with this girl online. Then he started to develop feelings for Macie despite how much he denied it. She hadn't stood him up at Spoons. She. Had. Been. There. She'd known for weeks. He faced her again, the reality of situation falling into perfect place.

"Did you enjoy it?" he asked with pure venom in his voice. Macie stepped back, but she wasn't getting off that easily. Zac crossed the gazebo, each step raising his anger higher. "Did you enjoy watching me fall for you? Did you enjoy watching me tear myself apart this morning? Did you laugh at me when I left?"

"No," she whispered. "That's not—"

"Not what, Chomper?" he yelled. "Not the way you wanted me to react to your grand joke. Well guess what, I don't find it fucking funny at all."

"It—"

"And you know the worst part," he screamed. "I fell for it. I fell for this image you faked online. And I fell for this person you pretended to be. I should've known better. I should've known you'd stoop so low for revenge. It is a dish best served cold, isn't it? I finally get that one."

He pushed by her and headed toward his car. Not once did he look back. Not once did he wonder if she even cared about him. He knew she didn't. He knew she did this just for her own stupid pleasure. He didn't even glance her way before he backed his car out of the spot. Anger controlled him as he headed toward the driving range. He paid for unlimited balls and used his nine-iron to sail them as far as they would go.

All this time he'd fallen in love with someone who was incapable of feeling anything but hate.

CHAPTER TWENTY-TWO

Macie didn't know how she got home. She didn't remember getting back into her wreck of a car or driving to her building. She didn't remember changing out of the carefully selected sundress or putting on her oversized Lafayette t-shirt. She didn't remember eating an entire carton of Ben & Jerry's, either.

The one thing she did remember was the expression on Zac's face. The confusion. The hurt. The understanding. Then the anger. He was so angry. This was unlike anything she'd ever seen from him before. After he found out his girlfriend had been sleeping with a professor during their freshman year, he was pissed. Not like this. After he was accused of cheating on a mid-term, he was ready to take down the school. Still not as angry as this.

She wasn't sure what to do next. How could she fix it?

The lightbulb went off in her head. A note, a message, a letter. Reconnect the same way they'd originally found each other. She'd explain everything. That was the only way to do it. The only way to make him see that she wasn't duping him. Macie grabbed her tablet and logged in to Blind Friends. Her mailbox didn't show a message. As much as she hadn't expected one, it still sent her heart on a downward spiral. She pressed the envelope to open her inbox.

Nothing was there.

None of the messages from the past several months existed anymore. Macie checked her trash bin. The ones she had deleted were still there, but not a single one she'd shared with Zac. Swallowing hard, she searched for his screen name.

User not found.

No. That couldn't be right. Maybe she typed it wrong.

User not found.

She hadn't typed it wrong that time. He'd deleted his profile. Macie thought she'd hit rock bottom before. She was wrong. Deleting his account forced her lower. He hadn't even wanted the memory of their conversations. Fortunately for Macie, she had a habit of backing everything up on her desktop. She turned it on, waiting impatiently for the old thing to boot up. Once she got her life on track financially, a new system was necessary. Especially if her online design business took off.

The file was still there on the desktop. She heaved a sigh of relief. Logically she knew it would be there, but that didn't stop the fear from building. She'd downloaded the messages for prosperity. When they were old and gray, she planned on laughing with Zac about how they fell in love. It seemed stupid in light of his reaction. She printed them out. Maybe if she showed him the past, he'd realize she wasn't doing this for some weird revenge.

That didn't mean he'd read them, though.

She needed something bigger. A grand gesture. Like in the movies when the guy does something incredible to make the girl realize he's not the asshole she thought he was. Of course, that was fiction. And the roles were reversed. Macie shook her head. The least she could do was try. If she failed, she failed. But if she didn't try, she would have failed far worse.

An idea began forming in her mind. She moved toward her closet, pulling her shirt off and tossing it on the futon. Inside, she dug through her art supplies and pulled out everything that caught her eye. Something was missing. Wire. She needed wire. Something she could bend easily to shape. Wood. She needed wood, too. It was almost ten, but Macie needed those things that moment. Or she'd lose the inspiration.

She quickly dressed and headed out into the night. First stop, the dumpster behind her building. Gross, yes, but effective at finding discarded items for her art. It was too tall for her to jump into, but luck was on her side. Someone threw out a perfectly good kitchen chair. Too bad she didn't have immediate need for it in her apartment or she'd lug it upstairs. She pulled it close to the dumpster and climbed onto the seat. A coil cut through the fabric and scratched her leg. No wonder it was thrown out. A box of wire hangers sat right at the top. Macie couldn't believe another round of good fortune. She hauled her bounty to her apartment. An idea struck her again.

She didn't need the wood. She had something much better.

Three hours later, the wire hangers twisted into shape. She mixed the paste and began to cover the wire with strips of their messages, entire sentences clear until parts were covered. Macie carefully placed the strips, wrapping them around the wire. The night disappeared into dawn. Macie had worked straight through without stopping. It was almost done. Almost. It still needed the proper base, but that would come later. First she needed to shower and down a couple of energy drinks just to make it to work.

For once, she didn't even bother with eyeliner or mascara. She pulled her hair back into a messy bun, too messy to be stylish. Macie rushed out the door in jeans and a Linkin Park t-shirt.

The work kept her busy until lunch. Another energy drink might have given her a heart attack, but some real food would help wake her up, too. She hadn't eaten since a quick dinner before she met Zac at the gazebo, and that had only been a small salad. She'd been too nervous to eat.

But she could close her eyes for a moment. Just a moment.

Macie started awake at the sound of someone clearing their throat.

"Late night?" Alex asked.

"No night." Macie stretched her arms above her head and yawned. "What time is it?"

"One." Alex sat on the edge of her desk. He'd toned down the attitude and his strict dress code of suits and power ties. His white button down and jeans was too casual for anyone in front of the camera. Unless he was working on a story that required research. It didn't matter. Macie just liked Alex as a normal person not trying to be a controlling asshole.

"Shit. I slept through my lunch. I'm starving." Macie reached for her phone, hoping for any message from Zac. Nothing but several unanswered texts from Lauren. She'd have to respond soon. The wedding was this weekend. She'd have to come clean about everything then. "Guess it's vending machine junk for me."

"Just order in. It's not like we don't eat at our desks, anyway."

Alex tapped on her computer screen, pulling up the video she'd been working on before lunch. "How's Nancy's new promo coming along?"

"So far, so good. What's new with you?" Macie opened her browser and ordered a sandwich from a deli down the street. It was too expensive, but she was moving toward hangry and their delivery was known for speed.

Alex shrugged. "Trying this not being the asshole of the office thing. It's not easy."

Macie laughed, drawing a glare from Alex. "Sorry."

"Yeah, well, you try changing your reputation overnight. It's not exactly a walk in the park." Alex reached over and grabbed Macie's mouse. He added a turkey on wheat to her order. "So, that guy the other night. That the boyfriend?"

"It's more complicated than that." Macie turned in her chair and faced him. "And I do know what it's like. To change people's perception of you."

"Guess we've got more in common than we thought." Alex stood and tossed twenty-five dollars on her desk. "Let me know when the food gets here, and I'm buying. It's the least I could do after the shit I gave you."

Macie smiled. "Thanks."

Alex nodded and left her alone. The video sat frozen on a clip of a hurricane. Wildly appropriate for her life at the moment. Alex's words rang in her ears. She wasn't changing who she was for Zac as much as changing his perception of her. Years of hatred didn't wash away overnight. Or even over a few weeks.

Macie needed more than just her grand gesture. She needed to make Zac understand.

She needed to write him.

Four days. Zac threw himself into work during the day and worked on detailing the business plan at night. It kept him occupied, but not nearly enough. He couldn't stop thinking about Macie. After she revealed herself, he had deleted every digital aspect of her from his life. The first being his Blind Friends account. A tiny part of him, the part that loved the girl he'd met online, regretted that. He also deleted her from his social media, which quite frankly she'd only been a part of because of Lauren and Ford, and from his contact list. He'd done everything he could to erase Macie Regan from his life.

But he couldn't get the memory of her from his mind.

Ford stopped asking. So did Lauren. They knew something was wrong, but they both had enough sense to stop bringing her up.

It helped that work had been overwhelming. Zac brought in more clients, much to the new partners joy. He went in at six and left well after five in the evening. What else did he have to do? Nothing but brood.

He unlocked the door to his empty apartment and stepped inside. The silence deafened him. She'd never been here, but he felt her presence nonetheless. Actually, if he was honest, he felt her absence. Macie had let him into her world with what he had thought were open arms. He had a hard time believing it wasn't an elaborate ruse to get back at him for years of torment.

The table had become his work space. Papers spread across the top in chaotic piles. He set his laptop bag on the chair and headed toward the fridge. It lacked food, but not beer. He opened a local microbrew and sat at the table, preparing for another round of planning. At this point, there wasn't much left to do. His plan was solid. There was no way he couldn't be successful at it. Sparks Consulting could be off the ground by the end of the year, turning a steady profit in less than five years. He just needed to pitch the idea to his father.

His phone vibrated in his pocket. He fished it out just as the call went to voice mail. Lauren. He waited to see if she left a message. When it vibrated again, he put her on speaker to listen.

"Hey, Zac. It's Lauren. I just…" She sighed heavily. "Look, I don't know what's going on with you and Macie. She's not talking. You're not talking. We just ask that you put your differences aside for this weekend. After Saturday, you can hate each other all you want, okay? Just … just fake it for one day."

The message ended and Zac wanted to laugh. Fake it. Macie had been doing a great job at that. He hadn't. That cut him more than anything. Not only had he fallen for this invisible image of her, he had started to fall for the person she'd pretended to be. The night of the party, he felt a primal need to claim her. When she danced with that pretty boy, he didn't think. He acted. When they'd gotten back to her apartment, he didn't think. He acted again. The complete lack of use of his brain sent him into this downward spiral. Just like Macie's painting.

He debated on whether to respond to Lauren or let it go. Then his stomach rumbled. When was the last time he had a decent meal? That he couldn't remember. He hadn't eaten much over the last few days. Mostly junk food or pizza. He needed something with substance. That left two options. Order delivery or go out. He opted for delivery. Sitting at a restaurant by himself didn't sound like a good time, or even an okay time. It sounded miserable. Zac was tired of being miserable. The quickest option was Chinese. He pulled up the app and ordered beef lo mein, pork fried rice with no onion, and General Tsao's chicken. That should last him a few days until he could get to the store. After he pressed send, he questioned his choice of the pork fried rice. He didn't even care for it. Why did he even bother? It hit him like a hammer to the chest. Macie loved it. Even subconsciously he couldn't get her out of his head.

Frustrated, more at himself than at her, he opened his laptop to iron out a few tiny details of his plan. A light rapping pulled him from the business world twenty minutes later. His stomach growled with anticipation. Zac hurried to the door, his hunger getting the best of him. When he opened it, nobody was there. There was a large white box with an envelope bearing his name. He glanced down the hall, seeing only the wisp of her hair. He knew without a doubt that this was from Macie.

Curiosity got the better of him and he brought it inside. He pulled the envelope free, tossing it onto the table. The paper tore like Christmas wrapping. He tugged at the flaps of the box and peered inside. It took his breath away. Careful not to break it, he pulled the rest of the box apart.

A papier-mâché couple in the shape of a heart jutted from the screen of a laptop. He turned it around, trying to figure out how she'd managed to do it. The top of the laptop was smooth. He looked at the paper couple again, shocked by the detail involved. She must've been working on this for days. Weeks, even. He glanced at the keyboard. The original letters were gone, replaced by a message or a title spelled out in what appeared to be a random pattern—Beginnings. It was spectacular. But something else gnawed at him.

He looked at the couple again. Then he realized. He should've seen it first. She'd printed their messages to each other and created this.

He sat back and stared at it, biting his thumbnail.

A knock at the door ripped him from his thoughts, or lack thereof. Zac opened the door, hoping to see Macie but was greeted by his forgotten dinner. He tipped the delivery guy and sat the paper bag on the coffee table, pulling out his meal as he glanced at the sculpture. It was powerful and intricate and unique and … so Macie. Under pieces of discarded box, the edge of the envelope poked out. He'd already forgotten about that, too. He freed it from the trash and sat in on the coffee table. His stomach growled and the rich smells of the beef drew his attention away again. He took his time eating, then he stored the leftovers in the fridge. He picked up the trash and broke down the box.

If he was honest with himself, he was really just avoiding the envelope. Forty minutes later, he couldn't avoid it anymore. Zac grabbed a microbrew from his fridge and sat back on his couch. The envelope lay on the coffee table, his name in calligraphy. Even that was a work of art for Macie.

It's like ripping off a Band-Aid, he thought. That was one cliché he truly understood. He picked it up and slid his finger under the flap to open it. One page of white paper, tri-folded. That was it. He didn't know what he was expecting. Pictures of their past when they'd gotten along? But a letter was how this started. It was how it would end.

Zac unfolded the paper and began reading.

> *Dear Zac,*
>
> *This is probably my tenth draft of this. It took less time to make Beginnings.*
>
> *Saying how I feel has never been easy. So, here we go.*
>
> *When we first started chatting on Blind Friends, I did not know it was you. I can't stress that enough. We started exchanging messages and I thought 'this guy's great'. We grew with each letter. I let my guard down. I let you see me. The real me. The one only my mother knows. The anonymity made it easier, but it was all for you.*
>
> *Obviously, you know I didn't stand you up the first time we agreed to meet. I was late because of work and I saw you sitting*

there. My world stopped. I almost kept walking. I almost shut everything down. But I couldn't. Not after learning you were Guy. I'd see you every day until the wedding and probably after, and I couldn't go through my life wondering about what might have happened if I didn't try to put the past behind us. We spent so much time hating each other that we never got to know each other. And Lauren and Ford gave me the perfect cover.

So, I decided to see what would happen between us. I opened myself up to you in person. I reigned in my temper. I told you things about me I hadn't shared with anyone else, and I think you did, too. I never realized how passionate you are, how caring, and how kind. You aren't who I thought you were. You're so much more, so much better than I will ever be. I fell hard and fast. And I don't regret it. I regret lying, but I don't regret falling in love with you. And I don't regret the night we spent together.

I wish I could make it up to you. I wish you'd let me. But if you won't, please treasure this small piece of my heart. Let it remind you of us even if you do regret it. Because some of us was pretty fucking great.

    Love,
    Chomper

CHAPTER TWENTY-THREE

Macie worked at station the until two in the morning. Lauren was getting married in eleven hours and Macie had to be at the salon in eight. She looked like hell. The bags under her bloodshot eyes grew bigger each day. She'd actually lost a few pounds since Sunday, mainly because of a complete lack of subsistence. The last real meal she had was the sandwich Alex bought her.

And she would see Zac for the first time since he left her at the gazebo. As much as she loved her best friend and wanted to see her happy, the last thing Macie wanted to do was go to a fucking wedding, stand at the altar with Zac opposite of her, and walk down the aisle with him. Her chest ached thinking about how it would feel. How much worse would it be when it happened.

It didn't help that Lauren had pestered her every single day about what took place at the party. Macie kept her mouth shut. It wasn't anyone's business. Besides, if Zac had told Ford, then Ford would've told Lauren. He clearly didn't want anyone to know. She had to respect that and respect his silence.

The only way to avoid thinking about him was to either live in a drunken stupor or work as much as she could. The drunken stupor was appealing, but that would only send her down a bad road. She needed to make up for missing two weekends in a row, anyway, and the overtime would help her check. Fortunately, Nancy approved the overtime and the days off, but after the wedding it would be back to a straight forty. When she wasn't at the station, she was working on her freelance business. Over the past week, she'd gotten three more orders for custom wedding invitations.

The work helped with her new-found insomnia, but it didn't stop her from thinking. All she'd done was replay the last several months in her head. She focused on where she went wrong and how she might've done it differently. In the end, it didn't matter. That only added to her misery. There was nothing she could do to fix what happened. It was over. The wedding, the reception, after it was done, she'd make sure Lauren knew everything so Macie would never have to see Zac again.

Her apartment was eerily quiet, more so than usual. Or she was just that tired. Macie settled into her chair and stared out the window at the crescent moon. She didn't know how long she sat there, only that she fell into some sort of trance. It wasn't sleep, by any means. Unless she dreamed of sleeping in the exact same position she was in and dreamed about the exact same moon. Macie jolted back to reality when the sun started to crest the horizon. She showered and lay down on her futon, setting her alarm for seven forty-five. Maybe she could salvage a few hours of real sleep before the wedding. Before she had her heart broken all over again.

✏ ✏ ✏

Getting drunk alone at his apartment the night before his best friend's wedding wasn't the best thing. Zac had never sunk so low. At least he'd laid off the tequila and vodka, sticking instead to the case of caffeinated brew in his fridge. It was enough to get him drunk and keep him awake. Again, not his best decision.

Not that sleep had been much of an option lately, anyway.

The sculpture sat on his coffee table. He didn't know where else to put it. There wasn't any other place to keep it other than the dining room table, and he didn't want it right in front of him while he worked and ate. It was too distracting no matter where it would sit. Even if he threw it in a closet, he'd think about it.

That was probably Macie's goal. He wouldn't know. He didn't bother to call or text her. He didn't know what to say.

In a few hours he would see her, walk down the aisle with her, smile as if there was nothing wrong. Everything was wrong. He wanted to fix this.

And he didn't.

He wanted to at least have peace for the wedding and reception. Macie wouldn't ruin Lauren's wedding. She would keep the peace, too. Then maybe he could figure out what to do. Figure out if there was anything to do.

/ / /

Lauren looked like a model, and Macie's heart swelled with happiness for her friend. For the first time in almost a week, Macie smiled a real smile. Not the fake ones she gave her coworkers. Lauren's cousins kept the conversation going, but Macie knew Lauren was dying to interrogate her about Zac. It didn't help that in less than ten minutes he would be standing at the altar beside Ford. Macie promised herself not to look at him, not to see him in his tux until she had no choice. Because she didn't want to cry. She didn't want to ruin her makeup before the photos.

"Are you ready?" Lauren's father asked through the door. He beamed with pride at his daughter. "You look beautiful."

"Thanks, Dad," Lauren said. She glanced at her small bridal party. "Ready?"

"This is it," squealed Keisha. At sixteen, Lauren's youngest cousin still believed in fairy tales, in happily ever afters.

Macie smiled, faking the brightness as she tugged the too loose dress. She changed the streak into her hair to match the plum color. The flower girl, Ford's niece, raced out the door followed by the other two bridesmaids, and Macie moved to follow but Lauren's father closed the door and Lauren put a hand on Macie's arm.

"You need to let me in, Mace," Lauren said. Fine lines cracked her face in concern. "What's going on?"

Macie swallowed hard and reached for Lauren's hand, squeezing it in promise. "Not now. Please. I just need to get through today. Then I'll tell you everything. I promise. I …. I can't ruin your wedding with my emotional bullshit."

"I love your emotional bullshit." Lauren squeezed Macie's hand back. "I'm worried about you. You're paler than normal and your dress is too big. Talk to me, please?"

Macie closed her eyes, forcing back the tears. "Give me a few days. It's too... raw."

"When you're ready?"

"I promise."

Lauren nodded and let go of Macie's hand. "Can you believe this is happening?"

"Yes," Macie said point blank. "You guys were meant for each other."

"He wants to wait....to start a family," Lauren said, the joy glowing on her skin. "He's got a big surprise coming in about seven months."

"Wait. What?" Macie's jaw dropped. "Are you serious?"

"Yeah, I'm serious." Lauren bounced in excitement. "I found out yesterday for sure. I wanted to tell you earlier, but the chatty twins wouldn't leave us alone."

"Ford doesn't know?" Macie needed to sit down. This was too much too fast. They didn't need to rush, but that was Lauren. Full steam ahead on anything and everything.

"Nah. I'm going to tell him tonight after we get home. He'd freak right now, and he's nervous enough as it is." Lauren laughed, her own nerves showing through. "We'll be fine. He's spent too much time talking to Zac about financial security over the years. That's set him on edge. People have made it with less."

"My mom made it okay," Macie said.

Lauren smiled. "And you turned out somewhat normal."

"Meh, normal's overrated." Macie smirked.

Someone knocked at the door. Lauren's father peeked in. "Okay, the bridal party is getting restless now. You ready?"

"Yeah, Dad, I'm totally ready." Lauren linked her arm through Macie's and whispered, "I've been ready for this since the day I met him."

Macie squeezed her friend's arm as they strode out the door. Lauren wasn't wrong. It was love at first sight. For her and Zac, it had been the opposite. It was strange how things worked out. Maybe getting her heart broken by him was the only way this thing was going to play. Tears began to well in Macie's eyes, but she blinked them away. If she cried at all today, it would be for Lauren's happiness.

They stopped at the end of the procession line. Macie kissed

Lauren on the cheek and let go of her arm. The flower girls and bridesmaids entered. Then it was Macie's turn. She took a deep breath and stepped into the chapel as Frank Sinatra crooned about doing it his way. Macie's smile widened. She'd always joked with Lauren that she'd only walk down the aisle to this song. Of course Lauren would take it too far and have Macie do just that.

Macie focused on Ford. He shuffled on his feet a bit, enough to be noticeable to his closest family and friends. Macie's smile widened. He was nervous. Even though Lauren had said so, it still took Macie off guard. A hand fell on Ford's shoulder, calming him instantly. Macie knew that hand, and knew she couldn't look there. She turned her head toward Lauren's mother who beamed like she was the bride. Lauren's grandparents smiled politely, one grandma dabbing the fake tears.

Then she glanced at Ford again, and instead landed on Zac. His gaze was hard and cold, staring through her completely. She tripped over her own two feet, catching herself before she fell and brought a trickle of laughter to the occasion. Great, that was just what Macie was. A joke. She glanced at him again, pleading with her gaze for some response other than hatred. His expression never wavered. Tears welled in her eyes again as she took her place opposite Zac and forced herself to stare toward the doors where Lauren would make her grand entrance. If she held off crying until Lauren walked in with her father, then the tears would at least be justified.

✐ ✐ ✐

Zac's heart stopped beating the minute Macie stepped into the chapel. When she finally looked at him, he froze. When she tripped, he stood beside Ford like a jerk and didn't rush to help her. But Macie never needed his help. She'd never needed anybody's help. That was one of the reasons Lauren had the violin player switch songs to Sinatra when Macie took the aisle. And she commanded it. There wasn't a single eye on her that couldn't see how beautiful she looked. The plum dress hugged every curve to the point of pornography. Her smooth bare shoulders, her gorgeous hair cascading down her back. He wanted to get on his knee and beg for forgiveness.

Macie took her place across the aisle, where she would be in his peripheral vision for mass. He could see her chest heaving, her eyes brimming with tears. As much as he wanted it to be for him, which was a horrible thing to wish for, he knew this was all about Lauren and Ford. Macie would do nothing to ruin their wedding. If she could control herself, so could he.

The music changed, and Lauren entered with her father. Zac's chest swelled with pride. She was perfect today. He heard Ford's sharp intake of breath and knew his buddy felt the same. Lauren didn't wear a veil, nor did she wear a white dress. Not that anybody would know. He only knew because Macie had told him. Macie. He needed to get her out of his head until all the pomp and circumstance was over. After the ceremony, after the photos, after the reception, then they'd talk.

Mass took forever. Zac stood when required and followed instructions, but he didn't pay too much attention. Ford and Lauren nudged each other at the alter like two school kids. He glanced toward Macie. Her face glowed. Waiting until after everything was done was going to take the will of a hundred men, but Zac needed to do right by his friends.

When the priest called for the rings, Zac and Macie set them on the open bible. Zac grinned as they said their vows, and grinned as they kissed for the first time as man and wife. He grinned as the congregation cheered. Ford and Lauren smiled at everyone and began the march back down the aisle to a song Zac didn't recognize. His grin dropped when he turned toward Macie and offered his arm. Without looking at him, she took it, and a part of him became whole again. He couldn't go on like this any longer.

Macie's body tensed. He wanted to tell her to relax, or how perfect she looked. But he couldn't talk. How was he going to make this right, when he couldn't even open his mouth? The minute they stepped through the doors, Macie dropped his arm like a hot potato and bolted down the hall toward the bride's dressing room.

He never got to say a word.

CHAPTER TWENTY-FOUR

The wedding party filed in, crowding the room. Macie moved to a corner to get out of the way of the chaos. Why Lauren decided to have the photos done between the ceremony and reception was beyond Macie. Logistically it didn't make sense. Had they done this earlier, it would've been out of the way. They would've had time to relax before the reception. But Ford was a traditionalist and Lauren liked a little chaos. It actually fit them.

Macie planned her avoidance techniques while she watched the aunts clean up and the rest of the women retouch their makeup. It was simple really, just stay away from Zac. There were moments where she wouldn't be able to. The first was when they walked back down the aisle together. She'd barely kept it together. Zac was as hard as granite. He couldn't stand to be in the same room with her, let alone touch her. The next problem would be the photos. They'd do all the traditional ones, but she knew Lauren had some whimsical ideas for the fun photos. Macie had no doubt that they'd push her and Zac together multiple times. Then the limo to the reception. She'd just have to sit as far from him as possible. The biggest challenge would be the wedding party dance. She couldn't even think about that. Considering what happened the last time they danced together.

A cold hand landed on her bare arm. Macie glanced up to the face of Lauren's mother.

"Macie, I just wanted to thank you for helping Lauren plan today," Sylvia said. Her smile saddened. "I wish I could've been here more to help."

Macie snorted. "You could've, Sylvia. You chose not to."

"Excuse me?" Sylvia put her hand to her chest as if she was truly offended.

And Macie gave zero shits if she was. "You heard me. You put your career first. You always have. So, do me a favor. When your first grandchild comes, make time for them." Macie pushed off the wall, leaving a slack jawed Sylvia behind. "That felt good," she muttered under her breath.

The photographer herded everyone into the chapel for the first round of photos. Macie sat in a pew, staring off into space and keeping a good distance between herself and pretty much everyone else. She couldn't stand talking to anyone. When she had to smile, she smiled. Once those photos were done, the photographer moved the wedding party outside. They trudged up a small incline and stopped at the top of the hill. Behind them, a small meadow rolled along the earth. It was beautiful.

"Okay, everyone," Lauren announced. "We're going to have some fun."

Fuck, here we go. Macie plastered on another fake smile.

The first photo was the bridesmaids and groomsmen pretending to keep a desperate Lauren and Ford apart. Macie doubted that would look good in the long run, but she wasn't paying for the photos so it was none of her business. The next one was similar. The bridesmaids gathered around Lauren and pretended to gossip while Lauren looked toward Ford. The groomsmen slapped each other on the back in fake conversation while Ford looked around them toward Lauren. Macie tried to hide her disdain for the stereotypes. At least, she hoped she did.

The next photo was the one she'd been dreading. The bridesmaids sitting on the bended knees of the groomsmen, pretending to be happy. She waited until she had no choice to sit on Zac's lap. His arm wrapped around her waist, squeezing her against his chest. She savored the feel of his touch, the smell of his skin, the heat of his body.

"Excuse me, Maid of Honor," the photographer said. Macie's eyes snapped open. "Could you smile?"

Macie tried. She really did. But she couldn't.

"I'm sorry," the photographer said as he stopped beside them.

"But you're going to ruin the picture if you don't smile more."

Tears filled her eyes. Ruin. That's all she every did. She ruined everything.

Macie pushed herself free of Zac's grip. "I can't do this anymore."

Then she ran as fast as her heels and dress would take her. She didn't get very far before a hand clamped around her arm, spinning her around to face her assaulter.

"What're you doing?" Zac dropped her arm as if it burned him. "You're screwing up—"

Macie felt everything inside her break, including her careful control. "That's what I do, Zac," she said. "I ruin everything."

"That's not what I meant and you know it." He shoved his hands into his pockets. "I meant the pictures."

"Right. Sure. That's exactly what you meant." Macie turned away from him so he wouldn't see her cry. But, damn it, why shouldn't he see her cry? She'd poured her heart out to him and he still rejected her based on some dumbass idea she wanted revenge on him. She spun back around and jabbed her finger into his chest. "Just say it. Come right out and say what you want to say, Zac. We might as well do this now."

"This isn't the time or the place to have this discussion." Zac took a hand out of his pocket and ran it through his hair.

"Yes, it is," Lauren shouted from where the wedding party stood watching the showdown.

"Shhh," Ford ordered.

"What? It's true," Lauren said.

"Just say it, Zac. Put a damn fork it me, I'm done." Macie shook her head at his continued silence. "You say I ruin everything? Well you ruined me."

"What's that supposed to mean?" he snapped.

"I love you, you jackass. That's what that's supposed to mean," Macie shouted. Macie's tears flowed freely, and she gave exactly zero shits about ruining her makeup. This ended here and now. "So just say it. Say you hate me. Say what a horrible bitch I am. Say you don't love me so I can move on with my fucking life."

"I can't say that," Zac yelled back.

"Why not? It's the truth. You're too damn noble to—"

"Jesus, Macie, do you ever shut up?" Zac's voice echoed off the rolling hill. "It's not the truth. I love you, too. Feel better?"

"Yes," Macie shouted. The words hit her like a jackhammer in the chest and she stumbled back. Zac's arm wrapped around her, pulling her close. Her entire body heated, and she could barely ask, "What're you doing?"

Zac trailed his fingers down her cheek. "This," he whispered before pressing his lips to hers.

"It's about damn time," Lauren shouted. "Now get back here so we can finish our photos. You'll have time to kiss and make up later."

Macie and Zac broke away from each other.

"You mean it?" Macie asked. She needed to hear it one more time to believe it.

"That I love you? Yes," Zac said before planting another quick kiss on her cheek. "And that I still want to kill you? That, too."

Macie laughed as they walked back toward the wedding party. "Well, let's just take that aggression out in the bedroom."

"Or in my car at the reception."

"If we even make it out of the building."

Zac laughed, lifting Macie off her feet and spinning her around. "You drive me crazy, you know that?"

"I hope to for a very long time."

EPILOGUE

Lauren fake sipped her champagne. It barely touched her lips, but she was determined not to let any of it down her throat. Just the thought of a baby growing inside her made her heart race and her cheeks warm. She had The Glow.

Ford kissed her cheek as he sat beside her.

"Hey," she said, not taking her gaze off the dancing couple in front of them. The DJ changed the song to YMCA, which got the crowd really going, but the couple didn't let go of each other as they swayed.

Ford nudged her arm. "You ever going to tell them?"

Lauren laughed, louder than she intended.

"What?" Ford lifted his champagne flute to his lips and drained the glass.

"Tell them what? That we knew they were each other's pen pal?" Lauren raised her eyebrows and stared at her new husband. "Are you insane? They'd never talk to us again."

"Well, to be fair, we didn't know until the end of the semester when you moved the app to a different server. They were the only two active accounts." Ford smiled, then glanced at her champagne flute. He raised an eyebrow. "Not in the mood to celebrate?"

Lauren leaned in and pressed her lips against his. "I'm in the mood to celebrate in a different way, husband."

"Then let's start the honeymoon, wife."

ABOUT THE AUTHOR

Lynn Stevens flunked out of college writing her first novel. Yes, she still has it and no, you can't read it. Surprisingly, she graduated with honors at her third school. A former farm girl turned city slicker, Lynn lives in the Midwest where she drinks coffee she can't pronounce and sips tea when she's out of coffee. When she's out of both, just stay away.

www.lstevensbooks.com